LEGACY:

SHADOW WATCH

LEGACY:

SHADOW WATCH

Book one of the Brotherhood of the Star trilogy.

By Andrew Lawrenson

Published by Pyrian Publishing

Legacy: Shadow Watch

ISBN 978-1-910980-00-2 (Kindle)
ISBN 978-1-910980-01-9 (Paperback)
ISBN 978-1-910980-02-6 (Hardback)

Published by Pyrian Publishing
info@pyrian.co.uk

2 4 6 8 10 9 7 5 3

For Karen

"They worshipped, so they said, the Great Old
Ones who lived ages before there were any men,
and who came to the young world out of the sky.
Those Old Ones were gone now, inside the earth
and under the sea; but their dead bodies had told
their secrets in dreams to the first men, who
formed a cult which had never died"

– H.P. Lovecraft, "The Call of Cthulhu"

Chapter 1.

November 4th, 1918. Novéant-sur-Meuse, Northern France.

Robert Knight knew he was lucky to still be alive. Whether he would make it through the night was another matter. He had been in desperate situations before, although never as bad as this, but he still held on to a smaller glimmer of hope. They had been on their way through the woods when it had all gone to hell. His unit had run into a squad of German infantry; a frantic fire-fight had ensued in the dark, and he alone had escaped alive.

The rain was coming down hard now, but accompanied by the sound of distant gunfire rather than thunder. In the darkness of the night, he lay in a shallow ditch overlooking the small village of Novéant-sur-Meuse. He was just outside Verdun, a couple of miles past the front-line into German-held territory, and he felt tired, afraid and quite, quite alone. He was soaked through from the rain and shivering from the cold, his uniform covered in mud. There was blood on his face; he no longer knew nor cared whether it was his or not. He took a deep breath, steadied himself and then wiped the mud from the face of his watch, looking at the hands in the pale moonlight. He still had time to complete their mission – barely – but he would have to get going.

With a supreme effort, he picked himself up from the floor, his tired muscles aching in the bitter cold, and started to creep slowly down the hill.

He stayed close to the tree-line for cover, keeping his head low in case of further soldiers hiding in the vicinity. His target was clearly visible to him in the distance – the old medieval church standing tall on the far side of the village. It was a solid stone structure, consisting of a single large hall with stained-glass windows and a three-storey bell tower rising from the front. It stood out along the skyline, standing proud above the other buildings of the town. With all the shelling that had been going on, it was a miracle it still appeared undamaged.

The village was eerily quiet as he made his way down the slope. As he got closer and reached the outskirts at the foot of the hill, he could see it was practically deserted; the only sounds were the falling of the rain and the distant sounds of gunfire from fighting over the nearby hills, carried by the wind. He could see now that the roofs of many nearby buildings had collapsed – brought down, no doubt, by the recent shelling. He cast his eye over other signs of warfare. There were craters in the road and cartridge shells lying in the street. He drew his pistol from its holster and slowly advanced. As he crept cautiously from street to street through the village, no lights were visible in any of the houses. Occasionally doors and windows hung open, banging in the heavy wind. There were no signs of human life here any more, and whoever used to live here had left in a hurry. Carefully, he advanced from building to building, taking cover behind walls and vehicles at every opportunity, growing ever closer to the small graveyard at the rear of the church.

As he reached the edge of the graveyard, he stopped briefly behind a low stone wall, which crumbled as he leant against it. He peered over the top of the wall, scanning the surrounding area for any activity, before he jumped over into the graveyard, taking cover behind a small marble crypt. Now that he was closer, he could see that although the main building had initially appeared dark and deserted, there was a faint glow visible through the stained-glass windows at the rear. It looked like some kind of open flame flickering in the darkness – candles maybe, or a small fire. He could also see a smaller chapel of more recent construction attached to the rear of the main church, a sturdy wooden door visible in the wall that faced him. He wiped the rain from his face, and then hurried towards the door, keeping his head low and using the tombstones for cover. As he moved from grave to grave, he prayed to God that he wouldn't be joining their ranks soon.

As he neared the door, he realized he could just hear sounds, distant and remote. He stopped and strained to hear them over the noise of the wind and the rain, struggling to distinguish them. They sounded like they might be human voices, calling out in strange rhythmic patterns, but if so, they were using a language unlike any language he had ever heard. That was when he realized he had almost certainly failed. He was too late.

He stepped over to the door, standing with his back against the wall and re-checked his pistol. There were only five bullets left in the chamber; his rifle and bayonet were long gone, lost in the melee in the woods. He put his ear to the door and listened carefully, but could only hear his own heart, pumping vigorously from the adrenaline coursing through his veins. The moon had retreated behind the clouds; there was now almost no light except for the faint flickering he could still see through the stained-glass windows in the main church.

Holding the pistol in his right hand, he grasped the door handle in his left and slowly, cautiously, turned it. The handle turned smoothly, the door opening a crack – it wasn't locked. He closed his eyes and readied himself, gathering his inner strength. He desperately wanted to rest, to wait, to put this off until later, but he knew he was out of time. Nervously, he opened the door and stepped into the darkness within.

Chapter 2.

November 1ˢᵗ, 2012. Bristol, England.

The door opened, and Jennifer Miller stepped out of the steamy bathroom. She was tall and slim with piercing blue eyes, and had long dark hair running down her back, which was still damp from the shower. She looked to be in her late thirties; the reality was a well-maintained forty-two. Wrapped around her was a thick blue dressing gown, with a matching towel across her shoulders to absorb the water from her hair. She walked down the stairs of their small flat, pausing momentarily to check herself in the mirror before continuing towards the kitchen. As she passed the front door, she bent down and picked up the mail lying on the floor. She walked down the hallway, leafing through the letters absent-mindedly as she opened the kitchen door and stepped through.

'Junk... junk... bill,' she muttered to herself, and then stopped. 'Hmm,' she murmured. She reached over the kitchen table and passed the letter to her partner, Jack Knight, who was reading a newspaper that lay on the table. He was drinking a cup of coffee and messily eating toast; more crumbs were on the newspaper than on his plate. 'There's some mail for you here – it's from some solicitors in London. The name doesn't look familiar to me.'

Without looking up from the paper, Jack reached out to take the letter with one hand, while still nibbling on the toast held in the other. He was a freelance reporter who was the same age as Jennifer, but was showing his age more. He was still in reasonable physical shape, but his short black hair was thinning on top and now included a noticeable amount of grey. There were wrinkles on his forehead and around his eyes.

'Hmm,' he muttered in surprise as he looked at the envelope. 'You're right – it's not from our usual solicitors.' He put down the toast, and picked up a knife from the table, wiping the butter off it onto a piece of paper towel. He sliced open the letter and read quietly for a few moments, before putting it down, and exhaling a long breath.

'What is it?' asked Jennifer, sitting down at the table to face him.

'It's my Uncle Stephen,' replied Jack. 'He's died. The letter is from his solicitors, informing me about the reading of his will.'

'You've never spoken about an Uncle Stephen,' she said, a slightly confused look on her face. 'You can't have been close.'

'That would be an understatement,' said Jack. 'The old bastard hated me as far back as I can remember. I can't recall him ever saying a nice word about me – so I stopped giving him the opportunity. I haven't seen or spoken to him for...' He thought for a moment. 'Well, it was before I met you – it must be at least ten years.' He picked up his coffee, took a large swig and then grimaced – it was lukewarm. 'You'll have noticed I wasn't invited to the funeral.'

'Why the hatred?' asked Jennifer, curious. 'It must have been something pretty serious.'

'I never knew. It wasn't just me – he and my father were never close either. There was some kind of bad blood between our two families. I think my father may have resented my uncle because he was the older brother. He inherited the family house and the bulk of my grandfather's estate – that made quite a difference to the lifestyle of our two families. I don't know what caused my uncle to dislike our side of the family so much though.' He stood up and walked over to the kettle, refilling it with cold water from the tap and putting it on again.

'And you never asked your father about it?' she asked, picking up his toast and taking a large bite while he wasn't looking.

'Well, my dad died when I was young, as you know, and I was too afraid and intimidated by my uncle at that age to ask him. And as an adult... well, you know what men are like for discussing their feelings.'

'If he's included you in his will, maybe he changed?' she suggested. 'Maybe he wanted to make up for the way he treated you.'

'Not knowing him – you never met the man. Would it be possible for him to leave his house and money to his daughters, and leave the tax and bills to me?'

'I don't think it quite works like that,' grinned Jennifer.

'Anyway, he's probably left me something terrible.' He looked down at his plate. 'And where's my toast?'

They sat in silence for a short while, Jack occasionally drumming his fingers on the table, obviously deep in thought. Jennifer presumed he was thinking back to his childhood memories of his father and uncle. She decided to break the silence.

'You mentioned daughters?' she asked.

'Three of them, all younger than me,' he replied, looking up at her again. 'They all inherited their father's dislike of our family. We don't keep in touch, not even cards at Christmas. Anyway, it doesn't matter – I'm not going.'

'Oh, don't be so petty,' she said. 'Besides, I want to know what you've inherited. You mentioned a house?'

'It'll be something hideous,' he replied with a sigh. 'Some final insult from beyond the grave. He probably plans to get me there in front of his daughters and then humiliate me.'

'I've never seen you so bitter before. He must have had quite an effect on you.'

'Like I said – you never met the man...' The kettle on the worktop was now boiling; he stood up and walked over to the sink, where he poured away the remains of his cold coffee.

'Get me a cup while you're up, will you?'

'I'm not travelling all the way to London for it.'

'It's only over there on the counter.'

He gave her a condescending look. 'I meant the will, and you know it. If it's important, I'm sure they'll let me know.' He went over to the cupboard and took out a second mug for Jennifer from the back of the shelf.

He grimaced as he read the slogan on the side – *Keep Calm and Drink Coffee*; it must have been a gift, he thought, as he put some coffee in both mugs. He walked back to the kettle and added the freshly boiling water, then passed one back to Jennifer.

'Well, I think you ought to just grow a pair and go,' said Jennifer. 'I'll go with you for support if you like.'

Jack sighed, a miserable look on his face. 'I suppose you're right. It's only half a day out of our lives.'

'Exactly. I think you're over-reacting to all of this. You're all grown adults. I mean, how bad could it be?'

Chapter 3.

December 13th, 1919. Latchmere House Hospital, England.

The patient sat in the middle of the room, facing three doctors in white coats who sat behind a plain wooden table. A single light-bulb hung overhead, not doing much to add to the meagre amount of light that came in through the two barred windows. The man was pale and gaunt, sitting restlessly and fiddling with his fingers in nervous anticipation.

The central doctor finished the hushed conversation he had been having with one of his colleagues, and picked up the paperwork that lay on the table in front of him. He scanned through it quickly, peering over the top of his glasses, before laying it back down in front of him.

'So – how do you feel these days?' he asked.

'Much better,' replied the patient eagerly. He looked across at the panel of doctors sitting in front of him, trying to make eye contact. 'I haven't had any episodes for a while now, and I've been taken off most of my meds.'

'How do you feel about what happened to you now?' asked the doctor on the left.

'I know now that what I saw wasn't real,' he replied nervously. 'I understand now that it was just a way for my mind to cope with the horrors of what I experienced in the war.'

'And can you remember what you truly experienced that day? The day when the rest of your unit was killed?'

'Only fragments. Some of the events earlier that day that happened in the run up to... well, the incident that caused my breakdown.'

'What about your sleeping?' asked the doctor on the right.

'I still have occasional bad dreams, but nothing like I used to. It's been a long time since I last had to be restrained.'

'I see,' said the doctor. 'When the time comes for your release and rehabilitation back into society, what are you planning to do? Do you have any family to stay with?'

'No, no family, at least not here. My only son now lives in America, and my wife died several years ago, just after the start of the war. I'm not sure how well I'd reconnect with those from my old life now. I was planning on selling my house in London and moving to the country – make a clean break of it and start a new life.'

The central doctor looked down at his notes. 'And how do you feel about losing your wife? I believe you were on active duty at the time, and weren't around to say goodbye properly.'

'Obviously I was very sad at the time – distraught.' He reached into a pocket and pulled out a photograph, taking a moment to look at it. 'When I first arrived here, many of my nightmares involved her, but those are long behind me now. These days, the memories of her help me find strength in myself – I have a much more positive attitude now.'

'Yes, I see. Thank you,' said the central doctor. He turned to each of his colleagues in turn, muttering something quietly to each, before returning to face the patient. He raised his hand, indicating to an orderly standing by the door. 'Thank you for your time. That will be all for now. If you could return to your room now with Mr Jacobs...' The orderly stepped forwards and touched the patient on the shoulder. He stood up and the orderly escorted him quietly back out of the room, shutting the door behind them.

The central doctor turned to face his colleagues. 'What do you think? Do you believe him when he talks about his improvement?'

'No,' said the doctor to his left. 'I don't believe he's being entirely truthful with us.'

'I agree,' said the doctor to his right. 'But he *is* significantly improved. He no longer needs most of the medications he was on, and I don't believe him to be a danger to himself or to others. There are others more in need of our help.'

'Agreed,' said the doctor in the centre. If he wants to leave, he should be free to do so. But I feel he is no longer mentally fit to serve in the army.' The others nodded in agreement.

The doctor pulled out the patient's medical record and struck it with a stamp. Fresh red ink on the top of the page read *Discharged*. The name of the patient written underneath it was *Robert Knight*.

Chapter 4.

November 15th, 2012. London, England.

Two weeks after they had received the letter from the solicitors, Jack and Jennifer found themselves stepping out of a black cab in a small back street in Soho, London. Jack gave the taxi driver a twenty-pound note and told him to keep the change. They walked up to the front door as the taxi drove swiftly off, heading to another fare.

The sky was dark and grey, bringing an air of gloominess down on them, not helped by the shabbiness of the street they stood in. Litter blew along the pavement, which sported a large number of broken and cracked paving stones, while busy Londoners bustled along it, doing their best to ignore each other. Jack looked at the building they stood in front of; it was a grubby red-brick establishment, one of many similar anonymous terraced offices along the street. The white paint was starting to peel from the old wooden window frames and the drain-pipe that ran down the front was smashed and broken just before it reached the street. A discreet brass plate by the door read 'Gingham & Rutherford, Solicitors.'

'Well, this is the place – shall we go in?' asked Jack, and Jennifer smiled politely back at him. He hesitated only momentarily, and then opened the door, allowing her to enter first before following her inside. They entered a small reception area, brightly lit by fluorescent lights hanging from the ceiling. It had obviously not been redecorated for a while; the brown carpet was worn, almost threadbare by the door, and the wallpaper was faded. Jack wondered what colour it would be underneath the various cheap reproduction paintings that hung on the wall – probably several shades darker.

To their left, behind a plain wooden desk and working at a computer, sat a middle-aged receptionist wearing a smart skirt and jacket combination. There were several plain wooden chairs around the edge of the room, next to coffee tables with an assortment of magazines on them. Across the room from the receptionist sat three women, all obviously from the same family – Jack's cousins. They were different ages, although all looked to be in their forties. They looked up at him as he entered, with various looks of contempt clearly visible on their faces.

'I see they still recognize you,' Jennifer whispered discretely to Jack.

'We're here for the reading of Simon Knight's will,' he said to the receptionist, who had stopped typing and turned to face them. 'Jack Knight. With these three fine ladies,' he said, gesturing towards his cousins.

'Of course, take a chair, Mr Knight,' said the receptionist, standing up and walking out from behind her desk. 'I'll let Mr Rutherford know you're here. Would either of you care for a tea or coffee?'

'Not me, I'm fine,' replied Jack.

'Me neither,' said Jennifer.

They both sat down in chairs at the other end of the room, a discreet distance from his cousins, while the receptionist walked across the room, knocking briefly on a door and then putting her head through. She withdrew her head a few moments later, and turned to face Jack and Jennifer. 'He'll be with you shortly,' she said, returning to her desk and resuming her work at the computer.

The next few minutes felt like an eternity as they all sat there politely, not saying anything, the silence only punctuated by the secretary typing at her keyboard. It reminded Jack of when he had been caught smoking at school, sitting outside the headmaster's office, nervously waiting to find out what his fate would be. He was just about to try and break the tension by saying something, when the silence was finally broken by the door opening and an old man with grey hair and a pin-striped suit emerging. He was elderly and moved slowly enough that Jack thought he ought to be using a walking stick.

'Good afternoon all, and thank you for coming today,' he said in an old frail voice. He looked towards Jack. 'I must admit I wasn't sure whether you would join us today or not, Mr Knight.' The cousin in the middle leant over to mutter something into the ear of her sister sitting on her right, who sniggered in response. She tried to conceal it by covering her mouth with her hand, but she didn't do a very good job. Jack did his best to ignore them. 'Anyway, please come in and take a seat, all of you,' he said, turning and slowly shuffling back into his office.

As Jack and Jennifer walked into his office, they saw it was a dark and cramped affair. Three of the walls were covered in book shelves, and the two windows at the rear had sprawling potted plants on the windowsills, blocking out much of the small amount of daylight there was today. A single underpowered energy-saving light-bulb was aglow in the ceiling, providing the rest of the illumination in the room. The solicitor's desk was covered in books and papers, his in-tray overflowing with correspondence. A computer sat on the desk, powered off. Jack wasn't surprised to see a walking stick resting in the corner behind his desk. Now that he was seated, Jack could smell a faint musty aroma in the room. He didn't know how much this solicitor charged, but based on his own experiences, he was sure he could have afforded a better class of cleaner than he clearly employed at the moment. The solicitor sat down behind his desk with an audible groan, and picked up a few of the papers on his desk, which he shuffled in his hands.

'Now, as some of you may be aware,' he began, 'I have been Simon Knight's solicitor for many years now, and he has appointed me to be the executor of his will. It was his request that you four be here for the reading, as the main recipients of his estate.' Jack gave Jennifer a puzzled look. She shrugged her shoulders back at him. Again, one of the sisters muttered something; the other two looked as if they desperately wanted to laugh, but were trying to hold it in, in respect of the solemnity of the occasion. He looked down at the papers he was holding, and then picked up a pair of thick spectacles from his desk, which he put on. 'That's better,' he said to himself, and then cleared his throat. 'Now then...' he said, beginning to read from the papers. 'There are several small bequests to charity and for small individual items to specific relatives – I'll skip over those for now if you're all in agreement?' he asked, looking up. The cousins all murmured in anxious agreement. Jack nodded along.

'Let me see,' he said, running his finger along the papers. 'Here we are. I, Simon Knight, being of sound mind and body, do declare that this document is my last will and testament. In executing such a document, I hereby declare that I revoke all other wills that I have previously made. I instruct my executor to distribute my estate the following way...' The solicitor here cleared his throat again, and took sip of water from a glass on his desk. He timidly looked up at the eldest daughter over the top of his glasses, and then rapidly looked back down at his papers. 'To my three daughters, I leave the sum of fifty thousand pounds each.' He paused again. The three sisters were looking at each other, slightly confused.

'To my nephew, Jack Knight,' he continued, reading slightly faster now, 'I leave my home, Ash House in Dartmoor, along with the bulk of my estate, notwithstanding the individual items detailed below.'

'What the fuck?' murmured Jack under his breath.

'WHAT THE FUCK!' screamed the eldest daughter, shooting to her feet. She turned to face Jack. 'What did you do to him? Did you blackmail him, you bastard?' she shouted, her face turning scarlet.

'Nothing... I... I didn't do anything. I haven't even seen him for years,' stammered Jack, standing up to face her. Jennifer stood up next to him, for moral support if nothing else. The eldest sister was tall and well built; Jennifer thought she could probably throw a fair punch. Mind you, so could she, if it came to it.

'He must have been senile!' exclaimed another sister, although she remained seated. 'I'll contest the will! Surely he couldn't have been in his right mind!'

'Now, now,' uttered the solicitor timidly, holding out his hands and standing up behind his desk. He looked glad to have it between him and the three daughters. Jack wondered if it would be strong enough if they all charged him. 'If I could have your attention, ladies, I'm afraid any kind of blackmail or senility is out of the question. As would be your success in challenging the will, I'm afraid, my dear. These main elements of his will were put in place over thirty years ago, not long after the death of your mother, when Mr Knight was but a small boy, and quite incapable of blackmail, I'm sure. Several minor details have been changed over the years, but he has never contemplated changing the main clauses. You see, his intentions were quite clear – as was his mind.'

'But... He... You...' the oldest daughter stuttered, her face going even redder. Jack wondered if she was going to have a heart attack – if this was a cartoon, he thought, there would be steam coming out of her ears at this point. She pointed a bony finger at the solicitor. 'You'll see... I'll be back!' And with that, she grabbed the door handle, violently yanking the door open. The door hit the wall with a loud band, knocking a couple of small books from the bookshelf onto the floor, and she stormed out, leaving the door swinging on its hinges. A few seconds later, they heard the front door opening and then that too was slammed shut, the Venetian blinds on it rattling back and forth. The other two daughters looked at each other, then the solicitor, and then they stood up and hurried out of the room, calling after their sister.

'If you could sit down,' the solicitor asked Jack, as he withdrew a handkerchief from a breast pocket and wiped his forehead. 'Perhaps I could try to explain,' he said, sitting back down into his own chair again with another small groan.

'That would be helpful,' said Jack, taking his own seat again. He had begun to feel a little light-headed.

The receptionist appeared in the doorway. 'Is there a problem?' she asked timidly.

'No, no, everything's fine now' replied the solicitor. 'If you could just close the door please, my dear?' The receptionist backed out, gently shutting the door as she went.

The solicitor cleared his throat, and took another sip of water. 'I could not explain in front of your cousins, but there is a reason behind your uncle's bequest – in fact, you could say a *requirement*. And one that you yourself must abide by if you wish to inherit your uncle's estate.'

'What do you mean?' asked Jack, confused now.

'Ever since the house came into your family in the 1920s, there has been a condition laid down along with its inheritance. A *condition of acceptance*, shall we say, that has been easier for some than for others. Since Robert Knight first left the house and the bulk of his estate to his eldest son, it has always been a requirement that you do the same and leave the house to your eldest son.'

'But Uncle Stephen–' began Jack.

'–had no sons, no. In that scenario, the requirement is that the house and bulk of the estate go to the oldest nephew. Only in the case of no sons or nephews are the requirements released.'

'But what's to stop me changing my mind – and changing my will later?'

'Technically, nothing. I would, of course, be willing to draw up a new will for yourselves, following these requirements, should you wish to go ahead. Agreeing to the terms of such a will is a requirement for the inheritance to be released to yourself. Technically, there is nothing stopping you drawing up a new will elsewhere later, but all the members of the Knight family have been... shall we say... *gentlemen* so far. Plus it would be possible for the err... *rightful heir*... to contest the will at a later date.'

'I see. Or at least I think I do,' said Jack. He thought silently for a moment. 'I suppose that's why he's always hated me...'

'I imagine so,' stated the solicitor. 'With only daughters of his own, he would have known he was obligated to leave his estate to you and not to his own children. After his wife died, he knew it was almost a certainty.'

'He may not have liked me, but I have to admit – he seems to have been a man of his word,' murmured Jack. He undid the top button of his shirt and loosened his tie; it suddenly seemed much hotter and more airless in there. 'But why? Why this tradition?'

'Why *any* tradition?' replied the solicitor. 'Because it has always been this way. I cannot claim to know the mind of Robert Knight all those generations ago. Perhaps he thought it was fair – he was an eldest son himself. Perhaps he was a misogynist. Whatever the reason, it is not my place to speculate.' He shook his head gently. 'Or to judge. In any case, assuming you're happy with these requirements, and wish to proceed... *Do* you wish to proceed?'

'Er... Yes,' spluttered Jack; then turning to Jennifer, 'We do, don't we?'

'It's not really my decision Jack, but yes – I don't see why not,' she replied.

'As I understand it, you don't have any children yourself?' asked the solicitor.

'That's correct,' said Jack. 'We've tried, but Jennifer's unable to have children... Ow!' Jennifer had kicked him in the shin, annoyance obvious on her face. 'Sorry,' he muttered by way of apology.

There was a look of slight embarrassment on the solicitor's face. 'That may at least make it easier for you in the future – you won't have to go through what your uncle did.'

'I guess that's true,' agreed Jack.

'Very good. You stand to inherit a significant amount, Mr Knight,' said the solicitor.

'How much, exactly?' Jack was starting to lean forwards in his chair. He noticed that Jennifer was leaning forwards too.

'Let me see here.' He rummaged through various papers on his desk. 'Yes... that... less that... less inheritance tax...' He made a few scribbles on a piece of paper with a pencil.

'Yes, here we are. After inheritance tax, you stand to inherit the house – which along with its grounds is worth in excess of two million pounds, and just shy of half a million, in cash, stocks and other liquid assets.' Jack had been leaning further and further forwards in his chair, but now collapsed backwards into it. 'There is also the not-inconsiderable value of the contents of the house; I believe your family has amassed quite a few paintings, sculptures and other *objet d'art* over the years. I'm afraid I don't appear to have an exact figure for that here. Would you like me to arrange to have them appraised for you?'

'No – no, that's okay,' said Jack. His head was really starting to spin now.

'That's fine,' said the solicitor, 'although professionally, I would advise you to get it done at some point, if only for insurance purposes. They like to have up-to-date values, and these things can accumulate quite a lot in value over the years.' He removed his glasses, and looked at Jack. 'I'm sorry,' he said. 'Would you like a glass of water?' Jack nodded. The solicitor looked around his desk for a few seconds before giving up and picking up his own half-empty bottle of mineral water from the table, which he passed to Jack. Jack accepted it gracefully and took a large gulp. 'Now, there are the details of the few personal items bequeathed to other family members. And of course, there is a fair amount of paperwork, both of which I can take care of, unless you'd rather...?'

'No, no, that's fine,' said Jack, still feeling somewhat dazed.

'Very good. If I sort that out, shall I arrange to have the final paperwork and keys brought round to your house in, say, a week?'

'A week?' Jack looked at Jennifer, who shrugged her shoulders and nodded, as if to say *I don't know why not*. 'Yes that ought to be fine.' He looked at the solicitor and wondered if he was planning on making the journey himself – he wasn't sure if he would make it in his state.

'Very good. My secretary has your number, I'm sure. I'll give you a ring to confirm before someone comes around.'

'That's very considerate of you.'

'Not at all, not at all, least I can do,' he said, seemingly as a reflex. He slowly stood up and stepped out from behind the desk and towards the door. 'Now, if you don't mind, I have another client in just a few minutes. Something to do with a dog, I believe...' Jack and Jennifer stood up, and were gently ushered out of the room, where the receptionist greeted them again. 'Oh, and Mr Knight...'

'Yes?' they both said in unison.

'Congratulations to you. Both of you.'

And with that, they stepped out into the cold autumn morning, still slightly bewildered, but a good deal richer than when they had arrived.

'So... What now?' asked Jack as they stood in the street looking at each other.

'Well, I don't know about you,' said Jennifer, 'but I'm going to go in to work on Monday and tell my boss where he can stick his job.'

'I'm not sure that will work for me,' said Jack. 'That's a lot less fun when you're self-employed.'

Chapter 5.

February 10th, 1920. Dartmoor, England.

Robert Knight opened the door and stepped off the street into the estate agents. He was thin and gaunt with white stubble covering his face, and was wearing a smart tweed suit. A small bell rang above the door as he opened it, announcing his entrance. Moments later, a small middle-aged man in a grey suit and tie stepped out of a back room to greet him.

'Good afternoon. Allow me to introduce myself. I'm Charles Hill, the proprietor. How can I help you today?'

'Well,' replied Robert, 'I'm looking for a property around here.'

Charles Hill nodded. 'I see. Are you thinking about buying, or renting?'

'Buying. I'm after something rural, isolated.'

'I've certainly got a few of those,' said the estate agent. 'Why don't you come in and have a seat?' Robert walked over and sat down in a wooden chair in front of his desk. Charles Hill walked over to a metal filing cabinet that was situated at the rear of the office. He opened the top drawer, and started shuffling through manila folders with his fingertips. 'Are you looking for anything in particular?' he called out.

'I've got a rough idea in mind,' said Robert. 'I'd quite like something late Georgian in style, and I was thinking about maybe four bedrooms, with room for a study and library. I'm looking for somewhere peaceful and quiet to do some study and research, so ideally it would have no neighbours nearby and generous grounds.'

'Sure... I've got a few that could meet your needs,' said the estate agent, rifling through the papers in the filing cabinet and pulling out several sheets of paper, which he brought back over to his desk. He laid them on the desk in front of Robert, spreading them out in a semi-circle, like a magician asking him to pick a card.

Robert leant forwards, and quickly skimmed through them. He passed over several properties, before stopping and pointing to one of them with his finger. 'This one here looks perfect. What can you tell me about it?'

'Ah – a very shrewd choice, sir. That one is Ash House in Dartmoor. It just came on the market recently, and it sounds like a perfect house to meet your needs – four bedrooms, two reception rooms, with rooms suitable for both a study *and* a library. Let me see here – yes, as I thought, it's quite isolated, with farms and fields on all sides. Quite a reasonable price too – the current owner is looking for a quick sale.'

Robert looked again at the picture of the house lying on the desk in front of him. 'Yes, that looks like exactly what I'm looking for,' he said, a wide smile across his face.

Chapter 6.

November 25ᵗʰ, 2012. Dartmoor, England.

They had been driving through the country lanes for just over two hours.

'Just admit it,' said Jennifer. 'We're lost.'

'We're not completely lost,' said Jack. 'We passed through that village just a few minutes ago. We can't be too far from there.'

'We've been going around in circles for hours,' pleaded Jennifer. 'Can we not just stop and ask someone?'

'Who?' said Jack. 'There's nobody out here.'

'Wait!' said Jennifer. 'What's that over there?' Just visible further down the road was a large house set back from the road.

'I think you may be right,' said Jack. 'If that is the place, they certainly picked the middle of nowhere to build it.'

Two minutes later, they pulled up on a short dirt path. In front of them was a pair of large wrought-iron gates mounted in a tall brick wall. A small metal plaque on the wall next to the gates read *Ash House*.

Jack pulled the handbrake on, and put the car in neutral. 'Well, this is finally it,' he said. 'Are you ready?'

'Ready when you are...' replied Jennifer.

Jack fished a set of keys out of his pocket, and pressed a button on a remote fob. For a second nothing happened; then, with a clunk and a creak, the metal gates begun to swing inwards. Jack passed the keys to Jennifer, then put the car back in first gear and they slowly crawled up the long gravel driveway. As they drove up the shallow hill, around the grounds they could make out a small orchard and a rose garden. In the far corner, behind a low hill, they could just make out a small marble building, which at that distance looked like a small crypt.

'Oh, do tell me your uncle isn't buried in there,' said Jennifer with a shiver.

'Not to worry – his solicitor said he was cremated. I don't believe anyone has been *interred* out there for a few generations.'

Jack pulled the car to a stop in front of the house and turned the engine off. He drummed his fingers on the steering wheel and looked at Jennifer.

'Shall we?' he asked.

Jennifer nodded back at him. He nervously opened the door and stepped out. The night was calm and quiet; there were no other houses for miles around, with only the distant sound of birds chirping in the air. He walked around the car to the steps in front of the house, his feet making conspicuously loud crunches in the gravel compared with the quiet of the night. He heard the sound of the passenger door closing behind him.

He turned round to see Jennifer holding the keys, which she offered to him. 'It's your house – you do the honours,' she said.

Jack took the keys and started up the steps to the porch. A sudden shiver flowed over his body despite the relative warmth of the evening; he took half a step back and the keys slipped out of his fingers, falling to the floor with a small clatter.

'What is it?' asked Jennifer.

'I don't know... I feel like someone just walked over my grave...' he said, shaking his head. He bent down and picked the keys up, cursing to himself. As he stood up, he looked back towards the main road. A black car was stopped outside the main gates, but took off again as he watched.

'Did you see that?' he asked her.

'See what?' she said, turning to look down the drive in the direction he was looking.

'There was a car stopped by our gates. It's gone now.'

'Probably someone lost and looking for directions. God knows *we* were stopping all over the place on the way here. Or maybe a local, curious about the new owners.'

Putting it to the back of his mind, Jack found the key to the front door and put it in the lock, twisting it firmly and then pushing on the door. It swung open to reveal the floorboards of a large, dark entrance hall, a shaft of light coming in through the door illuminating the dust hanging in the air. He stepped inside to take a closer look. The air inside was dusty and stale, and it was dark – all the curtains were drawn. Two closed doors flanked either side of the hall, with another door at the rear, half hidden by a large wide staircase. The stairs led up to a mid-level landing, before turning and leading to the first floor. Various works of art were tastefully placed around the hall – Jack could see at least three paintings and a statue on a pedestal. Hanging over the landing half way up the stairs was a large oil painting of a middle-aged man with short grey hair and a thick grey beard. He was wearing a brown suit with a purple bow-tie, along with round wire spectacles.

Jennifer followed him into the hall, looking around. 'Who's the portrait of?' she asked, walking to the base of the stairs to get a better view of the painting.

'I'm not sure' said Jack, switching the main lights on at the wall. He walked over to Jennifer at the base of the stairs and then walked up them to where the painting was hanging. A small plaque at the bottom of the frame read *Robert Knight*.

'My great-grandfather, Robert Knight,' said Jack. 'He was the one who originally bought the house into the family back in the '20s. He looks quite old here. This must have been painted near the end of his life.'

Jennifer walked up to him and looked the painting over. 'Well, you can certainly see the family resemblance,' she said, 'despite the generations.' She looked back and forth between the portrait and Jack. 'I never considered you with a beard before, but I don't know...' she said, trailing off. She gave him a serious look up and down. 'Might make you look quite handsome when you're his age. The grey almost makes him look distinguished...'

'What do you mean *when*?' he retorted. 'You don't think I'm handsome already?'

'Oh dear, you *know* I've only got eyes for you,' she said in a patronizing tone, fluttering her eyelashes at him. 'And at least you haven't gone *fully* grey yet,' she said, continuing to mock him. 'What do you know about him?' she asked, cocking her head towards the portrait, her tone serious again.

'Not too much,' he replied, racking his brain for any scraps of information. 'The solicitor who handled the inheritance told me what history he knew about the house. He said that Robert spent time in the army during World War One, and bought this house shortly afterwards. His son left for America before the war, to search for his fame and fortune, and only returned after his father's death when he inherited this house. His wife died of an illness at some point during the war. He never got to say goodbye properly – took her death pretty badly by all accounts.' He returned his view to Jennifer, and then looked around him at the house. 'When Robert returned from the war, he turned his back on his old life, moved out of London and lived here, all alone. It's pretty large for one person... It must have been lonely, isolated out here, all on his own – but I'm guessing that was what he was after.'

'Well, if we're going to be living in his house, with him looking over us every time we go up and down the stairs, maybe we ought to find out some more about him,' suggested Jennifer.

'Or we could just take the painting down,' mumbled Jack, but Jennifer didn't seem to hear him. He wasn't really paying attention any more either – he was already distracted by several expensive-looking vases on the upstairs landing.

They spent the next few hours unpacking the few things they had brought with them from their car and exploring the house. They started downstairs. The first door on the left as you came into the house was a spacious study; it contained recessed oak bookcases and a large antique wooden desk, which was paired with a modern office setup – a computer underneath the desk, a large monitor on top and a high-tech leather office chair behind it. Large bay windows overlooked the grounds, with two leather armchairs and a chaise longue next to them, a drinks cabinet standing in the corner. The next door along the hallway led into the kitchen, which was similarly spacious with large stone flagstones covering the floor. It contained a large range cooker flanked by two sinks at one end, and a black granite countertop stood in the middle of the room. A door at one end of the room led to a large pantry, its stone floor raised slightly above that of the kitchen; it was stocked with a large selection of tinned and boxed food. Another door led through to the dining room, where a long wooden dining table was surrounded by ten antique chairs. Two display cabinets were on one wall, either side of the windows, and a large fireplace was in the other, a chandelier hanging from the ceiling above the table. The two final rooms on the ground floor were a games room complete with pool table, and a luxurious living room with two leather sofas either side of a large fireplace, a huge flat-screen TV hanging above it.

Upstairs, they found three bedrooms, two bathrooms and a library. All the rooms were lavishly decorated and furnished with outstanding taste. Works of art decorated most of the walls. Jack didn't recognize any of the signatures on the paintings, but that didn't mean anything; when it came to the world of art, he was quite ignorant. One final door on the landing, however, was locked.

'Have you got a key for this?' Jennifer asked Jack. He took out the key-ring for the house and had a look.

'I don't think so,' he replied. He tried the only key that was roughly the right size, which he thought was for the back door. It didn't work. 'No, I don't' he finally confirmed, putting the keys back in his pocket.

'What do you reckon is in there?' she asked him.

'I've got no idea. He lived on his own. He shouldn't have needed to keep anyone out.' He thought for a second. 'The key's probably in the house *somewhere*. Where do you normally keep keys?'

Jennifer checked the drawers in the table by the front door and the study. Jack tried the kitchen. Before long he found a large key-ring with over a dozen keys on it – probably the keys to every lock in the house and grounds. Together, they walked back up to the landing, the keys jingling as they went, and Jack worked his way through them. On his third attempt, the key worked, unlocking the door with a dull click. Jack turned the handle and opened the door.

He stepped into what must have once been the master bedroom – it was larger and grander than the other three they had examined. However, it was also clear that this room hadn't been lived in – or possibly even visited – for quite a few years. A thin layer of dust rested on the polished floorboards, perfectly undisturbed. The two sets of curtains were closed, leaving the room dark and mysterious; a large ornate dresser stood between them. A large wooden bed lay against one wall, covered with a white blanket.

'Why would you keep a room like this locked?' asked Jennifer. She walked over to the window and drew back the curtains. Light streamed into the room, already making it feel more friendly and hospitable. She looked out over the hill-side in front of her. 'The view's easily the nicest of the four bedrooms.'

'The house is large for just the two of us,' pondered Jack. 'It must have been huge for my uncle living here on his own. He must have just made use of one of the smaller rooms.'

'Well, we can make use of this one,' said Jennifer, making her mind up for both of them. 'We can move some of the furniture in from the other rooms.' She went over to the bed and pulled the blanket off the bed. Underneath it was made up with sheets, but had no pillows. She crawled onto the bed, lying on her back and stretching, testing the mattress for comfort.

Jack walked over to the window to look out over the grounds. 'I really am going to have to take that solicitor's advice and get this lot appraised,' he said to Jennifer, as he looked at a jewellery box that stood on the dresser. He opened the lid of the box, but it was empty inside. 'Who knows what this lot is worth?'

'Well, I reckon we don't need to worry about moving any of the furniture from our flat,' said Jennifer, as she stretched out on the bed, kicking her shoes off. 'We don't have a single item that's better than anything here.'

'You're right. We should just sell it all,' conceded Jack.

'Sell it? It's not valuable enough to be worth the hassle. Just get a charity to come round and clear the place, once we've removed anything we care about.'

'I suppose you're right,' he said, grinning at her, 'as usual.' He climbed onto the bed and crawled over her, kissing her gently on the forehead.

'We'll have to go shopping for supplies tomorrow,' said Jennifer. 'There are some staples in the pantry plus what we brought, but not much fresh food. We can make do for tonight though.'

'I didn't see much in the way of local shops. We may have to go and stock up at one of the larger towns. I don't reckon Tesco would do home delivery all the way out here... even if they could find it.'

'Darling – you're a man of means now,' she replied, smirking. 'At the very least, you should be aiming for Waitrose.'

'Even *less* likely,' he muttered to himself.

'Come on,' she said, pushing him off her and rolling off the bed. 'Let's go make some dinner.'

Chapter 7.

He was lying on his back, gazing up at the stars above. They swirled around him in the sky, moving slowly and gracefully as time passed; exactly how much time had passed he could not tell. The pattern of the stars was familiar from the night sky, save for one large red star, which sat stationary as the others traced arcs through the heavens. This particular star stood out despite its relative dimness; it seemed to be flickering, almost pulsing to a strange rhythmic pattern. Staring at its pale red glow brought upon him feelings of bitter cold and loneliness.

Then he was drifting downwards. At first, he felt like he was falling gently through the skies, but then he realized he was sinking slowly through water, although he felt neither cold nor wet. As he descended, and the light of the stars grew pale and then dark; he could see fish swimming around him in the distance, recognizable at first, and then becoming more strange and unfamiliar in their appearance as he slipped deeper and deeper into the murky depths. As curious creatures came closer to investigate, he could make out vicious teeth, strange piercing eyes and slithering tentacles. As the depth increased and he sank deeper and deeper into the inky void, the creatures swirling around him grew monstrous and unrecognizable. Large shadows lurked just outside the range of his vision.

Down and down he sank, until he found himself standing on the ocean bed, but what he saw around him was not stone and sand, but some alien landscape; there were colossal stone ruins of some ancient civilization, their gigantic structures crumbling and dilapidated, seemingly lost to the oceans aeons ago. Huge pillars and monstrous towers loomed over him in the dark. The only light was a pale green glow, which came from all around, but from no light source in particular. Maybe it was distortions from the water, but as he drifted through the streets of this alien civilization, sandwiched between giant stone constructions, the geometry of the buildings seemed all wrong; there were walls whose edges were not curved but neither did they appear straight, constructions leered overhead at impossible angles, and buildings in the distance seemed to simultaneously be behind *and* in front of other buildings.

He drifted through the streets for what seemed like miles, but any sense of scale and distance was impossible among these Cyclopean structures. All he could see through the ebony waters were ruins, the leftover remnants of some impossibly old and immense civilization. No signs of life were present; not even fish dared to swim among the rubble of these remains.

He came to rest in front of two obscenely large metal doors, built into the side of a black stone wall that stretched as far as he could see in all directions. The door's thick metal handles were bound in heavy, rusty chains. As he stood there, the chains began to unwind and fall from the doors, moved by some unknown force; falling to the ground with dull thuds, raising clouds of dark debris into the already gloomy water. As the water slowly cleared, the doors swung silently outwards. Inside, through the murky gloom, he could only make out two glowing red orbs, distant in the darkness. He was powerless to stop himself from slowly drawing closer, across the threshold and through the darkness within, the orbs growing in size and intensity until they became two insanely large eyes, visible now atop a deathly green face, its complexion that of a forest at midnight. Beneath the eyes, a yawning chasm opened, the dark green flesh pulling apart to reveal a cavernous mouth surrounded by glutinous tentacles, which probed and caressed everything around them. They were seeking *him* out now, the eyes facing him, the tentacles reaching and stretching closer and closer towards him. He was drawn in, helpless, unable to run or even scream, ever closer and closer to that monstrous visage.

And then he was awake, lying in his bed, his eyes wide open, sweating and breathing hard. Jennifer lay next to him, snoring gently. Jack's heart was racing. He took a sip of water from a glass on the night stand, clutching at the memories like a drowning man clutching at straws, but as the dawn light crept between the windows, they were already fading away, like cobwebs being dusted from an empty room.

Chapter 8.

Jack came down in the morning to find Jennifer busy cooking in the kitchen, the aroma of bacon and sausages wafting gently through the air. The clock on the wall read a quarter past eight.

'Smells good,' he said, 'and as a bonus, we should find out shortly whether the smoke alarms here still work...' She turned and shot him a withering glance, and then resumed her cooking without a word.

'Sleep okay?' he asked.

'Not too bad,' she replied. 'I couldn't go back to sleep once I'd woken up. Probably just not used to the new bed yet. I thought I'd get up and get on with things.' She turned around to face him and took a better look at him. 'Are you okay? You look pretty rough.'

'I didn't sleep very well. I had the weirdest dream.'

'Well, while you've been asleep, I've been busy. Do you remember my friend Sarah?'

'I don't think so. Should I?'

'Probably not. Sarah Cousins from work. Her husband Douglas is in personnel – or I should say, *human resources* – for the Ministry of Defence in Gloucestershire. I've been having a chat with her online, and she reckons she can get him to have a look for any records for old Robert. War record, military history and all that stuff.'

'And it's okay, giving out those details?'

'It's all old enough. I'm sure most of it's in the public domain now. And we are family, or at least *you* are.' She waggled a ringless ring finger at him. 'At least for now...' she teased.

'You're really starting to take my family history to heart, aren't you?' he said, ignoring her waving hand.

'It just intrigues me, that's all,' she explained. 'The history of the house, the inheritance, all that business with your uncle – it's...' She searched for the right work. 'Unusual, that's all. Intriguing. You really ought to take more interest yourself – it's *your* family. And being a journalist – who knows, there may be a story in it. Your parents never talked about it?'

'We were never really into genealogy or family trees as a family. When we were young, we were busy enough looking after ourselves, and then when Dad died... As I said before, there wasn't a good relationship between our side of the family and my uncle's. My mother didn't get a lot of help from Simon, even after my dad's death, but I suppose he'd had enough issues of his own with his wife dying just a few years previously. I don't know if they blamed my mother for my dad's death, but, well, Mum didn't really like to talk about Dad and his family after that. There were just too many sad memories for her.'

'I understand,' said Jennifer, sympathetically. She put down the frying pan and looked at him. 'Are you okay?'

Jack paused for a moment, as if remembering something. 'I'm fine,' he swallowed. 'It's all ancient history now.'

They stood there for a moment, looking at each other across the kitchen, before Jennifer broke the silence. 'Anyway, Sarah said she'd get back to us in a day or two. I'd better get back to the breakfast before it burns.'

Sarah called back late the following evening. Jack sat in the living room, lying back on the sofa and watching the television while Jennifer had a long chat with her in another room. He was just contemplating turning off the television and going to bed when Jennifer walked back into the room.

'That was Sarah on the phone,' she said.

'So I gathered.'

'She's made an appointment for you to come and see her husband, Douglas, tomorrow at three in the afternoon.'

'Couldn't we just do it over the phone?' he asked. It seemed like a long way to go for a few bits of family history.

'She said there were some things he'd prefer to do face to face.'

'Is that unusual?'

'I really don't know – she didn't say.'

'Well, okay I suppose,' he shrugged. 'I'll check out train times in the morning. What about you?'

'I thought I'd go back to our house and pick up all the bits and pieces that we haven't brought over. I'll drop you off at the station if you like?'

Jennifer dropped Jack off at Bristol Temple Meads train station just after two in the afternoon, before heading into Bristol to pick up the last of the remaining possessions from their flat.

It was windy, with dark clouds overhead as Jack stepped off the train at Filton Abbey Wood station half an hour later; it hadn't started raining yet, but it was surely only a matter of time. As he made his way across to the Ministry of Defence complex, he pulled his coat collar up tight around his neck to keep out the wind.

He followed the signs for visitors until he arrived in reception. Once inside, he introduced himself to the receptionist, explaining that he had an appointment to see Douglas Cousins. The receptionist checked his ID, and a serious-looking security guard had him step through a metal detector before leading him into a waiting room. It reminded Jack of being at the airport.

He sat on a wooden chair in the windowless waiting room for several minutes, with nothing to do. They didn't even have the out-of-date magazines that traditionally belong in a doctor's surgery. He decided to check the latest news on his phone to try and alleviate the boredom; it didn't really help.

The door eventually opened, and a middle-aged man in a suit and tie poked his head in. 'Mr Knight?' he asked. Jack nodded. 'Good to meet you,' he said, extending his hand towards Jack, 'I'm Douglas.' They shook hands, and then Douglas Cousins led Jack down a corridor and into his office, where he motioned towards a chair opposite his desk. 'Please, take a seat,' he offered.

Jack sat down, and shuffled the chair towards his desk. Douglas Cousins took his seat behind it.

'Firstly, Sarah sends her love to Jennifer – says they really ought to get together for a girl's night out again sometime.'

'I'll let her know.'

'Would you like a cup of tea? Or coffee?' asked Douglas.

'No, I'm fine' replied Jack.

'Well then, let's get down to business shall we?' began Douglas, leaning forwards on his desk and clasping his hands together. 'Now, about your great-grandfather. I'm afraid I have some good news and some bad news... According to my initial inquiries, your great-grandfather signed up for the army in 1912, a couple of years before the outbreak of World War One. When the war broke out, he was a member of the Grenadier Guards – the most senior of all the infantry regiments, and quite an achievement. Here – let me show you.'

He passed a sheet of paper across the desk. It didn't contain anything interesting; name, rank, date of birth, and a faded head and shoulders photograph of Robert Knight looking like he was in his late twenties or early thirties. He looked quite different here from his portrait in Ash House – younger and happier, before the terrors of the war had got to him.

'During his time in the army, he was also a highly decorated officer,' he continued.

'Decorated?' inquired Jack.

'Oh yes – he received several standard campaign medals – the British War Medal, the Silver War Badge and so on. However, he was also awarded the Military Cross – quite a senior award given for gallantry; acts of bravery or self-sacrifice in the presence of the enemy.' He passed another sheet of paper over the desk, which Jack took. It detailed the decorations that had been awarded to Robert Knight during his time in the military.

'I see,' said Jack, looking through the list.

'Now – this is where it gets a bit strange...' continued Douglas. 'There are records of the decorations being awarded. However, for most of them, there seems to be no record of *why*.'

'What do you mean?'

'Well, this is what I meant when I said there was also bad news,' said Douglas, grimacing slightly. He took off his glasses and wiped them with a handkerchief. As far as Jack could tell, this made no difference to their clean-liness. 'According to the military records you have in front of you, your great-grandfather was a member of the Grenadier Guards. However, when I checked with the Grenadier Guards themselves, they have no record of him ever being part of their unit. It seems to be similar with the records of the decorations.'

'You mean that his records have been lost?'

'That's always a possibility, but as far as I can tell, it's more likely that no such records were ever kept – or created.'

'So, what are you trying to tell me? *Was* he a member of the Grenadier Guards or not?' asked Jack, frowning at Douglas. He was starting to get confused.

'It's impossible to say with one hundred percent certainty,' said Douglas, 'but I'm inclined to say not.'

'Then...?'

'This is all highly unusual, but I've spoken to several colleagues here at the M.O.D., and this kind of situation is not totally without precedent.' He paused for a second. 'This may have been a bit like a spy being given a cover story, where he would appear to be an employee of some normal company, but where that company is really just a front for MI5 or MI6.'

'Are you trying to tell me that Robert was a *spy*?' said Jack, incredulous now.

'Oh no – nothing quite as cloak and dagger as that,' chuckled Douglas. 'I only said it was a bit *like* a spy. But it is possible that he was part of some kind of military unit that was involved in highly sensitive operations.'

'What do you mean sensitive?'

'You're aware of what are generally called Special Forces?'

'You mean the S.A.S?'

'The S.A.S. are one form of Special Forces – although they didn't come about until long after your great-grandfather's time. In fact, what we now think of as Special Forces didn't really come into existence until the *Second World War*. However, as far as I can tell, that is what your great-grandfather was involved in. In trying to find his history, I came across a reference to something called the *Shadow Watch* that he appears to be part of, although again I can find no official record of a unit with that name. It may have been some kind of informal nickname or impromptu group.'

'So what are you telling me here?' asked Jack. He was really getting confused now.

'I believe your great-grandfather may have been part of this *Shadow Watch*, which was some kind of early Special Forces unit carrying out reconnaissance, covert operations, sabotage – that kind of thing.'

'Wow...' exclaimed Jack. He had never suspected that Robert had been involved in anything like that.

'If it was a secret unit, they've done a bloody good job of hiding it too, if you ask me. No one here knows anything about it. Not anyone at *my* rank, anyway,' he chuckled to himself. 'From what little I did find, he appears to have been active for most of the war, some of it in occupied France and Germany. His final mission was near the end of war. He was the only survivor of his unit, found by the French army in an occupied part of northern France. He was suffering from severe shell shock and they kept him in France for several months for treatment, until he was returned after the end of the war. After that, he underwent a year of rehabilitation at a hospital called Latchmere House back in Surrey. It's where they tended to a lot of officers with shell shock.' He removed his glasses and laid them on the desk. 'I'm afraid that's all I've been able to find.'

'Well, thank you. It's more than I was expecting and very...' He thought for the right word. '...illuminating. You've been very thorough. I'd never have guessed there was anything so special about his time in the war. I'd have thought it would have been better known in my family.'

'Well, many people were quite shy about their times in the war. Many men did horrible things; not because they *wanted* to – but because they *had* to. And in this case, it would appear that your great-grandfather may well have also suffered severe mental issues, given his time in the military hospital. That could also make him quite reluctant to bring up past histories; not something he'd want to discuss at family holidays and so forth. He may not even have remembered much of it, I'm afraid. Post-traumatic amnesia is quite common in many cases.'

'I understand.' Jack stood up. 'Well, thank you for your time. I'm certain you must be very busy.'

'Not at all. It's always good to let people understand the sacrifices the soldiers of that time went through, especially when it affects their own family.' Douglas stood up from behind his desk and led Jack to the door. 'If there's anything else I can help you with, do please feel free to get in contact. Although in this case, I'm not sure there's much more I can find out.'

'I understand,' Jack repeated. 'And once again, thank you.'

* * *

Jennifer picked Jack up from the train station on her way back from their flat, and together they discussed what Douglas had told him.

By the time they pulled up in front of Ash House it was evening, and the sun had gone down. Jack passed Jennifer a box of books from the boot of the car, and he took a box of papers for the study. In their driveway, it was pitch black except for the lights from the car and the moon whenever it appeared from behind the clouds. Jack walked up the steps and put his box of papers on the porch while he opened the front door and turned on the hallway lights.

'We really are going to have to get some motion-sensing floodlights put in out there,' he called to Jennifer. 'Otherwise, one of us is going to break their necks before long.' He picked up the box of papers from the floor. 'I'll put these papers in the study.'

'I'll put these in the library – I'll unpack them in the morning,' replied Jennifer, walking in behind him. She kicked the front door closed with her feet, then started up the staircase towards the library. Jack shuffled into the study, carrying the box in both hands, before dropping it onto the desk. He thought about filing the papers away now, but then decided that these too could wait until the morning. There was nothing urgent here. He looked towards the drinks cabinet in the corner of the room.

'Do you want a nightcap?' he called out to Jennifer. When there was no reply, he called out her name. Again, there was only silence.

Suddenly there came a frightened cry from upstairs. 'Jack!' Jack hurried back out into the hall and stopped. Standing at the top of the stairs was a man dressed all in black: black sneakers, black combat fatigues and a black hoodie, which was over his head, obscuring his face. With his left hand he held Jennifer by her shoulder; in his right, he held a gun, pointing it into Jennifer's ribs.

Chapter 9.

'Don't do anything sudden if you want your wife to live,' growled the intruder, his voice low and gravelly.

'Actually, I'm not his—' started Jennifer. The man pushed the gun harder into her ribs and she stopped.

'What... what do you want?' stuttered Jack.

'Where is it?' he growled down at him.

'Where's what?' he managed to reply. His head was reeling as he struggled to think what the man might be seeking. 'Is it money you're after?'

'Don't play dumb with me!'

'I'm not playing dumb – I really don't know what you're after.'

'We all know,' started the man, moving the gun to point towards Jack. 'According to the pro...' Without warning, Jennifer's elbow flew backwards and up, hitting the man in his nose with a sharp crunch. In a fluid movement, she spun around, bringing a knee up in between his legs. With a loud grunt, he doubled over, the gun slipping from his hand to the floor. It slid across the pol-ished floorboards, sliding down several steps with a bump, ending up on a step behind Jennifer.

Jennifer turned around to check on Jack. 'Are you okay?' she called down.

'Jenn! Look out!' he called back. The intruder had recovered more quickly than she had expected. Jennifer turned around to see him lurching towards her.

Blood was running from his nose, and an angry snarl was across his face. As his outstretched hands lunged towards her, she ducked down, reaching for the gun but coming up short, losing her footing and slipping down a step. The man stumbled clumsily into her as she crouched. As their bodies made contact, she instinctively pushed up with her legs, lifting him up, trying to push him off her. Carried by his momentum, he rolled over her back – and over the banister. With a loud, sickening thud, she heard him land in their hallway. She turned and bent over the banister to look down at him. He was lying on his back on the floor; he wasn't moving.

'Is he...?' asked Jennifer nervously. She was suspecting the worst – she hadn't liked the sound of that thud one bit. Slowly and cautiously, as if he expected him to jump to his feet at any moment, Jack walked towards the body on the floor. He bent over, intending to check his pulse, but as he got closer he could tell by the angle of his neck and the look on his face that it wasn't going to be necessary.

'Oh, he's dead,' he said.

'What should we do?' asked Jennifer. She started to walk down the stairs on trembling legs, which promptly collapsed under her. She decided to take a seat on the stairs instead. She was pale and trembling. Jack kneeled down, to take a better look at the man who had invaded their house. The hood had fallen back to reveal a rough face, covered with stubble. On his left cheek was a long scar, and he could make out a star-shaped tattoo on the palm of his left hand.

'We haven't done anything wrong. We should call the police,' said Jack, pulling his mobile from his pocket. He looked up at Jennifer, her face white with fear and nerves. 'I bet you could do with that nightcap now!'

An hour later, they were sitting in their Study with Detective Inspector Cross – a serious middle-aged woman, her brown hair tied back into a tight pony-tail. The first police car had taken just over ten minutes to arrive – which Jack reckoned was pretty impressive considering their remoteness. It had been closely followed by an ambulance and more police. Their driveway was still full of vehicles, but at least it had calmed down now – most of the emergency services had left, and all the flashing lights and sirens had been turned off those vehicles that still remained. The body had been removed, but a white outline was still drawn on the floor where it had lain, the area around it busy with crime-scene investigators dressed in white coveralls. Looking at it, Jennifer felt like this was all part of some bizarre television crime drama.

'Well, your story appears to check out, as far as I can tell,' said Detective Inspector Cross, closing her notebook. 'Looks to me like a burglary gone wrong. There'll need to be a coroner's inquest to decide whether any charges need to be brought against you, but based upon what I've seen and heard, as long as the forensics back up your story I wouldn't worry about that too much. You're within your rights to defend yourself, and if he was armed with a gun and threatening you, then you certainly weren't using unreasonable force.'

'That's good to know,' said Jennifer.

'And you're sure you don't know what it was that he was after?'

'No. But he was definitely after something specific,' said Jack.

'And you'd been out for a while?'

'Since the early afternoon. I don't know when he broke in, but he must have had quite a while to look around. There are signs of him having searched through most of the rooms in the house.'

'Is there anything particularly valuable here?'

'Lots of things. There are several works of art all about the house, as well as jewellery and a small amount of cash, but he seems to have ignored all of it. I'm not sure how much any specific items here are worth – I only inherited the house and its contents recently, and I haven't had it all valued yet. But as far as I'm aware, they're all on display, out in the open.'

'You haven't removed anything significant? Moved anything to another property, or hidden anything in a safe?'

'No, but we didn't inherit everything that used to be in the house. Some items went to other relatives. It's possible–'

'Yes, I see,' interrupted the detective. 'I'm sure this was just a solitary burglar, but we ought to warn them, just in case. Do you have their details?'

'No. But I can give you the details of the solicitor who handled it all – he must have all their contact details.' Jack grabbed a pen and a sheet of paper from his desk and hastily jotted down the name and address of the solicitors.

'Very good,' said the detective, folding the sheet of paper and then inserting it into her notebook. 'Now, the crime-scene guys will take a few hours to finish – it may be easiest to spend the night at a hotel.'

'We'll be fine,' said Jack, looking at Jennifer, 'I don't think either of us will be getting much sleep tonight anyway.' She nodded back at him.

'That will be fine with us – just check with them before going into any room. They'll need to have completed their examinations before you can go back in. I'll ask them to finish with your bedroom first.' She stood up. 'We'll need you to come to the station in the morning to make an official statement – both of you.' She passed Jack a business card.

'Do you know who he is? Was?' Jennifer asked the detective.

'No, not yet – I don't recognize him as anyone I've run across before, and he wasn't carrying any ID. We'll run his prints through the system and see what comes up. Check with any missing persons cropping up in the next few days, that kind of thing. He's got some distinguishing features, which always helps.'

'What about how he got in?' asked Jack.

'We found a set of lock picks on him. I'd suggest putting in a better set of locks – the one's you've got look quite old. Officially, we're not allowed to recommend anyone…' Cross smiled at them. 'But personally, I'd use these guys.' She took back the business card and jotted a name on the back. 'I used them for my house. If you'd like it done sooner for peace of mind, explain the situation to them and tell them I sent you – I'm sure they'd prioritize the job.'

'Thank you,' said Jack. 'I'll call them first thing in the morning.'

'It's also possible you'll get a few reporters calling over the next couple of days,' said the detective. 'I'd advise you just to keep the gates shut and ignore them. Once the official report comes out, any interest will probably die down a bit.'

'Good to know. Thanks.'

'Now, I'd better be going. Paperwork to fill out before I can retire for the evening – you know how it is. I'll see you tomorrow for your statement.' She walked out into the hall, where she started talking to the other policemen and crime-scene specialists. Once she had left, Jack went over to the liquor cabinet and took out a bottle of Scotch. He proffered a glass to Jennifer. She nodded, and he poured them each a large measure.

'What have we got ourselves into?' he muttered softly to himself.

Jennifer awoke late the next morning. When she looked in the bed next to her, Jack wasn't there. She got up and put a dressing gown on, before descending the stairs to the kitchen. As she reached the hallway, she saw Jack in the study, hanging up the phone.

'It's not like you to be out of bed before me,' she said. 'What's up?'

'I had trouble sleeping,' he said. 'Weird dreams again. Not entirely surprising, I suppose, given what happened last night.'

'Is that coffee I smell?' she asked.

'Yeah – the machine's on. Grab me another cup, will you?' Jennifer trotted off towards to the kitchen.

'I spoke with the locksmith,' he called after her. 'If we drop a key off with them when we're in town today, they'll pop round tomorrow and fit new locks. They'll give us a new key beforehand, in case we're not around when they finish the work.' Jennifer returned to the study and handed him a cup of hot coffee. 'Cheers!' he thanked her, and looked at his watch. 'I thought I'd let you sleep, but we ought to be going before long if we're going to meet Detective Inspector Cross this morning. It'll probably take an hour to get there and park.'

'I suppose you're right,' she replied. 'Just let me have a quick shower first.' She jumped over to Jack, and gave him a peck on the cheek. 'Ten minutes – I promise!'

✳ ✳ ✳

When they arrived at the police station in Exeter, they were taken through to an interview room, where Detective Inspector Cross met them again. They both wrote down their description of the events, and once they had checked and double-checked them, they signed and dated them.

'And you haven't remembered anything else since we spoke last night? You're both sure you don't have any idea who he was, or what he was after?' asked Cross.

'No – none,' said Jack. 'Do *you* know who he was yet?'

'Not yet,' she replied. 'But these things are normally just a matter of time.'

After she had shown them out, Cross wandered across to see her partner, Detective Sergeant Brooks, who was sitting at his desk, looking through some crime reports. He was a short and stocky man, with a thin moustache.

'Any luck with that John Doe yet?' she asked.

'Not yet,' he replied. 'No match on the prints, no ID and no matching missing persons yet.'

'Anything interesting in the post-mortem?'

'No. The only distinguishing features were his facial scar and a small tattoo on the palm of the hand – a star.'

'Okay,' she said. 'Run it around the other forces – see if they know anything about him.'

Chapter 10.

Jack and Jennifer lay in bed the next morning. The dawn sunlight was only just creeping in through a gap in the curtains, but they were already both awake.

'You know what really bugs me?' asked Jack.

'You mean more than an intruder coming into your house and poking a gun in my ribs?'

'Yeah – more than that. What I mean is – what was he after? He was clearly after something specific – and was quite intent on getting it.'

'I *had* noticed.'

'So what was it?'

'I guess we'll never know...'

'Until his friends and partners turn up looking for it.'

She gave him a stern look. 'Please don't joke about that.'

'Okay, okay. But just suppose. Imagine there is some great treasure hidden somewhere in the house. Something of unimaginable wealth and beauty...'

She raised one eyebrow. 'I'm listening.'

'Well... I don't know. I'm just rambling here. I don't have a master plan.'

'How about we get up and search the house?' she suggested. 'How's about that for a plan?'

'I could go with that,' he shrugged. He rolled out of bed, pulling on a dressing gown.

Jennifer slipped out of her nighty and pulled on some underwear. 'How about I do downstairs, you search upstairs?' she suggested, lying on her back and wriggling her legs into a tight pair of jeans.

'Sounds good to me,' Jack replied, shuffling out of the room.

Jennifer checked through each of the downstairs rooms in turn. She started with the games and living rooms, looking behind the paintings for safes, knocking on the walls to check for hollow spaces, checking for loose floorboards under rugs. She found nothing. She even checked under the cushions in the sofas, but wasn't surprised not to find anything.

Next, she tried the study. Again, she checked behind paintings, and then started to go through all the bookshelves in turn, starting at the top. On each shelf, she removed the books, checking for hidden spaces behind or below, before then checking each book itself, looking for anything hidden inside. Many of the books were old; many leather-bound. Some looked like antiques and were almost certainly valuable, but being in plain sight they were unlikely to be what the intruder was after. The only vaguely interesting thing she found was an old receipt from an antique store, used as a bookmark.

'Jenn?' came a call from upstairs.

'Yes?' she called back.

'Do you want to come and have a look at this?' called Jack. Jennifer put the book she was looking at back onto the shelf and then jogged up the stairs. She found Jack in the master bedroom, kneeling on the floor by the head of the bed. 'There's something odd here,' he said. 'Give me a hand pulling the bed out, will you?' Jack pulled the bed from the bottom, while Jennifer helped push it away from the wall. The bed was solid wood and heavier than they expected. When it was out a couple of feet, Jennifer squatted down against the wall to look at it. Jack came over and crouched next to her. Carved into the wooden headboard was a series of peculiar lines and curves. No writing, no symbols; just lines and curves. Jennifer touched the lines with her finger. 'They're smooth – and not deep,' she said, running her fingertips along them.

'They look man-made. *Deliberate*, I mean,' said Jack. 'Not just some random scratches.'

'Yes,' agreed Jennifer slowly, almost hypnotized as she moved her fingers up and down the lines. She snapped out of it and stood up. 'But it's not going to be what we're looking for. Is it?'

'I don't think so,' agreed Jack. 'Give me a hand to push the bed back.'

After several hours of searching, they stood in the study, ready to give up. They had turned the house upside down and were no better off for it.

'Damn it...' spat Jack. 'I was so sure.'

'There's either nothing in the house, or else it's very well hidden,' agreed Jennifer. 'If there *is* anything here, we're not going to find it without some kind of help.' She exhaled noisily and flopped down into one of the chairs. 'All this work's made me hungry,' she said.

'Do you fancy something to eat?' Jack offered.

'Yeah, I could do with a sandwich or something,' she replied.

'Make me one while you're at it then,' said Jack, sitting down at the desk and opening his laptop. He smiled over the top of it at her. 'I was going to do some quick research online – see what I could find.'

Jennifer sighed and stood up, grumbling under her breath as she walked into the kitchen. Ten minutes later she came back in carrying a tray with a sandwich and a glass of orange juice. 'I've brought you something to eat,' she said, depositing the tray precariously on the clearest spot she could find on the desk – a rough pile of papers at one end.

'Huh?' said Jack, looking up from the laptop. 'Oh. Thanks.' He took the glass from the tray before it slipped off, and cleared a space to put it down.

'Found anything?' she enquired.

Jack took a bite of his sandwich and washed it down with some of the juice. 'I've been looking online for anyone who might have knowledge of this *Shadow Watch*,' he told her. 'I can't find anything explicit, but I've found this guy.' He rotated the laptop around to show her a website. 'Ian Williams. He claims to be a military historian. According to his own rhetoric, he's a bit of an expert in the history of Special Forces, clandestine and covert operations – all that stuff.'

'And you believe him? Some random guy with a website?'

'Have you got any better ideas?'

'I guess not. I suppose anything is better than nothing.'

'There's a landline number for him under the contact details on his website. I'll try giving him a ring.' Jack picked up his phone, double-checked the number on his screen and dialled. They waited while the phone rang. Jack listened some more. 'It's gone to voice mail,' he explained to Jennifer as he stood there with the phone to his ear. He left a brief message explaining their interest in *Shadow Watch*, leaving his contact details and then hung up.

'Nothing to do now, but wait and see if he rings back,' he said.

Chapter 11.

September 8th, 1928. London, England.

Robert Knight stepped out of the busy Kensington street and into the small antique shop. He removed his hat, and shook the rain from his jacket. It was quiet and peaceful as he glanced around; the air was warm and smelled of old wood and paper. The inside of the shop was cramped, packed with items both large and small. Many of the larger goods were items of furniture – some were locked display cabinets, protecting the precious goods within; others items of furniture were themselves antiques for sale. A layer of dust was visible on the tops of many of the items further from the aisles – they obviously didn't get a huge trade through here.

He stepped slowly and carefully through the store, looking inside the various display cabinets scattered along the aisles. Many marvels were on display: old books and statues, weapons and jewellery. Stuffed animal heads leered from the walls and assorted pieces of metal-ware hung from the ceiling. None of it was visibly priced, and much of it looked like genuine antiques, as opposed to what he normally found in these shops – mere trinkets to capture the attention of wealthy tourists. However, none of what he saw was what he had come here looking for, until he stopped in front of the counter, looking through the glass lid at what lay within.

'May I help you?' came a male voice from behind the counter – the owner presumably, or one of his assistants. Robert looked up into the face of an old man, smiling at him from behind a pair of spectacles.

'Yes – may I have a look at those?' said Robert, pointing to a pair of items below the glass. The owner smiled and reached under the counter, pulling them out and placing them on top. 'May I touch them?' asked Robert.

'Certainly.'

On the counter lay a purple velvet cloth. On top of this lay two stone cubes, milky white in colour. They were engraved with a symbol on each of their faces, like some type of esoteric dice. They looked like they were made from marble, but Robert knew they were made out of a much rarer stone than that. He picked one up and laid it on the palm of one hand. He could feel a sensation in his fingers like static electricity, and a shiver ran down his spine.

'Quite something, aren't they?' said the shopkeeper. Robert nodded. He had spent a lot of time and money tracking these down, but there was no doubt in his mind – these were the real deal. 'They're believed to be very old,' he said. 'Possibly dating as far back as the eighteenth century. These two were found buried in India a decade ago.'

'How much?' asked Robert.

The shopkeeper nervously licked his lips. 'Twenty pounds for the pair.'

Robert looked at him. It was a huge amount of money. Robert was sure that the shopkeeper would have believed he was overcharging him, but he would have gladly paid ten times that.

'I'll throw in a box and the cloth for free!' added the shopkeeper.

Robert took his wallet out of his pocket. 'I'll take them.'

Chapter 12.

November 30th, 2012. Dartmoor, England.

Jack awoke in darkness. He was instantly struck by the absolute blackness that lay in front of him – this was more than the normal night-time darkness of their bedroom. His first thought was that there had been a power-cut, eliminating the myriad of little lights and LEDs on the clocks and devices around the room. This darkness was total, absolute, with not a hint of light anywhere. He tried to sit up, but smashed his forehead onto something solid.

'Fuck!' he exclaimed. 'What the hell?' He felt above him – it felt like a solid stone wall, cold and damp, just inches above his head. He tried to feel next to him, but there were solid stone walls to either side of him too, and he had trouble moving in the confined area. He had never suffered from claustrophobia before, but the oppressiveness of the stone walls so close around him and the pitch-black nature of his surroundings was making his heart beat faster, his breathing more rapid.

Then, his location suddenly hit him. He had been buried alive somewhere, trapped in a stone coffin. Panic overwhelmed him. His lungs were starting to burn, fighting to take in oxygen as the air supply grew low. He opened his mouth to scream, but nothing came out.

He awoke from the nightmare violently, sitting bolt upright in bed. His head was spinning, his heart pounding. He closed his eyes and counted to five; when he opened them again, he felt slightly better. He looked around the dark bedroom. The clock on the table next to him read 02:13. The weather had worsened while he had been asleep; heavy rain was lashing against the windows and the wind was howling down the chimney.

'Jennifer! Wake up!' he called, his heart beating in his throat. She mumbled something unintelligibly into the pillow. He shook her gently. 'Jenn. I've had an idea.'

'Couldn't it wait until morning?' she muttered without lifting her head, still speaking into the pillow.

'What if we've been looking in the wrong place all along?'

'What do you mean?' she asked, rolling over and rubbing her eyes.

Jack jumped out of bed, stripping off his pyjamas. 'Get dressed and meet me downstairs in the kitchen,' he said, pulling on a pair of jeans. He grabbed a T-shirt and jumper and scampered out of the door.

Really? she asked the empty room. She rolled over and looked at the clock next to the bed. 'Good grief...' she sighed.

Three minutes later, they met in the kitchen. She was a dishevelled mess, wearing jeans, mismatched socks and an old jumper; her hair was desperately in need of a brush. He wasn't looking much better; he was wearing a raincoat and Wellington boots, holding a torch and crowbar. He gestured towards another torch and raincoat that he had put on the kitchen table for her. 'Put that on,' he suggested. 'You're going to need it.'

'Where are we going?' she asked, failing to suppress a yawn. He opened the back door and triumphantly thrust out an arm to point across the lawns. Through the heavy rain, by the light of the moon, they could just make out the family crypt in the corner of the grounds.

'Jennifer, I give you the location of Robert's legacy. Maybe...' His voice wasn't entirely convincing. Jennifer looked out through the dark and the rain. As they stood there, a fork of lightning shot through the sky, accompanied by an ominous clap of thunder.

'Are you fucking kidding me?' she exclaimed.

Jack took the big ring of keys from a peg in the kitchen cupboard, and together they ran through the rain. By the time they reached the crypt, they were already quite wet despite their coats. The crypt was a white marble building, about the size of a large shed, positioned behind a small hill in the corner of the grounds. The large wooden door was guarded by a wrought-iron gate; in the middle was a solid metal lock.

'Hurry up!' urged Jennifer, shivering in the torrential downpour, as Jack fumbled his way through the keys on the chain until he found ones that look suitable. On the third attempt, the lock opened, and he pulled the stiff rusty gate open. He went to open the door, but found that that door too was locked.

'Damn!' he uttered as again he fished through the set of keys. This time he was luckier; the first key he guessed at fitted the lock and the door swung inwards. They quickly hurried in, out of the storm. The crypt was even smaller on the inside than it looked from outside, and sported a damp, musty smell. A white stone coffin was on a pedestal in the centre. Six other stone coffins were present, stacked two high around the side and rear walls. Jack turned on his torch.

'So this is Robert's last resting place,' he said, shining the torch onto a small plaque on the side of the coffin. 'Robert Knight. 1875 to 1929.'

Jennifer prowled around the rest of the crypt. 'This one here is David Knight. 1895 to 1961. His son?'

'That's the one,' replied Jack.

It didn't take them long to search the crypt; apart from the coffins, some garden detritus and spider webs, it was empty. Jack lifted up his crowbar and squeezed the end into the gap beneath the body and lid of Robert's coffin.

'Wait? Are you kidding?' shouted Jennifer over the noise of the wind and rain.

'What?'

'You think this is the perfect time to go opening coffins? At the dead of night. In a thunderstorm. Have you never seen any horror movies?'

'I never took you for the superstitious type,' he laughed. 'You can't hon-estly tell me that you think we're going to find anything–' He searched for the right word. '–*supernatural* in there?'

'It's not that. It's just...'

'Well?' he asked, exasperated.

'Whatever is in there can surely wait until the morning, which is almost certainly just a rotting skeleton anyway.'

'He'll be just as dead in the morning. And I...' he heaved on the crowbar, '...want to know...' he heaved again, as the lid creaked and slowly lifted up, '...now!' With a final groan, the lid slid up and across, almost, but not quite toppling to the floor. Jack picked up the torch and peered in. 'Well, I wasn't expecting *that*,' he said.

'What?'

'Come take a look.'

'Really? Can you not just tell me?' she pleaded.

'No. Come look.' Jennifer slowly shuffled forwards, took a deep breath and, expecting the worst, peered in. What she saw surprised her – the sarcophagus was empty, save for a thin layer of dust.

'Where is he?' she exclaimed.

'Damned if *I* know!' Jack replied.

'How did he die? Was he lost at sea?' she joked, a sarcastic tone in her voice.

'You know,' said Jack. 'Now you come to mention it, I'm really not sure. I always assumed that he died of natural causes.'

'All that for nothing,' said Jennifer with a sigh. 'Can we go back to bed now?'

'Yeah,' said Jack, resignedly. 'Give me a hand with the lid, will you?' He moved round to the bottom of the sarcophagus so he could push the lid back on more easily. 'Hang on...' he muttered. 'What's that?'

Jennifer's ears pricked up. 'What?' At the bottom of the sarcophagus was a small stone box, the letters 'RK' engraved on the lid. He reached in, and lifted it out carefully. Together, in the torch light, they stared at it.

'Go on then!' urged Jennifer. Jack lifted the lid. Inside was a purple velvet cloth. He unfolded it, and saw that within lay a stone cube and an old key on a fine silver chain. The key was about one inch wide and just over two inches long; the tip of the shaft was in the shape of a six-pointed star. The cube was about an inch across, made of a milky-white stone – Jack thought maybe marble. He picked it up and held it in the palm of his hand. It was polished smooth with rounded edges and on each side was engraved an unrecognizable glyph. As he held it, he felt a strange sensation running down his spine, making him shiver. He stared at it, captivated by the stone, running his fingers over the symbols etched on its surface, feeling a numb tingling sensation in his fingertips as he did so.

'What is it?' asked Jennifer, jolting him back to reality.

'I'm not sure,' replied Jack, snapping out of it. The sensation had gone now, as suddenly as it had arrived. 'Some kind of stone cube.' He put the cube back in the box and lifted the key out by the chain. It glimmered in the light of their torches. 'Here,' he said, beckoning to Jennifer. He took a step towards her, and placed the chain over her head, so the key hung down between her neck and breasts.

'Brrr,' she shivered, the cool metal resting against her skin. 'It's cold!'

'It *has* been sitting in a stone coffin for the best part of a century...' he started, but then saw the look on her face. 'Maybe it's best to try not to think about that,' he added.

'Easy for you to say,' she said. Jack picked the stone up again, turning it around in his fingers. 'What do you think it is?' asked Jennifer. 'Is there anything in there with it? Any kind of note?'

'I don't think so,' said Jack. He put the stone in his pocket and turned back to the box. He lifted out the cloth, revealing a folded sheet of paper underneath. 'No – wait a moment, there's something here.' He pulled it out, revealing a single type-written sheet of paper, which he held in front of him. They both read it by the light of the torches.

I am writing these notes for you, my descendants, following in my footsteps so many years from now. I am committing these thoughts to paper as I fear I will not be around much longer. I hope to offer you some guidance in what lies ahead for you, as I fear for your life as much as I fear for my own. It is now your time to take over the responsibility, and to protect those you love from the approaching darkness.

There will be three times in this millennium when the stars are aligned and the Great Old Ones can be allowed back to reclaim their place in the world – a place they will not deign to share with mankind. They have been around since before man first walked on this earth, and their followers are legion, waiting for an opportunity to serve their masters. On each occasion, they will try to unlock the shackles that keep their masters out of this world, and bring forth a new era of darkness.

The first was back in 1918. I stopped them then, barely, but ever since that night in France, I have been a different man; what happened to me there on that night changed me forever.

The second time is upon me now. I fear I may not live through it again, but it is time for me to try and complete what I started so many years ago.

As I write this, the final time will come 84 years from now — and on this occasion, it will be your duty as my heirs to act. For reasons I cannot explain now but will become clear to you eventually, it will be your responsibility to stop those who will try and bring about the end of us all. It will be hard, and you may suffer greatly upon the way, but I have faith in you and I know you will not be found wanting, for my blood flows in your veins.

By the time you read this, forces will already be under way to bring about the oncoming darkness. I have faced them once before, and must do so again. As you read this, it will be your turn, and you too will have to face your own adversaries, but with this note I have left you what you need to succeed — more than that, to survive! Keep it with you, and when the time is right it will protect you as it once protected me.

Be careful who you trust. Keep a low profile and your wits about you if you are to survive; the fate of us all now rests in your hands.

Robert Knight. Dartmoor, England. November 9th, 1929.

'What the hell?' muttered Jack.

'This just keeps getting weirder and weirder,' agreed Jennifer. 'And what the hell is *"the fate of us all now rests in your hands"* supposed to mean?'

'I don't know. I'm having a hard time believing any of this.'

'You don't believe him?'

'You've got to admit it sounds pretty far-fetched — and don't forget, he was committed after the war. He was *literally* insane at one point.'

'I'll grant you that,' she replied. 'But don't you feel that something strange is going on here, something bigger than just the two of us?'

'I must admit, I've had an odd feeling ever since we moved into this house. The guy that died in our hallway certainly seemed to think that something was going on.' He reached into his pocket and brought out the stone cube. 'Do you think this is what he was after?'

'Possibly. But how would he have known it even exists? It's not like we did – or presumably even your uncle.'

'What if he was one of them – the people Robert warned us about in this note?'

'Okay,' she said. 'I'm not saying that all the stuff in this note about monsters and the oncoming darkness is real, but...'

'But what?'

'I just think we should keep an open mind for now – and we should keep this key and stone with us at all times – just in case.'

'Okay, I can do that,' he agreed.

'Well then – let's get out of here,' she suggested. 'We can tidy up in the morning.'

'Agreed,' he said. He picked up the stone box, which was now empty, and placed it back into the vacant coffin, before sliding the lid back on again.

Together, they hurried out of the crypt, shutting the door and gate behind them, then running back to the house, where a warm fire and hot drink awaited them.

Chapter 13.

The next morning, Jennifer was woken by Jack pulling back the curtains, allowing the sunlight to come streaming into their bedroom. The storm had passed, revealing a bright clear sky.

'Wake up sleepy-head,' he said. 'Time to get up. We've got a busy day ahead of us.'

'What do you mean?' she yawned from under the covers, hiding her eyes from the bright sunlight.

'Get dressed and come downstairs,' he said. 'I'll explain over breakfast.'

Jennifer pulled on a pair of jeans and a blouse, and then came downstairs to the dining room. Jack had some toast and coffee waiting for her on the dining room table, as well as his laptop. She sat down and took a much-needed sip of the coffee. 'Got something to show me?' she asked.

'I've been looking into Latchmere House,' he said. 'It would appear that it was decommissioned as a hospital and converted to a prison shortly after World War Two – and even that was closed down two years ago. I doubt they'll have any medical records from the First World War there any more.'

'Oh well,' said Jennifer, sighing audibly. 'No point going to see them then.'

'However...' said Jack, drawing the word out to tease her. She leaned forwards in anticipation. 'The National Archives building in Richmond is the main source of historic records from that time,' he continued. 'It's open for public access, but they've put a fair amount of it online, including military medical records from the time.'

'And does it have anything for Latchmere House?'

'It certainly does,' he said, smiling at her. 'In fact, I've managed to find some records for Robert.' He turned the laptop around to face her. 'You remember how I said that Robert was found by the French army? Well, it says here that he was found outside a church in Novéant-sur-Meuse in November 1918. He needed urgent medical attention as he was in a bad way, both physically and mentally. He was in a near-catatonic state, unable to speak to them, unable to explain what had happened to him. They managed to get him back to one of their hospitals, where he stayed until the end of the war, which came soon after. Eventually he was shipped back to Latchmere House for hospitalization. His physical wounds healed relatively quickly, but he was hospitalized for over a year for a series of mental disorders. He was categorized as suffering from shell shock, but this included amnesia, night terrors and bouts of psychosis. He was eventually discharged, but was still suffering from some amnesia and anxiety.'

'That's great, but it doesn't really explain anything. I'd still like to know what the hell happened in France to do this to him,' said Jennifer. 'By all accounts he was an experienced officer who had seen action before this – it can't have been just a normal battle... Can it?'

'It was a pretty horrific war, by all accounts. Maybe it was just... I don't know, one battle too many for him?'

'I suppose so. But don't you want to know the truth about what happened to him?'

'Of course I do,' he said. 'That's why I suggest we take a trip.'

'To Novéant-sur-Meuse?'

'It's a small village. Presumably it only has one church. And France isn't that far away really. Not with the Eurotunnel.'

'What are you expecting to find? Whatever happened was almost a century ago.'

'I don't know – probably nothing.' He shrugged. 'But shouldn't we at least try? Go and have a look?'

'And what – you're suggesting we go today?'

'No time like the present,' he said. 'You'd better go pack an overnight bag, just in case. I'll see if I can book us a place on the shuttle.' He turned his laptop back to face himself, and starting typing on the keyboard.

Jennifer went upstairs to their bedroom, where she pulled a bag out from under the bed. She went to her chest of drawers and put a change of clothes for both of them into the bag, before heading to their en suite and adding various toiletries. When she had everything she thought they needed, she came down to the study, stopping off in the kitchen to pick up a torch.

'Where are our passports?' she called out to Jack, leaning through the doorway into the hallway.

'In the study. Top drawer of the desk, left-hand side,' he suggested. She opened the drawer – there they were, staring up at her.

'Don't you need stuff for driving in France?' she asked him. 'Warning triangles, breathalysers, that kind of thing?'

'Don't worry about it – there's a shop at the Eurotunnel terminal. We'll get it all there,' he told her. There were sounds of clicking and typing from the laptop. 'I can get us on a 2pm shuttle today,' he said after a few moments. 'Will that be okay?'

She looked at her watch. 'That gives us, what, almost five hours? That sounds fine.'

Chapter 14.

November 30th, 2012. Northern France.

They drove through the afternoon, going east across the north of France, first down the A26n then east along the E50. They stopped just outside Reims, for petrol and refreshments, where Jennifer also picked up a local guide book.

'There's a small section here on the village of Novéant-sur-Meuse,' said Jennifer, reading from the guide book. 'There's just the one church, like we thought. It was built back in the twelfth century, replacing a pagan temple that used to be on the grounds. Apparently, it was pretty common when everywhere was converting to Christianity.'

'Does it say how to find it?'

'No, but it shouldn't be hard. It's a small village and by the looks of it from the photo here, it's a fairly tall building.'

By the time they arrived in the village, the sun had gone down. It was a small community, and the streets were poorly lit with only the occasional street light, but it was a clear night. As they parked in a small lane behind the church and stepped out of their car, the gibbous moon provided sufficient light for them to make out their environment. Jennifer went to the boot of the car and searched through the bag she had placed in there, retrieving the torch she had packed earlier.

Together, they walked to the gate at the side of the lane. The gate was old and wooden, in a poor state of repair; as Jack touched it, some of the white paint flaked off onto the floor. It opened stiffly into the church grave-yard, which they started to walk through towards the main church building. The path they walked down was covered in weeds; the grass among the gravestones was long and unkempt. There were no fresh flowers visible on any of the graves. Even from a distance, they could tell the building was abandoned. The smaller ground floor windows were boarded over; the larger stained-glass ones were covered with metal grills. They walked around the side of the church through the long grass, until they reached the front of the building where the two main doors stood, huge, solid – and locked. There was no way in there. They retraced their steps around to the back of the church, where a slightly more recent chapel had been added – although it still looked several hundred years old. Its doors and windows were boarded up too.

Jack went up to the nearest window and gave the boards nailed over it a firm tug to test them – they were nailed on pretty well. 'You didn't pack a crowbar in that bag, did you?' he asked her. Jennifer ignored him and started to explore further along the perimeter of the building, examining it in the light of her torch.

'Hey, Jenn, come check this!' Jack called after her a few moments later. Jennifer walked back over to him, shining her torch in his direction. He had moved over to another boarded-up window and was gesturing towards the boards nailed over it. She shone the torch over them.

'The boards over this window are loose and rotting. And it looks like there's no glass in the frame behind them. Do you reckon we could prise them off and get in here?'

'It's worth a try, I suppose,' she said, shrugging her shoulders. Jack star-ted pulling on the boards with little success while Jennifer looked with her torch for something to lever the boards off with. Jack had made little pro-gress, and was already swearing and starting to sweat when Jennifer returned a few minutes later. 'Look what I found,' she said, handing him a piece of metal scaffolding. It was about a metre long and felt like it was made out of aluminium.

'Brilliant!' he replied, taking the bar of metal from her. He held it in the middle, lifted it up and brought the bottom of it down on the lowest board, like a man smashing rocks. The board cracked where he hit it, splinters of rotten wood falling to the floor. He struck it again. Larger pieces of the board split off now and fell to the floor. He continued striking the board, until it shattered into two pieces, which then dropped to hang from the nails pinning them to either side of the window, dangling in the breeze. Jack thrust the bar into the newly made space, and the two of them used the metal pole as a crowbar to lever off the rest of the boards. A few minutes later, they had cleared enough of a hole to climb through. Jack cleaned up as many sharp splinters around the frame as he could.

'After you?' he offered.

'Age before beauty,' she countered. He shrugged with a resigned sigh, and climbed through, pulling himself up on the window frame at the top of the window, then lifting and dropping his legs through.

'Okay, I'm in. Pass me the torch,' he called back quietly to Jennifer. She obliged and passed him the torch, before following him into the building.

The inside of the church was derelict, and had obviously been so for quite some time. Debris was all over the floor, along with a thick coating of dust and dirt. Broken furniture lined one of the walls, and spider webs were everywhere. It was also dark, with the only natural light coming in through the window they had removed the boards from. By the light of their torch, Jack could see graffiti spray-painted in black on the far wall – something in French that he couldn't understand.

'What exactly are we looking for?' asked Jennifer.

'I don't know, but I'm sure we'll know it when we see it,' said Jack.

'*If* we see it,' replied Jennifer, a more pessimistic tone to her voice.

With only a single torch, they had no choice but to search together. They went slowly and methodically through the room, fearful of what they might disturb in such an obviously decrepit structure; the last thing they wanted was to fall through a hole in the floor or get trapped under a pile of rubble. The small chapel had been cleared of any major furnishings or decorations – it didn't take them long to decide that there was no longer anything of interest there. From the chapel, they went though the only doorway – although there was no longer any door – into a vestry. This was also derelict, containing several cupboards and storage areas, but they contained nothing more interesting than a few mouldy robes and now-empty boxes that used to store communion wafers.

For a short while, they thought the door from here to the main church was locked; luckily, it was merely warped and stuck in its frame. With a few barges with his shoulder, Jack forced the door open, and they entered the main church building. The moonlight coming through the stained-glass windows cast eerily coloured shadows over the room. Several rows of wooden pews were still present to the left and right of the building. At the back of the church near where they stood was the chancel. They could see that there was still a solid stone altar there, although all other religious trappings had been removed.

Jennifer walked over to the aisle in the centre of the church. Looking towards the altar, he could see a large stone cross-beam above the altar. Carved into it was the phrase: *Regarder vers le ciel pour le salut.* 'What do you think it means?' she asked.

'Err...' he said, trying to remember what he knew of French, but it had all been a long time ago. 'Something to do with looking at something,' he said. 'Hold on a moment.' He got out his phone and starting typing the phrase into it. 'Look to the sky for salvation,' he finally replied.

Jennifer looked up at the ceiling. 'If they neglect this place any more, that's not going to be too tricky.' They both moved over to the altar and started looking around. Stained-glass windows on their left showed the temptation of Eve in the Garden of Eden; on their right was the crucifixion of Christ. Turning around, Jack could see that on the back of the altar was a mosaic tiling, mostly black with random flecks of white.

'Does that look familiar to you?' asked Jack.

'Are you trying to say I remind you of Eve?' replied Jennifer, still looking at the stained glass.

'No, not the windows – the altar,' said Jack. 'Do those patterns of white look familiar to you?'

'You're right!' said Jennifer, walking back towards the altar and shining her torch on it. 'Those pieces of white there look like the Big Dipper.'

'And that's Ursa Minor,' said Jack, pointing to another collection of small white tiles on the mosaic.

'It's the night sky,' she said, confirming his suspicions.

Jack stood there for a moment, looking at it closely. 'That red spot there! Look!'

'What's that?' asked Jennifer. In the middle of the black and white mosaic was a single red tile.

'I don't know. It just seems... familiar somehow,' said Jack. Then it came to him. 'I saw it in a dream.'

'A dream?'

'More of a nightmare really. I'd forgotten all about it until now.'

'What do you think it means?'

'I don't know,' he muttered. He got down on his knees next to the altar and ran his fingers over the tiles. 'Look to the sky for salvation,' he whispered to himself, examining the red tile with his fingertips. 'Shine the torch here,' he asked Jennifer, and she obliged, coming over and kneeling next to him. The tile was pale red, and about a centimetre across. As he felt it with his fingers, it sunk in, along with a tile below it; it was hinged like some kind of cover.

'I think there's a hole behind it,' he whispered to Jennifer. Jack peered closer by the light of the torch. 'There's something behind there,' he muttered. 'See if you can shine the light in.' Jennifer moved closer and lent over him, repositioning the torch. Jack again peered in. 'It looks like a star shape,' he said. He turned to face Jennifer, peering down her top as she leaned over him. A grin came over his face.

'Now is *not* the time,' she said sternly.

'No, not that – the key!'

'Oh, that.' She reached into her top and pulled it out, lifting the chain over her head to remove it. He took it from her and then pushed it gently into the hole, twisting it until the points of the star lined up. It went in about a centimetre and then stopped. He gave it a firm but gentle twist, and it rotated with a sharp click. From behind them came a deeper whir and then a thud. They turned around to see that one of the flagstones behind the altar had lifted up; about an inch of stone tile was lifted in the air, with a thin gap beneath one side where it had tilted out of the floor.

'Bingo!' muttered Jack. He shuffled over and felt the flagstone with his fingers. 'I think this will lift up.'

'A hidden trapdoor?' whispered Jennifer.

'Looks like it,' said Jack. 'I'll try and lift this – watch your fingers.' He crouched down next to it and gripped the edge of the flagstone with his fingertips. He groaned as he strained to lift the weight of it up. He raised it about an inch before it slipped and he let it fall.

'It's heavier than I thought!' he exclaimed. They both thought for a moment or two in silence.

'Wait here,' said Jennifer suddenly. 'I'll be right back!' she said, scampering back out into the vestry.

'Hey!' called Jack. He was alone in the darkness; she had taken the torch with her. 'It's a good thing I'm not afraid of the dark,' he grumbled to himself. The shadows seemed much deeper now that the room was only illuminated by the multi-coloured moonlight coming through the stained-glass windows. She returned about a minute later, holding the torch in one hand, and the metal scaffolding pole in the other.

'You lift again, I'll stick this in – then we can lever it,' she told him.

Once again Jack took hold of the flagstone with his fingers and pulled as hard as he could. It raised an inch. Two inches. Jennifer tried to insert the bar, but it was slightly too thick. 'A bit more!' she urged. Jack gave a grunt and pulled as hard as he could. The stone slab raised another half an inch and Jennifer slipped the scaffolding into the darkness beneath. 'That'll hold it open,' she said.

'Ugh!' exclaimed Jack, dropping the stone onto the metal bar with a deep *thud*. Jennifer put the torch on the floor facing the flagstone, and then together, silently, they both pulled on the flagstone, using all their strength to lift the slab of stone up. Slowly it rose, until it reached about a forty-five degree angle, and then all at once it came up easily, almost throwing the two of them to floor with the unexpected change in resistance. Jennifer picked the torch back up off the floor and pointed it down into the darkness below. They could make out rough stone walls descending vertically and a floor about twenty feet beneath; iron rungs were mounted on the wall that would allow them to climb down without too much difficulty.

'Okay. I think we've already set the precedent that you go first?' said Jennifer nervously.

'All right,' said Jack, gritting his teeth. 'We've come too far to stop now.' He sat on the side of the hole and lowered his feet in, before finding a rung a little way down with his feet. 'You shine the torch in, so I can see where I'm going.' Jennifer pointed the torch down the hole while Jack slowly climbed down into the darkness. 'Okay – I'm down,' he called up, once he had reached the bottom. 'There's another tunnel leading off from here. Can you pass me that bar of scaffolding?' he asked her, looking into the pitch black beyond. 'I'd feel a bit safer with a solid piece of metal in my hands...'

'Here it comes,' she said, lying down and holding on to it with one hand while lowering it into the hole. Jack grabbed it from below. 'Got it,' he said, holding it out in front of him like a club. Jennifer then held the torch between her teeth and slowly climbed down the rungs herself.

'What is this place?' she asked as they both stood at the bottom of the shaft. They were at the start of a rough tunnel channelled through the earth, disappearing into the darkness in front of them. They shone the torch around them and examined their surroundings. Black stone bricks lined the wall and rough wood planks lay on the floor; every so often, beams jutted out of the walls, bearing the load of the roof. Jennifer ran her hands along the stone of the wall – it was cold and damp, a light condensation present on it.

They both shuffled slowly down the tunnel. It carried on for about ten metres, before it opened out into a much rougher tunnel, bearing to the right. There were no supports here, only natural rock. The floor was rough, and on a slight but obvious incline downwards. No light or sound penetrated down here from above – it was eerily silent except for their breathing, and pitch black except for the light of their torch. Jack stopped next to Jennifer, taking the torch from her and shining it down the new tunnel, revealing nothing but rock walls and inky darkness.

'Are we sure about this?' asked Jack.

Jennifer nodded in agreement, and then realizing he probably couldn't see her added 'Yes. But let's go now, before I change my mind.' She took the torch back from Jack, firmly holding his arm with her other hand for encouragement as she did so. 'I'll lead the way.' They started off down the tunnel, Jennifer taking the lead, with Jack close behind.

'I'm no expert, but this looks like a natural formation to me,' whispered Jack. 'I can't see any evidence of mining here.'

'Do you think they built the church on top of this deliberately?' Jennifer whispered back.

'Quite possibly,' he replied. 'The site used to be a place of pagan worship, remember? Maybe they used to hold pagan rituals down here.'

They carried on down the tunnel for quite some time; it felt like at least a mile, but with nothing to help gauge their progress, it was impossible to tell exactly how far they had come. It twisted gently back and forth, turning back on itself at times, but always gently descending deeper into the earth. Eventually, the tunnel opened up into a larger cave; the floor looked like it had been manually flattened, but the walls and ceiling were rough stone, damp and shiny. From the back of the cave came the faint sound of water gently dripping.

'Where's that sound coming from?' he muttered, stopping just inside the entrance to the cave. Jennifer shone the torch around the walls of the cave; about ten metres away on the far side, they could make out another passageway leading out of the cave.

'I've got the strangest feeling right now,' he said.

'No shit,' she replied sarcastically. She took his hand in hers for support. 'You're shaking,' she said.

'It's... It's more than just nerves,' he replied in a sombre voice. 'Let's just keep going.'

They started off again towards the passageway at the rear of the cave, cautious of what might lie in their way. The passageway out of the room was much shorter – about twenty metres – before it opened up into a huge cave. There was perhaps twenty metres of ground, before it appeared to give way to a wide chasm stretching across the entire width of the cave. Beyond, by the light of the torch, they could just make out water trickling down the walls on the other side, the source of the noise they had heard. Apart from each other, this had been the only sound they had heard since they had started their descent.

'What's that over there?' Jack muttered. 'Point the torch over there,' he directed Jennifer, pointing towards the rear of the cave. 'No – right a bit.' By the light of the torch, they could make out some kind of dark rectangle about ten metres away, standing before the chasm – an obviously man-made object standing out against the natural backdrop of the cave. Slowly, they both started moving towards it. They had taken no more than ten steps when Jennifer's feet bumped into something, making her stumble and drop the torch. It rolled away slightly, pointing back towards them. With the torch on the floor, the room seemed darker, the light now a very murky black. Jennifer reached down to pick up the torch, and aimed it towards her feet to see what she had tripped on. She screamed briefly and very nearly dropped the torch again. On the floor by her feet was a human skeleton, its dry bones covered only in a few scraps of cloth. It had obviously been undisturbed for a very long time.

'Jesus!' she exclaimed. Jack knelt down next to her, and examined it by the light of the torch. 'Well?' she asked.

'I don't know,' he replied. 'I'm not a doctor – or an archaeologist. He – or she – didn't die from having their skull caved in, but apart from that... I just don't know.'

Jennifer scanned the torch around the floor of the cave near the body, looking for any clues. 'Over there!' she called, pointing the torch light about two metres further into the room; something metallic was shining dimly in the light, the metal still reflecting some of the light despite the layer of dust that covered it. Jack slowly walked over and crouched down to pick it up.

'It's a gun,' he called back, picking it up and brushing the dust from it. 'A revolver – an old one too.' He opened it and looked inside at the chamber. 'Only empty cartridges – the bullets have all been fired.' Jennifer moved slowly over to him, and Jack held the pistol in his left hand, the scaffolding in his right. He knew it was illogical, but even though he knew it was empty, just holding the gun in his hand made him feel less afraid.

Jennifer started to scan the rest of the floor with the torch. Together, they drew closer to the chasm, until they could make out what the dark rectangle was; it was obviously some kind of altar, made out of black stone. Jack thought it might be marble, although there was no way to be sure. A thick red candle stood at each end of the altar, held in place by melted wax that had run down their sides. A large leather-bound book lay open on the top; next to it was a metal bowl.

'I don't think this was ever part of any Christian ceremony, even one from the middle ages,' said Jennifer. Jack stuck the gun in the waist band of his trousers, rested the scaffolding on the altar and picked up the bowl. He blew hard on the bowl to remove the dust – he was rewarded with a face-full of the fine powder, causing him to cough momentarily. When he had regained his composure, he held it closely in his hands and examined it. The bowl appeared to be copper and was around six inches in diameter. It looked crude and old-fashioned; around the outside there was a patterned band and inside there was a deep, dark-red stain.

'I agree,' he replied. He put down the bowl gently, and turned to the book. Its leather cover bore no name; its pages were brown and aged, hand-written in a language unknown to him. As he flicked through the pages, there were several hand-drawn illustrations, disturbing in their nature. He shivered, and not just from the cold of the cave.

'Look,' said Jennifer, once again pointing the torch to the floor. Although the floor was rough and covered in a layer of dust and dirt, they could now see white marks on the floor where they had walked across it. She knelt down and rubbed away the dust and dirt with her hand to reveal lines and markings written on the floor. It looked to her like white paint, or possibly thick chalk. She shuffled around on her hands and knees, rubbing away the dust with her hands, until the whole pattern was visible. They could now make out a six-pointed star about three metres across; above each point was a symbol she did not recognize, and a further circular band of symbols was present inside the star, surrounding a smaller red star in the centre.

'Are you thinking what I'm thinking?' she asked.

'Yeah – I've seen enough horror movies to know where this is heading,' he said. 'The occult. Black magic. Whatever you want to call it, it's not good. And I'm guessing he was some kind of sacrificial victim.' He nodded back towards the body lying in the darkness on the other side of the cave.

'What now?' asked Jack. Jennifer shone the torch around the cave. She could make out other tunnels leading away from this cave, one either side of the passage they had come through, one higher up in the wall. Slowly, she walked past the altar towards the chasm, stopping as close as she dared. As she pointed the torch down, she could make out the opposite side of the chasm at first, but the light of the torch struggled to illuminate the other side as she peered deeper; she could not see the bottom. She bent over and felt for a rock. She picked up a few, until she found one of a size she liked – about the size of an egg. She stood up, holding the torch in her left hand, throwing and catching the rock gently in her right.

She gently threw the rock a few feet over the side into the darkness and started counting. 'One.... Two... Three...' she started. She gave up at ten.

'I don't think you're going to hear anything,' said Jack. She spun round, surprised to see him so close – she had been so intent on listening for the rock, she hadn't noticed him approach. 'If there was anything to hear, you'd have heard it a long time ago.'

'What does that mean?' she asked.

'Well... maybe it hit something soft. Mud perhaps, or some kind of vegetation. Either that or it's deep. *Really* deep.' They stood in the dark and silence for a few seconds, peering over the edge, and then Jennifer shone the torch back towards Jack and looked deep into his face.

'Should we search some of the other tunnels?' Jennifer suggested, somewhat half-heartedly. Jack could see from the look on her face that she wasn't too keen.

Jack still wanted more answers. All they had seemed to find so far were more questions. He was about to speak, to suggest they continue on for just a little longer, and then paused to reconsider. He wondered how long the batteries in the torch would last; he had no idea how old they were. He wasn't sure if it was his imagination, but the torch didn't seem quite as bright as when they had first entered. He had visions of endlessly wandering through long labyrinthine tunnels in absolute darkness. 'I think I've seen enough freaky shit for one night, and I really, *really* don't want to get lost in a maze of catacombs down here,' he eventually said.

'Agreed,' said Jennifer. 'Let's get the hell out of here.'

They turned and started to head back towards the entrance when from somewhere in front of them came a terrifying inhuman scream. Jennifer and Jack looked at each other. 'What the *fuck* was that?' asked Jack, his voice quivering with fear.

'Let's go,' whispered Jennifer. 'Now!' As quietly as they could, they retreated rapidly across the cave. They had only taken a few steps when from somewhere in the darkness ahead of them they heard the sound of something scraping along the floor.

'I don't think we're alone in here,' said Jennifer, fear audible in her voice.

Jack took a couple of steps back towards the altar and reached over and picked up the metal scaffolding from it. He held it in both hands like a base-ball bat and then stepped back in front of Jennifer. Once again they started moving back towards the entrance, Jennifer scanning in front of them with the torch.

They were approaching the edge of the cavern when out of the darkness came a terrifying growl; a creature suddenly flew through the air from above, leaping down from an alcove high in the wall and landing just a few feet in front of them. It was some kind of humanoid creature, towering over them, at least eight feet tall. Its sinewy body was largely composed of muscles covered in rubbery pale-white flesh; its grotesque nose-less face sported large yellow eyes and there were dirty fangs visible within its wide mouth as it growled at them. There was an overbearing stench emanating from the beast; the smell of decay and rotting meat – the smell of death. Jack had to fight back a wave of nausea as the creature took a step towards him. He briefly saw long claws on the ends of its fists as it lashed out towards him, bellowing a powerful roar. He instinctively brought the metal bar upwards to defend himself. He made contact with the creature as it lunged, the bar glancing off its powerful forearm, deflecting the blow but not harming the creature.

The beast lurched forwards, now swinging its other arm towards Jack. Jack stumbled backwards, tripping on the uneven floor of the cavern and falling to the ground, the creature's claws raking through the air above him. As he lay on the floor, the beast towered above him, bellowing and raising its arms in the air, about to strike again. Jennifer cursed that she didn't have a weapon to hand, but made do with what she had; she thrust the torch forwards, shining the light directly into its face and its large yellow eyes. It took a step backwards, hissing and shielding its face with its arms, its eyes unaccustomed to the bright light of the torch. Jack took the opportunity to scramble back to his feet, the scaffolding still in his hands.

With its arms covering its face, Jack swung the bar as hard as he could into the body of the beast, which staggered backwards with the force of the blow. Jack raised the bar back above his shoulder, then swung again with all his might, shouting a scream of primal rage; as he made contact, the beast opened its mouth wide to utter an inhuman howl, briefly showing a horrifying collection of fangs in the torchlight. It took another couple of steps backwards, shrinking into the corner of the cavern, away from the light and the pain.

'Let's go!' shouted Jack urgently. Jennifer didn't need to be told twice. They both ran as fast as they could in the darkness, stumbling down the dark passageways and bouncing off the walls. They didn't stop to look behind them until they had reached the place where they had first entered the tunnels. Jennifer scrambled up the rungs first, rolling out of the shaft onto the floor of the church, closely followed by Jack. As soon as Jack was back in the church, Jennifer started closing the trapdoor as fast as she could. Jack joined her, pushing it down and then kneeling on all fours on the flagstone, using his weight to push it back into place with a heavy click. The seal was amazingly tight – once closed, apart from the disturbances in the dust on the floor, it was impossible to distinguish between the hidden trapdoor and any of the other flagstones.

'What the *fuck* was that!' he shouted, collapsing onto the floor, his muscles aching.

'I don't know, and I don't intend to hang around to find out,' replied Jennifer, panting with exhaustion. 'Let's get the hell out of here, in case there are any more around. Who knows what other exits there may be around here from those tunnels.' She picked herself up and walked back over to the altar, where her key was still poking out from the mosaic. She pulled it out and placed it over her head again, before they both headed back out to the chapel.

As they crawled back out through the window, Jack's phone gave a short double beep. He pulled it out and glanced at it as they walked briskly through the graveyard.

'I've got voice mail,' he explained, the light from the screen illuminating the darkness around them. He stopped walking, about to dial up for his messages.

'Now?' exclaimed Jennifer. 'Come on – I'm sure it can wait.' She grabbed him by the hand and pulled him along.

'Okay, okay,' he said, putting the phone back into his pocket. 'I'll do it later.' He unlocked the car remotely as they reached the gate at the back of the graveyard, and they climbed in. 'Let's get the hell out of here,' he said, turning the ignition, and driving away at speed, happy to put some ground between themselves and those tunnels.

It was late when they gave up driving, and pulled into a hotel just off the motorway. Jack hid the pistol under the spare tyre in the boot of the car, and they checked in for the night. They both staggered into their room exhausted and collapsed onto the cheap double bed.

While Jennifer was getting ready in the bathroom, Jack took the opportunity to check his voice mail. He dialled the number and listened as it connected. 'It's that historian – Ian Williams,' he called to Jennifer through the thin door. 'He says he wants to meet us – well, me, technically – at a restaurant in Oxford, the day after tomorrow.' He looked at his watch – it was past midnight. 'I suppose it's just tomorrow now.' He hung up and put the phone back in his coat pocket. 'I wonder what he's got to say?'

'I don't know,' said Jennifer, coming out of the bathroom, wearing just her underwear. 'Maybe he can shed some light on whatever the hell Robert was doing at that church – although I doubt it.'

'We don't even know for sure that he ever made it into those caves.'

'It would have to be quite a coincidence if he didn't. Something around there drove him mad, and I can think of at least a couple of possibilities down there that would fit the bill.'

❋ ❋ ❋

Jennifer awoke late the next morning to find Jack browsing on his phone, the pistol lying on the bed next to him.

'Do you not know what roaming data costs?' she said, chuckling. He gave her a stern look. 'What are you looking at?' she asked.

'Guns. Pistols to be exact. Or to be completely accurate, different military pistols from World War One.'

'Then that gun we found last night?'

'A Webley Mk IV revolver. Issued to officers in World War One. *British* officers, to be exact.'

'So Robert Knight *was* down there – or at least someone from his unit.'

'It's not exactly conclusive. But as circumstantial evidence goes, put together with what else we already know from his medical report... If you ask me, it's pretty convincing,' he said.

'And whatever happened to him down there – it drove him mad.'

'I think so. That letter he left me is starting to sound a bit more plausible. At the very least, I'm convinced that he believed it all.'

'So, the million dollar question,' she said, 'is whether what happened to him back then is related to what's happening to us now?'

'Yeah, that's the question all right,' he confirmed. 'And my guess would be *yes*.'

'So what now?'

'Another *very* good question. C'mon – help me pack and we can get the hell out of here and head back home. We can discuss what to do in the car.'

'What shall we do with the pistol?' she asked, as they were putting their bags into the boot of the car.

'I don't know. We can't really take it with us,' he replied. 'It's old, but as far as I'm aware, that doesn't make it any less illegal. And if it's illegal in England, it's probably illegal here too, for all I know. I don't really want to be arrested at the border for gun-smuggling.'

'Agreed,' she said. 'We should dump it. Somewhere safe, where no one will find it.'

They took a scenic route back towards the motorway. As they drove through the countryside between villages, Jack stopped the car on a deserted bridge over a wide river – the water was flowing fast and looked deep. He went to the back of the car and opened the boot, removing the pistol hidden within. He felt the heft of it, weighing it in his hand, then threw it over his shoulder. The pistol flew through the air, tumbling end over end, before hitting the water with a splash and disappearing without a trace. He walked back around and got back into the car. 'Let's go,' he said.

Chapter 15.

December 2nd, 2012. Oxford.

They set off mid-morning for their meeting with Ian Williams. Traffic was light en route to Oxford, and the sky was clear and bright for a change, although there was still a crisp wintry wind.

After reaching Oxford, Jack had to deal with the one-way system, driving round and round the streets for what felt like an eternity. Eventually though, he found a parking spot just a couple of streets from the restaurant. He reversed the car into the tight space and turned off the engine. Jennifer investigated the parking restrictions, while Jack emptied all his loose change into the ticket machine – enough for two hours of parking, the maximum allowed. He thought that ought to be plenty.

As he locked the car, Jack checked his watch – they were late, but not by much. He took Jennifer by the arm, and they both hurried down the narrow side streets towards the restaurant, frequently having to dodge students on their bicycles – even at this time of year, there were still plenty around. It didn't take long to reach the restaurant, a modest affair hidden away below street level, down a set of steps in the pavement; it was almost unnoticeable among the other buildings unless you were looking for it. Jack walked down the stairs and pushed the door open; as he stepped in, he was greeted with a blast of warm, sweet-smelling air. It took his eyes a moment to adjust to the light within. Compared with the street outside, the restaurant was poorly lit with just a few dim bulbs illuminated on the ceiling, and the small amount of light coming in through the subterranean windows did little to improve the situation. Patrons mainly sat in isolated booths, quietly chatting with each other. A few small candles were present on the tables where couples were sitting and eating.

A waitress dressed in a formal uniform appeared in front of them, walking out from behind a counter. She was young and slim, with mousey brown hair, blue eyes and freckles on her cheeks. Jack found her surprisingly attractive and guessed she might be a student at the University when not working here – probably quite a popular one. 'Good afternoon,' she said politely. 'Do you have a reservation?'

'Err, yes,' said Jack, momentarily flustered. 'Ian Williams – that is, we should be meeting Ian Williams here.' Even without looking at Jennifer, he knew that she would be giving him a disapproving glance.

The waitress picked up a clipboard from the counter next to her, and scanned through it. 'Ah yes,' she said. 'This way, please.' She turned and walked away from them, deeper into the restaurant. Jack and Jennifer looked at each other wordlessly and then followed her. The waitress led them round a corner and past several empty tables to a small booth in a rear corner, where a small man was sitting nursing a glass of port. He was wearing a shirt that was noticeably grubby around the collar and round, wire-framed glasses. His dark, greasy hair looked overdue for a cut, and he already sported a five o'clock shadow, despite it only being lunchtime.

'Ian Williams?' asked Jack.

'Mr Knight?' he replied, standing up and offering his hand to Jack. He looked up and down at Jennifer. Jack wasn't sure whether he was unsure about her, or checking her out. 'I was expecting you to come alone,' he said.

'My partner,' said Jack by way of explanation, as he shook his hand. 'I trust that's okay?'

'Well, I wasn't–' began Ian.

'Good,' interrupted Jack, cutting off his reply. He pulled out a chair for Jennifer to sit down, and then joined her.

'Here are the menus for you,' said the hostess, handing out a pair of leather-bound menus. Would you care for a drink first, or to see the wine list?'

'Just a black coffee for me, please,' said Jack, taking both the menus, and passing one to Jennifer.

'And for me,' she added.

Ian Williams looked at his glass of port, now half empty. 'I assume you will be picking up the tab, Mr Knight?' he asked.

'Err, yes?' replied Jack, taken aback by the frankness of the question.

'Another port for me then,' Ian requested of the hostess. She gave him a reproachful glance, and then turned and left.

'So, I understand you may be able to help me with investigating our family's military history,' began Jack.

'Maybe,' replied Ian. 'On the phone, you mentioned the *Shadow Watch.*'

'Yes,' replied Jack. 'We're trying to get information about my great-grandfather's time in the army. I've been told that he may have been part of a group called the *Shadow Watch*, but we're having a hard time finding any information about them.'

Ian took a sip of his port. 'I'm not surprised,' he said. 'The *Shadow Watch* is one of the most secretive groups I've come across in my time. It would appear to have been more of an informal ad hoc team than a true military unit, gathering servicemen together from different regiments as needed. It was a team that has always been officially denied, and with a very specific purpose.'

'And do you know what that purpose was?' asked Jennifer.

'Have you heard of the *Germanenorden*?' he asked. Jack and Jennifer both shook their heads. '*The Thule Society*?' Again, they shook their heads. Ian Williams sighed. 'They are German occult societies, founded early in the twentieth century. You are presumably aware from modern films and novels that Adolf Hitler was very interested in the occult?'

'I've heard mention of it, but I've not really—' began Jack.

'What most people don't realize,' said Ian Williams, cutting him off, 'is that the Nazis' interest in using the occult to further their agenda started much earlier than the Second World War – before the First World War, to be exact. They had...' He paused momentarily, as the waitress returned with their drinks, depositing them gently on the table.

'Would you care to order?' she asked, smiling at Jack.

'Err,' hesitated Jack, hastily picking up the menu and scanning through it. 'I'll have... a BLT sandwich, please.'

'Make that two,' said Jennifer, not bothering to look at the menu. She didn't really feel that hungry any more anyway.

'I'll have the steak – rare, with peppercorn sauce,' said Ian Williams.

The waitress made notes on a small pad of paper that she took from a top pocket. 'I'll get right on it,' she said, turning and walking away again.

'As I was saying,' resumed Ian Williams, 'the German army had a branch investigating the occult as a potential source of power and influence. Some would say they were actively involved in occult practices.'

'And the *Shadow Watch*?' asked Jack.

'I believe they were the British army's unofficial response to the Germans' occult research. They were sent in to stop their activities when they were discovered, as far-fetched as that may sound.' Jack and Jennifer looked at each other in silence, remembering what they had seen beneath that church in France.

'Actually, I don't have too much trouble believing it,' muttered Jack. Ian raised an eyebrow, surprised.

'And did the Germans ever find anything?' asked Jennifer. 'Did they ever succeed with their research?'

'Into the occult?' scoffed Ian Williams. 'Of course not – load of stuff and nonsense, obviously. It didn't stop them from spending decades researching it, though.'

'Then you've never found any evidence?' she said.

'Oh, there's plenty of evidence of the Nazis' involvement in the occult.'

'Sorry,' said Jennifer. 'I meant evidence of any actual occult activity, such as—'

'I, madam, am a serious historian,' said Ian Williams. Jack looked at him. He didn't know what a serious historian usually looked like, but Ian Williams wasn't the first thing that came to mind. 'I deal in *facts*,' he continued, 'not preposterous works of fiction.' Suitably embarrassed, Jack and Jennifer sat in silence for a minute or two, sipping their drinks.

'Is there anything else you can tell me about the *Shadow Watch*?' asked Jack eventually.

Ian Williams closed his eyes and thought hard for a moment, biting on his thumb. 'Not much. As I said before, they worked in secret; no records were kept, at least not any that I'm aware of. Most of what I've found is hearsay and conjecture.' So much for dealing only in facts, thought Jack to himself, but he bit his tongue. 'From what I've seen before,' continued Ian, 'most of their active time was spent in France and Germany. After the end of World War One, they were disbanded – as much as any organization that never truly existed *can* be disbanded, anyway.'

They drank again in silence for a few minutes, until they were interrupted by the waitress bringing their food. Jack and Jennifer nibbled on their sandwiches, while Ian Williams gobbled down his steak like a man who hadn't eaten a decent hot meal for a while. Jack considered his meal; despite the lack of ambience in the restaurant, the food tasted surprisingly good.

When they had finished, Jack stood to go. 'Thank you for your time,' he said to Ian. 'I'll pay for the food on the way out – and order you another port.' Ian had his mouth full, but raised his empty glass as if to say thanks.

As Jennifer gathered her things, Ian put his knife and fork down. 'Mr Knight?' he asked.

'Yes?'

'If there is a particular individual you are interested in, I could attempt to perform some deeper, personal research. See if I could find anything in particular relating to him?'

Jack glanced at Jennifer, who shrugged and nodded back at him. 'Why, yes, that would be great,' he said.

'I will have to charge you for my time, of course,' said Ian, 'and expenses.'

Jack looked at the remains of the steak on his plate and empty port glasses on the table. He wondered how many of those he would be paying for as *expenses*. 'Yes, that'll be fine, I'm sure,' he said. Ian Williams picked up his coat from the seat next to him and retrieved a notebook and pen from the inside pocket. He opened the notebook and turned to a new page.

'What can you tell me about him?'

'His name was Robert Knight. He grew up in London, moved to the West Country after the war. Born in 1875 and died in 1929,' Jack said. He thought for a moment. 'He was possibly in the Grenadier Guards, and we know he was hospitalized after the war – in Latchmere House in Surrey.'

Ian Williams nodded. 'I'm aware of it. What was he in for?'

'Shell shock,' said Jack. He didn't feel a need to share the specifics with him at this stage.

'I think that will be enough to be getting on with,' said Ian. He pulled out a shabby leather wallet from his trouser pocket, and extracted a business card, which he passed to Jack. 'In case you need to contact me. If I need any more information, I have your mobile. I assume that's the best number to contact you on?'

'Yes,' agreed Jack, reaching for his coat, 'and thank you for your time.'

* * *

'Well, now we know what Robert was doing beneath that church,' said Jennifer, as they walked back out into the cold sunshine.

'I'm still not quite sure I believe it – but yeah, I think we do,' said Jack. 'His unit was there to stop some kind of occult ritual being carried out by the Nazis.'

'And if what he saw down there drove him insane–'

'–Then, despite Ian Williams' protestations – maybe they succeeded at whatever they were trying to do...'

Chapter 16.

December 4th, 2012. Ash House, Dartmoor.

It was late at night, and Jack was sitting slumped on the sofa in the living room, Jennifer having already gone to bed. The only light in the room was from the television playing above the fireplace, its volume turned all the way down. He had spent the last two days searching the internet for any more information about Robert Knight or the Shadow Watch, without any success. He was exhausted and just starting to drift off to sleep, his eyelids growing heavy, when he heard something buzzing. He looked up and saw his phone on the table, vibrating. He had turned the volume off but it was still noisily rattling around on the hard wooden surface. He shook his head to wake himself up a bit, and groggily stepped over to the table. Who could be calling at this hour, he wondered? He picked up the phone – the number looked vaguely familiar – an Oxford number. He swiped the screen to accept the call.

'Yes?' he asked sleepily.

'Mr Knight, it's Ian Williams here.' It sounded at first like there was some argument going on in the background – then Jack realized it was just the sound of his television. He looked up at his own silent television; it was turned to the same channel.

'Oh, hi Ian – what's up?'

'I've been talking to a contact of mine, Pete, and I think we've found some information about your great-grandfather.'

'Great, what is it?'

'It might be easier to talk face to face. Can you meet tomorrow?'

Jack thought for a moment, mentally flicking through his diary. *Every* day was clear as far as he knew. 'Yeah, that should be fine.'

'Shall we say 2pm?'

'Works for me.'

'Okay, I'll see you then.' The line went dead as Ian hung up. Jack put the phone back on the table and plugged it in to charge. He looked at the time showing on the screen of his phone; it was just past eleven o'clock. 'Time to go to bed,' he thought. 'At least now we might have a new lead.'

The next morning the sun had already risen when Jack got up and came down to make some breakfast. Jennifer was still dozing in bed, dribbling into her pillow. He put on the kettle, put some bread in the toaster and then went to go and check his phone. He had a nagging feeling at the back of his mind as he unplugged the phone from where it was charging, and started to scan through all the emails he had received overnight. When he could hear the kettle boiling, he carried the phone back into the kitchen and poured himself a strong black coffee. While he sipped on it, he scrolled quickly through the rest of his inbox – nothing but spam and the usual marketing messages. He checked his watch. It had only just gone nine – they had a good few hours yet until they had to meet Ian – no need to wake Jennifer. As he put his coffee down on the worktop, he suddenly realized what had been bugging him. He knew he was meeting Ian at two o'clock, but he hadn't asked him where they were to meet. He selected the call from last night and quickly added Ian to his contacts before dialling his number. He stood up and walked over to the window, looking out over the grounds while the phone rang in one hand, his mug of coffee in the other. The phone had rung a few times and he was just about to hang up, when it was answered.

'Hello?' came an unfamiliar voice.

'Is that Ian Williams?' asked Jack politely, knowing full well that it wasn't.

'Who is this calling, please?' asked the voice on the other end; male, fairly old, with a strict quality – like a teacher questioning a pupil.

'Err...' muttered Jack, momentarily confused. 'This is Jack Knight,' said Jack. 'Who am I speaking with?'

'This is Detective Inspector Harvey,' said the voice. 'I'm afraid you won't be able to talk to Mr Williams. There was a break-in at his flat last night. He's in the hospital.'

Jack walked to the kitchen table, and sat down. He was feeling faint. 'Is he okay?' he asked. There was a pause on the other end of the line, probably as the detective decided whether or not to release that information.

'I'm afraid it's not looking good. He's in intensive care and on life support. He's not expected to live out the day. It's a miracle he's alive at all, to be honest.' There was another pause as neither party spoke. 'Can I ask what your relationship is with Mr Williams?'

'It was professional. He was performing some research for me.'

'I see. Can I ask the nature of the research, please sir?'

'Err...' hesitated Jack, considering what to say. 'Just some family history. Military history,' he clarified, taking another sip of his coffee.

'I see, sir. Well, I hope you didn't pay him a big deposit.' Jack almost choked on his coffee. He was shocked by the callousness of the statement, but he supposed if you spent your life dealing with death, then you had to grow detached from it. There was another pause. When Jack didn't say anything, the detective continued. 'It's unlikely, but if we need to contact you about Mr Williams, can we contact you on this number?'

'Err, yes. Can I ask – when did this happen?' said Jack.

'Early this morning, we think at about five. The neighbours were woken by a gunshot and called us.'

'I see.'

'Very well, sir,' said the detective. 'Oh – and my deepest condolences on your loss,' he added as an afterthought, before he hung up the phone. Jack put the phone down on the table and stared at it. This couldn't be a coincidence. Just then, Jennifer walked into the kitchen, wearing a dressing gown and with her hair in a state, a toothbrush sticking out of her mouth.

'Who was that on the phone?' she mumbled with a mouth full of toothpaste.

'Ian Williams,' said Jack in a daze, not looking at her.

'Oh, did he tell you anything of interest?' she managed to mumble, momentarily taking the toothbrush out of her mouth to speak before continuing her brushing.

'No. Sorry. It wasn't Ian. Ian's dead.'

'Dead?' she half choked on her toothbrush. She spat into the kitchen sink. 'What do you mean, dead?'

'Well, not actually dead, but he's expected to be shortly. He was attacked by a burglar last night. I was just talking to the police.'

'Oh, that's horrible!' she exclaimed, and sat down opposite him. They both sat in silence, looking at each other for a moment. 'Do you suppose–'

'How could I not!' he blurted. 'Two burglaries. Two deaths. We ask him to look into our history and two days later he's dead! I think we're quite a long way past coincidence here. Especially just after he'd found something out for us...'

'What?' she exclaimed.

'I spoke to him late last night. Said he'd found something of interest. Now we'll never know what...'

'Whoa, whoa, whoa,' she said, holding up her hands. 'Don't be so hasty. We could always...'

'What?' he asked.

'I don't know. But what if he'd found some crucial information for us?'

'Then what do you suggest?'

'I don't know. How about we just turn up at his place. See if someone's in his flat to let us in. The landlord. The police?'

'Like they're just going to let us wander in and search through an active crime scene.'

'Well, have *you* got any better suggestions?' He had to admit, he didn't. 'He's not that far away. Maybe we go visit him in hospital. Maybe if he's feeling better we could talk to him ourselves? Ask him for his keys?'

'I think that's a bit optimistic. The detective didn't make his outlook seem very good. It sounds like he's on death's door. He's not expected to survive long.'

'All the more reason to go right now.'

Chapter 17.

They set off towards Oxford as soon as they were ready. Jack drove, going as fast as he felt he could get away with down the motorway. Jennifer browsed on her phone for the major hospitals in Oxford, ringing each to see if Ian Williams had been admitted to them. She got a hit on her second try. 'He's in the John Radcliffe Hospital,' she said. 'Should be well signposted when we get nearer, although if he's in intensive care, we may not be able to visit him.'

They drove for a while without talking, stopping at a petrol station to refuel and pick up a *Get Well Soon* card. When they arrived at the hospital, they parked in the visitor parking and then walked round to the reception, passing a small group of smokers standing outside the front door. The inside of the hospital was bright and clean, with lots of glass and metal. Various people walked back and forth in front of them, patients and staff alike. Sat behind a desk was a middle-aged receptionist who greeted them and confirmed that Ian Williams was a patient in their intensive care unit – and still alive. Jack and Jennifer breathed a collective sigh of relief.

'Are you relatives?' she asked.

'No,' said Jack, pausing momentarily. 'Friends.'

'*Close* friends,' corrected Jennifer.

'We generally try to restrict visitors for intensive care patients to their immediate family,' said the receptionist.

'I understand,' said Jennifer. 'But we understand he may not make it through the night. It would mean an awful lot to us – and him – if we could see him before...' To Jack's surprise, Jennifer began to weep gently. 'We have been good friends for *such* a long time...'

The receptionist smiled compassionately. 'I'm sure it would be okay, if you're brief.'

Jennifer pulled out a handkerchief and dabbed at her eyes. 'Oh, thank you so much.'

The receptionist proceeded to give them brief instructions on how to get to the ward. 'I'll ring ahead, and let them know you're coming,' she added. They thanked the receptionist again, and walked off towards the lifts, Jack with his arm around Jennifer's shoulders to console her.

'Impressed?' asked Jennifer.

'Have you ever thought about a career in acting?' replied Jack.

They signed in at the ICU reception, and were shown to the ward where he was being monitored. The room was long and wide, with ten beds stationed on either side, each occupied by a patient. The room was almost silent apart from the background noise of hospital machinery, and the curtains at either end were half drawn, leaving the large room dimly lit. A nurse took them over to a bed at the far end of the room. In the bed was a man who they could only assume was Ian Williams; physically he was about the right size, but his head was wrapped heavily in bandages, obscuring his face. A ventilator was in his mouth, a drip in his arm. Various wires and sensors were attached to his body, the other ends connected to an ECG and other monitors. Jack thanked the nurse, and they both pulled up a plastic chair from under the window and sat down next to the bed.

'I don't think he's going to be telling us anything soon,' sighed Jack dejectedly.

'No,' agreed Jennifer.

They sat there for a moment in silence, before Jennifer took the card out of her handbag and held it in her hand. Next to the bed was a small unit containing a couple of drawers and a small cupboard. She moved over to the unit to place the card on top of it, and as she did so, she quietly pulled the drawer open slightly. Inside she could just make out various personal effects including, to her surprise, a set of keys on a key-ring. She sat back down next to Jack and opened her handbag. It didn't take her long to find what she wanted – her house keys. Still on the key-ring was an old front-door key, useless now that the locks had been changed.

'What are you doing?' whispered Jack.

'I'm going to swap his door key for one of ours,' said Jennifer quietly. 'Unless anyone actually tries to use it, no one will ever spot the difference. And I don't *think* Ian's ever likely to use it again.' Jack stared at her, his mouth open. 'Sorry!' she mouthed back at him silently. Working with her hands out of sight in her handbag, she twisted the old key off her key-ring and held it in the palm of her hand.

'Create a distraction, will you?' she asked him under her breath.

'What?' he frowned back at her in confusion.

'Distraction! Go!' she whispered urgently.

Somewhat flustered, Jack stood up and started walking back towards the door where they had come in. A couple of beds down, a trolley stood in the aisle. On top of it sat a tray containing several medical instruments. He walked towards the trolley and as he approached he stumbled, knocking into it, sending the tray falling to the floor. The metal tray made an almighty crash as it clattered onto the tiles, immediately grabbing everybody's attention in the quiet room. Scissors and forceps flew from it, scattering all over the floor.

'Oh my God, I'm so sorry!' called out Jack, his face turning red as he bent down and starting to pick the items up off the floor. The two nurses who had been attending to the ward came over, also bending down to help.

Jennifer seized the opportunity while everyone was looking at Jack. She reached into the drawer, removing the set of keys, and quickly twisted the door key off the key-ring, before adding her own and shutting the drawer again. She sat down in her chair and looked around. No one seemed to have noticed.

With Jack's help, the two nurses had collected all the items from the floor and put them back on the tray. 'I'll go get these cleaned and get a fresh set,' said one of the nurses to the other. She stared at Jack, annoyance obvious on her face.

'Once again, I'm so, so sorry,' apologized Jack. He walked back to Jennifer. 'I think we may have outstayed our welcome. Shall we go?'

'I think that may be a good idea,' she said, giving him a knowing nod. She picked up her handbag and the two of them walked out of the ward, Jack mumbling his apologies to the nurse as he passed, unable to look her in he eye.

Half an hour later, they were sitting in their car as the sun went down, parked down the road from Ian Williams' flat. Jack was holding Ian's business card with his address on it in one hand. He looked down the busy street towards the large concrete block of flats where he lived. It was located on a busy main street; two lanes of rush-hour traffic sped along it noisily.

'Are we ready to do this?' he asked.

'I think so,' replied Jennifer. 'I'm a bit nervous – I don't think I've ever committed B and E before.'

'Technically, I don't think it's *breaking* and entering if you have the key – although taking that was theft.' He paused and looked at Jennifer. 'I'm not sure which is worse?'

She shrugged back at him. 'Are we sure about this?'

'Whoever nearly killed Ian sure as hell wasn't a random burglar. They've already come for us once, and I'm not going to sit around waiting for them to come a second time. If there's any chance of preparing ourselves, we ought to take it.' He waited until there was a break in the cars speeding along the street, then opened his door, and climbed out of the car. Jennifer was waiting for him by the side of the road; together they walked to the front door of the block of flats.

Across the street sat a man in a black car who had been watching the flat. He picked up his phone and typed in a number. It rang twice before it was picked up.

'You'll never guess who's just turned up,' he said. 'It's *them* again...'

The front door to the block of flats was ajar, leading into a drab and dreary foyer. Jack and Jennifer both entered and took a quick glance around. There was an old wooden desk in the corner, where in more prosperous times a receptionist or security guard must have sat. Jack looked at the lift, which had an Out of Order sign hung from it.

'I guess it's the stairs then,' he groaned to Jennifer.

Together, Jack and Jennifer traipsed up two flights of stairs, before they arrived at the front door of Ian's flat – a grubby grey door halfway down the hallway. It didn't look like a great neighbourhood to them; the old brown wallpaper was peeling off the walls and the threadbare carpet showed signs of damp. Jack didn't need to check the address on Ian's business card to make sure he had the right room – there were multiple strands of black and yellow tape stretched across the door frame: *Crime Scene. Do Not Enter.*

'Oh well, in for a penny, in for a pound,' said Jack pulling out the key and slipping it carefully into the lock. He could feel his heart beating in his chest, and slid his forearm across his forehead to wipe away the sweat. He had never felt so nervous; he wondered how Jennifer was doing behind him. He turned the key in the lock, and the door swung open to reveal a dark hallway. He ducked down under the tape and stepped in, closely followed by Jennifer.

Before them, lay the hallway; there was a door on either side and one at the end, all open. It wasn't a large flat. Looking around they could see a small kitchen at the end of the corridor, a living room to the left and a bedroom to the right. On the hallway floor in front of them was a small pile of free newspapers and leaflets for local fast-food shops. A couple of coats hung from a peg on the wall, and an umbrella leant against a small table with a phone and answering machine on it. A dim red zero was visible on the machine; no messages. Jennifer quietly pushed the door behind her, opening and shutting the lock manually so as to minimize the noise. Jack moved to switch on the lights.

'No!' whispered Jennifer. 'We don't want to draw any attention.'

'Did you bring a torch?' asked Jack.

Jennifer paused. 'No.'

Jack took out his phone and turned it on. Even with just the lock screen showing, it lit up the hallway by a significant amount. A small amount of light was also coming in through the windows in the other rooms. 'This will have to do then,' he said.

They walked down the hallway. Jack peered through the door to the bedroom on his right and then stepped through the doorway on his left into the living room. There was a two-seater sofa in there, facing a small flat-screen television. A desk in the corner had a printer and monitor on it, but there was no computer visible – just various cables hanging down and resting on the floor, presumably where a computer used to be. Scattered on top of the desk were several books and papers. On the floor, just in front of Jack, there was a dark-red stain on the carpet, almost black in the dim light. This was presumably where the attack had happened. There was a fetid smell in the air.

'Watch where you step,' advised Jack quietly.

Jennifer took hold of his shoulders and peered around him. 'Ugh. Is that...?' she asked, already knowing the answer to her half-question. Just the thought of it was starting to make her feel a bit queasy. Maybe it was just the light, but she thought Jack didn't look much better.

'Yes,' replied Jack solemnly. 'That'll be where...' he trailed off.

'I'll look in the bedroom, if it's all the same to you,' she said, stepping back into the hallway and getting her own phone out of her pocket for illumination.

Jack stepped over the blood stain and started to look around some more. Next to the sofa was a small coffee table, upon which were dirty plates and cups, piled on top of magazines, sheets of paper and receipts. Even allowing for what had happened to Ian in here, the environment was squalid and depressing. Being a military historian obviously didn't pay well, he thought.

He went over to the desk and looked at the space underneath where it looked like a computer used to live. Presumably whoever had attacked Ian Williams had taken it with them – either because there might have been some valuable information on there, or just to make it more convincing as a burglary. *Oh well*, he thought, *I hope you made a backup of whatever it was you found.* He leafed through the papers on the desk. Some were printed, mostly from websites: discussions on various military units and battles, as far as he could see. There was nothing dating as far back as the First World War, nothing of any relevance to them. Other papers were handwritten, and nearly illegible. He looked through them for any trace of Robert Knight's name, or the *Shadow Watch*, but came up blank. He scanned around the rest of the room – there was nowhere to hide anything else in here. He stepped back out into the hallway, mindful of the blood on the floor as he passed.

He poked his head into the kitchen. It was pretty minimal; a small old white cooker and slightly more recent microwave were against one wall, flanked by cabinets. The door of one was askew, hanging slightly off its hinges. A small table was in the centre, two plain wooden chairs facing one another around it. The only things on the table were dirty plates and cutlery; the same could be said for the sink. He walked over to the cupboards and opened them, but found merely crockery and food. He tried the drawers next, but they only contained cutlery and kitchen utensils. He turned around to find Jennifer coming out of the bedroom.

'Anything?' he called quietly to her.

'Nothing I'd care to think about. He's got a large collection of books and magazines – but his tastes extend only from guns and tanks to strong pornography. There's an en suite bathroom as well, but...' She shivered, recalling what she had seen.

'I guess that's that then,' he said. After all the adrenaline and anticipation, he was starting to come down now, starting to feel quite gloomy. All the risks they had taken, and for nothing. 'If there was anything here, it's gone now.'

Jennifer nodded and turned towards the front door. Jack followed her down the hallway and then stopped suddenly.

'Wait a second,' he said, as Jennifer reached for the door.

'What is it?'

Jack turned to the small table upon which the phone and answering machine sat. The table had a shallow drawer, which he pulled open. He rummaged through the drawer, discarding several fast-food fliers, before he pulled out a small black book. He scanned through it quickly; it was Ian's contact book, containing phone numbers for all of his contacts. He held it up to show Jennifer.

'This might be useful,' he whispered, slipping the book into his trouser pocket.

'Are we done?' asked Jennifer, her hand on the door handle.

'I think so,' confirmed Jack, and Jennifer quietly opened the door. They ducked under the police tape again, quietly shutting the door behind them.

They had just started to make their way down the corridor towards the stairs when a gravelly voice called out from behind them. 'Stop right there, you two!'

'Shit,' cursed Jack under his breath. He turned around, expecting to see a policeman or security guard. Instead, a man dressed all in black stood before them; he wore black boots, black combat fatigues and a black coat, its hood pulled up over his head. In his hand he held an automatic pistol, which he had trained on them.

'No sudden moves, either of you,' he said.

'What do you want?' asked Jack, eyeing the gun in his hand.

'Our leader wants a word with you – and your wife.' He gesticulated towards Jennifer with the gun.

'Err... we're not actually married,' interjected Jennifer.

The man ignored her. 'He'd prefer you alive,' he continued. 'However, it's also been made quite clear that both of you ending up dead is an acceptable alternative – so let's take it nice and easy, shall we?' He took a couple of steps towards them, closing the distance. 'Down the stairs, slowly,' he instructed. Jack and Jennifer looked at each other, and then started down the stairs, walking two abreast. They could hear the man following close behind them as they went.

'Stop here,' instructed the man when they reached the lobby. Jack and Jennifer drew to a halt in the centre of the room. The man had hidden his gun in the pocket of his coat, but he was clearly still pointing it at them. 'I like this coat, so I'd hate to ruin it by putting a bullet hole through it,' he growled, 'but I will if I have to.' He stepped over to the front of the lobby and peered out through the glass front doors. 'We're heading for my car on the opposite side of the street,' he said. 'A black Audi. Let's go.'

Jack opened the door, holding it open for Jennifer and then following her through, with the armed man behind him. Evening was fully upon them now, the sky dark; if anything, the street was even busier than before with the rush-hour traffic. Jack looked at the traffic rushing by at a dangerous speed, and then glanced up and down the road. There was no crossing in sight.

'Why doesn't Jennifer go across first and get in the car?' he suggested. 'You can keep me hostage – she won't do anything stupid.'

'Jack!' she cried.

'Just do what he says and no one will get hurt,' replied Jack.

'You should listen to your husband,' said the man in black. Jennifer grimaced, but said nothing. 'Go – now!'

Jennifer stood by the side of the road, and waited for the traffic to lighten. When there was a suitable gap, she managed to run across to the centre of the road. There, she had to wait again for a gap. As she darted across to the far side, the man in black reached into his pocket and pressed a button on his car keys. The indicators on the car flashed, indicating that the car was now unlocked. Jennifer pulled the door handle to open the door and climbed into the back seat, turning to look back out of the window at Jack and the man holding him hostage.

'Our turn now,' barked the man, giving Jack a slight nudge. Jack hesitantly walked to the edge of the curb, and then squeezed between two parked cars to reach the edge of the traffic. 'There's a gap after these three lorries,' said the man, indicating a convoy of three articulated lorries that were coming down the road towards them. Jack waited patiently and then as the lorries approached, he sprinted into the road without warning.

In the car, Jennifer was searching for anything of interest, anything they could use. Then, with horror, she heard a loud howl of air brakes and the screech of tyres skidding along the tarmac, followed by an intense crash of shattering glass and metal.

Chapter 18.

A plan had formed in Jack's mind; it was reckless, but it might just work. He would have to be fast and his timing would have to be perfect. Without warning, he ran into the road, planning to get the lorries between himself and the armed man. Separated, and with the lorries for cover, they might have a chance to make a run for it and escape. He made it past the front lorry with only feet to spare.

He expected to hear the blast of a horn, behind him. What he actually heard was far, far worse; the sickening thump of the lorry hitting a body, followed by the squeal of brakes and tyres. Looking over his shoulder, he realized that the man in black had tried to follow him; his timing had not been as lucky. The lorry had hit him while going at least forty miles per hour. There had been no time for the driver to brake, or even sound his horn. Then, there was another almighty smash; as the driver of the first lorry had stepped on the brakes – too late for whoever the man had been, – the second lorry had gone into the back of him. Jack looked along the road briefly. A body dressed in black lay on the bonnet of a parked car, its windscreen shattered; the body wasn't moving, its limbs lying at odd angles like a rag doll. He had been thrown a good twenty feet along the street. The lorry was still coming to a standstill, considerably further along the road. There were already screams from pedestrians, many of them taking out phones – some to call the emergency services, others to take photos. The cars on the other side of the road were reducing their speed now, so they could see what was going on. Jack took advantage of the slowing traffic to dash across to the other side, his legs unsteady. He could feel his heart beating in his chest, adrenaline coursing through his veins. As he reached the black Audi, Jennifer opened the door, and stood up in front of him. She looked into his face, which was white with shock. He was shaking.

'Let's go!' she said to him, looking firmly into his eyes. 'Before anyone stops us to ask any questions.' She took his hand and led him away, walking briskly, not looking back and trying not to draw any attention. 'We'll return for our car later.'

They walked through several side streets, Jennifer squeezing his hand for reassurance as they manoeuvred through the steady stream of pedestrians walking the other way. Before long, they found somewhere where they could hide out – a local cafe. They entered, and sat down at a small table at the back of the shop, as far away from the street as they could find. When a waitress came to their table, they both ordered a black coffee and a bacon sandwich, although neither of them was particularly hungry. Jack would have preferred a stiff drink to calm his nerves, but the cafe wasn't licensed.

'Who do you think he was?' asked Jennifer quietly, as they sat sipping their coffee.

'I don't know,' said Jack, 'but he definitely wasn't the police. I'm assuming he was another of the group Robert warned us about, just like the man who died in our house.'

Jennifer looked up from her coffee. 'Do you think he was the one who killed Ian?'

'That would make sense,' said Jack. 'If he was, then I guess he got what was coming to him. It's just a shame we won't have a chance to find out much about him now – or his boss.' Jack took another sip of his coffee. 'At least we can be certain now that it wasn't a random burglar that killed Ian, and we can be pretty sure that whoever his boss is, the man in our house was working for him too. It's a pity that with his death our hope for any answers has died too.'

Jennifer thought for a second, chewing on her bacon sandwich. 'Don't be so sure,' she said, after swallowing. 'I've been thinking. What about his car? It may still be unlocked. Who knows what might be in it?'

Jack nodded in agreement again. 'We'll have to wait until it all dies down though. I don't want to head back there until everything is back to normal, in case a witness recognizes me. Either of us,' he corrected himself. 'And that's likely to take a few hours.'

'Oh well,' sighed Jennifer, and turned to the waitress who was walking past her. 'Can I have another black coffee please?'

From the cafe, they moved to a pub just around the corner, where they could stay late into the night without drawing any attention. They sat in the corner and drank coffee and soft drinks, chatting occasionally and eating bar snacks. They had been there for a couple of hours, listening to the jukebox and watching the football that was playing silently on the TV in the corner, when the match finished and the programme changed to the local news. The sound was turned off, but the subtitles were turned on. In the headline story, the newsreader silently explained that an armed man had been killed in a traffic accident earlier that day – they were appealing for witnesses, in partic-ular a middle-aged man and woman who had been seen with the victim just before the accident.

'If that's the extent of their description, I think we'll be okay,' Jennifer told Jack.

They left the pub shortly after midnight, when it was starting to empty and headed back to the scene of the accident. The street was quieter now, more tranquil. The road had been re-opened but the traffic was light – at this time of night, only occasional vehicles moved calmly along it. Various lines and marks had been spray-painted on the road, and on either side was a yellow sign. It read: 'POLICE – CAN YOU HELP? – ACCIDENT HERE', followed by a phone number.

Jack walked casually up to the black Audi, looking over his shoulder as he reached it; no one seemed to be following them, no one was watching. He tried the driver's door; it was still unlocked, and so he opened it and climbed in. He heard Jennifer open the boot as he looked through the compartments in the doors and in front of the gear stick – a pack of chewing gum, some tissues – nothing of interest. After that, he opened the glove box and started rummaging inside.

He heard the boot shutting, and then the passenger side door opened and Jennifer stepped in, sitting down in the passenger seat. 'Look what I've found,' she said. In her hands, she held a leather satchel. She undid the buckles and reached inside, pulling out a handful of handwritten papers and a black smart-phone. Jack took the phone and turned it on; fortunately, it wasn't locked. He opened the list of contacts and scrolled through. He stopped when he reached the entry labelled *Home* and looked at the number – he recognized it as Ian's landline.

'I think we've found our answer as to whether he was involved in Ian's attack,' he said. 'This is his phone.'

Jennifer was looking through the papers; there were handwritten notes scrawled all over them. 'These seem to be notes from some research he'd been doing,' she said. 'The handwriting's practically illegible, but I can't see anything here that has any relevance to us.'

Jack looked at the notes. 'Yeah – they're Ian's. I recognize the handwriting from some of the other papers in his flat. We'll take them with us.' He pulled on the door handle, opening the door and climbing out. 'Come on, let's go.' He slung the strap of the satchel over his shoulder, putting the phone into his jacket pocket. They walked quickly back down the street to their car and climbed inside. Jack put Ian's phone into the glove compartment before putting the keys into the ignition. He was about to start the car when he stopped and turned to face Jennifer.

'Look, these guys – whoever they are – they obviously mean business. They almost killed Ian in his house, and they know we're involved – and where we live.'

'What are you saying?'

'Do you think it's safe to go back home?'

Jennifer thought for a moment. 'Probably not,' she sighed. 'We're responsible for the deaths of two of them now. They don't strike me as the type to back down.'

'No,' agreed Jack. 'They're only likely to get more serious – deadly serious.'

'So, where do we go? Back to our old flat?'

'I'm not sure we can risk that either. They seem to know a lot more about us than we know about them. If they know we only just moved in – and I think it's safe to assume they do – then surely they must be able to find our previous address. For tonight, I suggest we check into a hotel. We can plan properly in the morning.' Jack started the engine and pulled out into the street. They drove back towards the motorway in silent contemplation, heading for the safety and anonymity of the nearest cheap hotel they could find.

Chapter 19.

Jack awoke the next morning to find Jennifer sitting on the foot of the bed, holding Ian's phone. 'Anything on there?' he asked.

'Not really. None of the emails or messages seem relevant to us.'

'What about contacts?'

'Yeah, there's a few on there.'

'Pass it here,' asked Jack. He had an idea. Taking the phone, he opened the contacts. 'What was that name he mentioned,' he muttered to himself. 'Paul? No – Pete.' He scrolled through the contacts, but there was no one called Pete or Peter in there. He cursed quietly, and then remembered that they also had Ian's contacts book from his flat. He got out of bed and fished it out of his trouser pocket. He flicked through it until he found an entry under W – someone called Peter White.

He glanced at his watch; it was just after nine, not too early to call. 'Let's give this a go,' he said to Jennifer. 'Ian told me he had been talking to someone called Pete – let's see if he'll speak to us directly.' He pulled up the keypad and typed the number in. The phone rang a few times, and then was picked up.

'Hello again, Ian,' came an old male voice. 'How are you doing?'

'Err... actually, this isn't Ian,' said Jack awkwardly. There was a brief pause at the other end of the line.

'Who is this, and why do you have Ian's phone?' the man on the other end asked. The voice sounded cold and suspicious.

'I'm afraid Ian has been in an accident – a bad accident. My name's Jack Knight. I'm a friend of his – well, not actually a friend; I'd hired him to do some work.' Jack stopped, realizing he'd been gabbling on, his nerves getting to him. He paused and took a breath. 'I'm sorry – let me start again. I'm Jack Knight. I believe Ian had talked to you about a relative of mine – Robert Knight. Does this make any sense to you?'

There was another pause. Then there came a single word from the other end of the line. 'Yes.'

'I'm sorry to contact you like this, but the information you have is very important to us. At least, I hope it is. I'm presuming you did find out something about Robert Knight, Ian said you had...'

Again, a single word from the other end. 'Yes.'

'Can we meet you? Discuss this face to face?' There was a longer pause where no one spoke.

'Okay,' eventually came the reply. Peter White didn't appear to be keen on long conversations.

'One other thing...' said Jack, looking up at Jennifer. He dropped his head, closing his eyes; he hoped this was a wise move. 'We've reason to believe your life may be in danger.'

'Danger? What do you mean?' asked Peter White. Jack couldn't tell whether it was suspicion or curiosity in his voice.

'It wasn't just some random accident that Ian got himself into. He was attacked – and we're fairly certain it was deliberate. We've been attacked too. It could just be coincidence, but well... we don't think so. We think it was the same group of people. If Ian was attacked for something he found out – something about Robert Knight – then you too could be in danger.'

Silence from the other end. Then he spoke again. 'How do I know I can trust *you*?'

Jack thought for a moment. 'If we were trying to kill you, would I have warned you that your life was in danger?'

Peter White was silent, obviously thinking. 'Okay, but let's meet somewhere public. Do you know the Imperial Square and Gardens in Cheltenham?'

'No,' replied Jack.

'Well... find it. I'll be on a bench there at noon. Look for a man with...' he paused. 'Oh hell, just look for a man in a red jacket. If you're not there by quarter past, I'm gone.' And with that, he hung up.

Jack looked at the phone in his hand. 'Get dressed,' he said. 'Hopefully it's time to find out what the hell is going on.'

Chapter 20.

Detective Inspector Cross was sitting at her desk in the headquarters of the Devon Major Crime Branch. It wasn't even mid-morning yet, but she was already tired; too many late nights were getting to her. She was working through some paperwork, writing up an investigation report on her computer, when she was interrupted by a sharp knock on her door. The door opened, and her colleague Detective Sergeant Dave Brooks poked his head through. He was a short and stocky man with a thin moustache.

'Inspector,' he said, leaning through the doorway.' Have you got a minute?'

She put down the sheet of paper she was holding. 'Sure, Dave, what's up?'

'Well, you know that death you were looking into in Dartmoor? The burglary that ended in the accidental death?'

'The one in that country house? Yeah, what about it?'

'Well, take a look at this.' He stepped into the room and passed her an A4 printout of a photograph. She pushed the computer keyboard back along the desk to clear some space and took hold of it.

'What am I looking at here?' she asked.

'This was taken by a CCTV camera just before an RTA in Swindon last night. This guy here–' he pointed to a face in the picture, '–he was the victim. But these two, standing in front of him – do they look at all familiar to you?'

Cross put the photograph down on the desk in front of her and looked at it closely. It was blurred and grainy, taken by a cheap camera and illuminated only by streetlights, but now she was looking closer, she thought that she *could* recognize them.

'It's the same couple, isn't it?' asked Sergeant Brooks.

'I couldn't be one hundred per cent sure,' said Cross, 'but if I had to put money on it? Yeah, I'd say it was.' She looked up at her colleague. 'What's the story behind this?'

'The vic was hit by an articulated lorry at 45 miles per hour while crossing the road in rush hour.' Cross winced. 'Yeah, it wasn't pretty. CCTV footage caught these two with him shortly before, but they didn't stick around. A loaded gun was found at the scene, hence the greater level of investigation than you'd normally expect from a road accident. We believe the gun belongs to the stiff, but we're awaiting official confirmation on the prints from the lab guys.'

'So it's not just one dead guy they're involved with but two.'

'There's more,' said Brooks. Cross raised an eyebrow out of curiosity. 'Where the accident took place,' he continued, 'always assuming it *was* an accident – it was right outside some flats where there was a murder just the night before. The victim was attacked in his flat, and died in hospital last night.'

'Okay. That might be something, but it *could* just be coincidence.'

'Except that I've just spoken to the Detective in charge of that case, D.I. Harvey over at Thames Valley C.I.D.'

'What did he have to say?'

'When he was at the crime scene yesterday, the flat where the murder had been committed – also believed to be a burglary gone wrong, by the way – he answered a call that came in on the dead man's landline. Guess who the caller identified themself as?'

'You're not trying to tell me it was Jack Knight?'

'Bingo!'

She let out a low breath. 'So that's *three* dead bodies. What the hell are they involved in? Do you think they had anything to do with the death in the flat?'

'It's unlikely they were directly responsible. If they were, why would they ring him the next morning? D.I. Harvey said that he seemed quite shocked when he told him – unless it was all an act.'

'Nah – I've met him. He's not that good an actor.'

'It's still possible they're an innocent party in all this, the target of some person or persons unknown. I just don't know why.'

'No one with that many corpses lying at their feet is entirely innocent. They're involved in something. I don't know whether it's drugs, blackmail or what, but I reckon they know more than they're telling us.' She stood up. 'Good work, Dave. I think it's time we had another little chat with those two.'

Chapter 21.

Jack managed to find the Imperial Square and Gardens by searching online; it was a small public gardened area next to the Cheltenham town hall. Jack put the address into his phone's GPS and they checked out of the hotel.

It was a trouble-free journey, and just over an hour later they parked in a street just around the corner from the town hall. Jack looked at his watch; they still had a few minutes before noon. He put Ian's phone back in the glove compartment of the car and they headed over towards the town hall. They found the gardens right behind it, a large open area, quiet and peaceful at this time of year. There were several large areas of grass containing flower beds, although many were currently empty. Paved paths lay between the gardens, with benches placed at regular intervals along them. As they approached the centre of the gardens, they could see a middle-aged man dressed in jeans and a red windbreaker sitting on a park bench, his back to a statue standing in the centre of a small fountain. The statue was standing with its arms outstretched, as if beckoning them forwards. The sun was shining brightly, and the man was wearing wrap-around sunglasses in the bright light, his hands in his jacket pockets. They approached cautiously.

'Peter White?' asked Jack as they drew near. The man stood up and removed his sunglasses. Jack guessed that he was probably around sixty, although he looked fit and healthy for his age. He had piercing grey eyes in the middle of a weather-worn face and grey hair in a crew cut. He extended a hand towards them.

'Jack Knight, I assume?' Jack nodded, and shook hands with the man, as did Jennifer. 'Let's walk as we talk,' he said, pleasantries having been exchanged.

'How did you know Ian?' asked Jennifer, breaking the ice.

'Our fathers served together in the Special Forces,' he replied. 'It's where he got his interest in the military.'

'And you?' asked Jennifer.

'Well, let's just say that I have had more than a *passing* interest in the military myself. And you two – what have you got yourselves caught up in?'

'Robert Knight was my great-grandfather,' replied Jack. 'He was part of some kind of secret special ops group back in World War One – something called the *Shadow Watch*.' Peter nodded. 'You've heard of them, then?' asked Jack.

'Rumours... nothing more,' said Peter, shrugging his shoulders.

'It would appear that he was involved in something near the end of the war,' continued Jack, 'something that drove him insane and very nearly killed him. We think it finally caught up with him a decade later, and now, it looks as if the same forces have returned to continue with us, for reasons we're only just beginning to understand.'

Peter raised an eyebrow. 'The sins of the father being visited on the children, eh? Or in your case, the great-grandchildren. But why not just go to the police?'

'I'm not sure they'd be able to help us,' said Jack.

'Or even believe us,' added Jennifer. 'I don't think you'd believe us if we told you.'

'You'd be surprised,' said Peter. 'I've seen some weird shit in my time.' Jack wondered whether he was ex-military himself; he had the right air and confidence about him.

'This is more than just weird,' said Jack. 'What happened back then with Robert, and what we now seem to be involved in – I know this is going to sound mad, but it seems to be related to the occult.' He smiled nervously. Peter stopped walking momentarily and looked at them. This is it, thought Jack – where he either laughs at us, or walks away. Instead, Peter hesitated, as if about to say something, and then changed his mind. He started walking again, beckoning Jack to continue with a wave of his hand.

'We also think time may be a factor,' continued Jack. 'There seemed to be an urgency behind the people who attacked Ian and us, and I've got a feeling this is all leading towards something that is going to happen soon. We can't afford to be locked up in jail – whether for our own safety or not.'

Peter stopped, and bent down to look at a bed of crocuses. When he stood up, he looked them both in the face. 'Let me guess. The stakes are high, the situation dire? And you two are the only ones who can stop it?'

'Something like that...' agreed Jack with a shrug. Jennifer nodded in agreement.

'How much do the police know about your activities?' he asked them.

'Well, I ended up killing the first one of them we met. The attackers, not the police,' she clarified. Peter smiled at her. 'They know all about that,' said Jennifer.

Jack thought for a second. 'And when I tried to ring Ian the morning after he was attacked, I spoke to another detective,' he added. 'Then we had a run-in with another of them last night – he ended up dying too.' Peter looked at him with a curious expression on his face. Jack wasn't sure, but thought he looked impressed. 'I'm not sure whether they know we had anything to do with that,' he concluded.

Peter nodded and reached into his inside jacket pocket. For a hideous second, Jack thought he was reaching for a gun. What he actually brought out was a mobile phone – an old-style Nokia model. 'The police will probably be looking for you before too long,' he said. 'I'd advise you to turn your phone off and remove the battery; otherwise they might track you with it. If you need to use it as a camera or browser, at least remove the SIM card – that would make it harder for them. This phone is clean, untraceable.' He held it out towards them.

'Thanks,' said Jack, taking the phone and slipping into his jacket pocket.

'This is what I found out about your great-grandfather,' he said, reaching into another pocket and removing a couple of sheets of folded paper. 'Here,' he said, holding them out to Jack, who took the sheets and opened them. The first was a photocopy of an outgoing passenger manifest for the *RMS Caronia* from Liverpool to Boston, dated the 10th November, 1929. Highlighted on the page with a yellow marker was a Robert Knight, his occupation listed as Army (Retired). 'I believe that's your great-grandfather,' said Peter. 'The date of birth is correct as far as I'm aware.' Jack looked at the paper again and nodded.

'Although I could find him listed as an outgoing passenger, I couldn't find him anywhere on a ship back to Britain again. That's when I found what's on the next sheet.' Jack swapped to the second sheet of paper. This one was again a photocopy; across the top it read *The Commonwealth of Massachusetts, Copy of Record of Death*. This was dated just a few days later, and the name at the top was Robert Knight.

Several phrases jumped out at Jack. 'What exactly do "death in abscentia" and "imminent peril" mean?' he asked.

'It means no body was ever found, but he was believed to have been involved in some life-or-death situation – typically a plane crash or boat sinking with no survivors, that kind of thing. Not the *RMS Caronia* though – that arrived fine.'

'You don't know what exactly what happened to him then?' asked Jack.

'No, I hadn't got that far yet. Just that he died shortly after he arrived in Boston. But in doing some background research, I did manage to dig up some other records. In late 1919, Robert Knight purchased a house in Dartmoor.'

'I know,' said Jack. 'Ash House – I inherited it recently. That's when this whole nightmare started happening to us.'

Peter nodded. 'Well, you may find this interesting then,' he said. He pulled another couple of sheets of paper from his pocket and handed the first to Jack. It was a larger piece of paper this time. Jack unfolded it, revealing blueprints for a house – Ash House, dated 1905. 'Those are the original blueprints for the house.'

'Okay...' said Jack.

'Now, here are the updated blueprints from 1929 when he had some extra work done, including putting the family crypt into the grounds.' He passed the second sheet to Jack. 'Notice anything interesting?'

Jack held the two sets of blueprints in his hands next to each other. Jennifer peered over his shoulder to look. 'The first one has a cellar,' she said, 'but it's gone in the later one.'

'Correct,' said Peter. 'It looks like there was originally a small cellar under the pantry, which was missing from the later blueprints.'

'Why would anyone remove it from the blueprints?' asked Jack.

'Maybe it was unstable or kept flooding, and they filled it in,' replied Peter. 'Or maybe, just maybe, it's still there, hidden away for all these years.'

Jack looked at Jennifer, a smile on his face, then again at the blueprints.

'This says November 1929. That's when he went to America, when he died. Do you know when exactly the work was carried out?'

'No.'

'So it could be either before or after he left?' asked Jennifer.

'I guess so.'

Jack folded the sheets of paper back up again and slipped them inside his jacket pocket. 'Well, thank you for getting all this for us – it sounds like it could be really useful.'

'Not at all. Glad I could help fight the good fight one more time,' he chuckled.

'And look – please be careful,' pleaded Jack. 'If whoever is behind this knows you gave this information to Ian or us, your life may be in danger too.'

'Oh, I wouldn't worry too much about me,' said Peter. 'I still know a few tricks. If anyone comes after me... well, they're in for quite a surprise.' And with that, he turned and walked into the midday sun, not looking back.

They walked back to their car in nervous silence, and climbed back inside. Jack pulled his keys from his pocket and slipped the car key into the ignition. He was just about to turn the key when they both heard an unfamiliar beep from somewhere in the car.

'What the fuck was that?' asked Jack, panic in his voice. The sound had rattled him. Too many Hollywood action movies brought images of car bombs into his mind, their car being engulfed in an enormous fireball.

'I think it was from in here,' said Jennifer, reaching for the glove box.

'Careful!' blurted Jack. 'It could be a bomb!'

Jennifer laughed. 'I know there may be people out to kill us, but now you're getting paranoid,' she said. 'Besides, whoever heard of anyone hiding a car-bomb in the glove compartment?'

'And you got your qualifications in bomb disposal from...?' asked Jack sarcastically.

'Oh for heaven's sake,' she said, 'get a grip man!' She pulled the latch to open the small door in front of her. Jack winced and closed his eyes. In front of her was a black phone, a small light flashing on it to indicate a new message.

'It's just Ian's phone,' she said. 'He's got a new message.' She picked it up and swiped the screen. 'It's just an insurance reminder,' she said. 'Nothing important.' She turned to look at Jack. 'So – is it time to head back home?' she asked.

'I reckon so. We need to know what's in that cellar. From what he said in his note, I don't think Robert was planning to return from America. I think he was expecting whatever happened to him over there.'

'And you think he deliberately hid the cellar before he left?' she asked.

'I'd put money on it. If he was expecting to die, then putting in a crypt makes some kind of sense – and we know he left something for us there. His son who inherited the house had never been there before. He wouldn't know there had ever been a cellar. I doubt it's been disturbed in all this time.'

'And you think he left something down there?'

'There's only one way to find out. There's just one problem – what if somebody is waiting there for us?'

'Well, we knew we'd have to go back sooner or later. We'll just have to be careful.'

'Talking of being careful, I think we ought to turn this phone off too,' said Peter, taking Ian's phone from Jennifer. 'It's evidence from a crime scene – we don't want anyone tracking its location.' He turned it off and put it back in the glove box. He hesitated, before taking it out again. Heeding the advice from Peter White, he took the back off and removed the battery. 'You never can be too careful,' he said.

Chapter 22.

Jack and Jennifer slowly walked across the field in the darkness. They had parked their car in a country lane about a mile from their house, and now they were trudging through the mud of a neighbouring field towards the wall at the rear of their property. From this direction, some light woods would provide cover as they neared the wall; their small orchard would help once on the other side.

They reached the wall with their boots covered in mud, but otherwise undisturbed. It was a cemented limestone wall, around five feet tall with rough stone blocks jutting out at irregular intervals. It was obviously built for privacy and to delineate the edge of the property, rather than to keep anyone out.

'This shouldn't be too hard,' said Jack. 'Here, after you!' He crouched down next to the wall, bending over so that Jennifer could use him as a step. She wiped the worst of the mud off her boots and then climbed up onto his back, before she effortlessly jumped up, pulling herself onto the top of the wall. She reached down and gave him a hand up, before jumping down onto the other side.

Their house was a couple of hundred feet in front of them, clearly visible beyond the trees. It appeared deserted; all the lights were out, everything quiet and still. Together, they crept towards the back of the house. Jack was suddenly very glad that he'd never had any motion-detecting floodlights installed. Together, they stepped onto the porch by the kitchen back door and Jack tried the door handle. Unsurprisingly, it was locked.

'Do you have a key?' he asked Jennifer.

'Sorry – front door only,' she said, grinning sheepishly.

'Damn it – me too,' he grimaced. 'Okay, you wait here. I'll slip in the front and then let you in.' He crept off around the corner of the house. As he approached the front, he stopped and cautiously peered round the edge. All was deserted. He couldn't see anyone, but he knew that didn't mean anything – there could still be someone there, lurking in the shadows.

Around the porch was a patch of gravel next to the drive. He carefully stepped through it, the quiet crunching of the stones impossibly loud to his ears in the silence of the night. As he reached the front door, he checked over his shoulder. It still appeared all clear. He slipped his key into the lock, turned it and slid through the doorway into the house, shutting it quietly behind him. He hurried to the rear door. The key was in the lock, and he opened the door to let Jennifer in. Inside, everything appeared grey in the pale light of the evening. Jack went over to the pantry, opening the door. They looked down at the floor, which was covered with large stone flagstones. The floor of the pantry was slightly higher than that of the kitchen.

'I reckon they've laid these flagstones on top of the previous floor,' Jack said to Jennifer. 'Wait here – I'll be right back.' He hurried off out of the door into the hallway. When he returned, he was carrying his toolbox in one hand. He laid it on the floor and knelt down next to it. Then he lifted the lid and rummaged through it, first removing a crowbar, which he laid on the floor next to the toolbox, followed by a hammer and chisel, which he held in his hands.

'Where do you reckon?' he asked.

Jennifer looked at the blueprints in the dim light. 'Dead centre, I reckon. Try that big stone, there.'

Jack shuffled over to the centre of the room. A large flagstone, approximately a metre across, sat in the centre of the floor. He placed the chisel over the cement surrounding it and brought the hammer down on it. In the silent house, the sound of it was unnaturally loud, echoing noisily in the small room.

'Can't you do that any quieter?' asked Jennifer.

'I don't see how,' said Jack. 'Let's just get it done quickly.'

The cement was old and dry, and cracked easily under the blows of the hammer. Jennifer went around after Jack pulling the broken chunks out from between the tiles. When they had finished, he put down the hammer and chisel and picked up the crowbar.

'Are you ready to see if there's anything under there?' he asked. Jennifer nodded back at him. He sunk the crowbar into the gap in front of him, and together they pushed down on it, edging the crowbar under the stone as they levered the large slab upwards. It rose without much difficultly, and together they slid it to the side. Underneath they could see a thin rim of stone and concrete around the outside of the hole. This had held the flagstone in place, while sunk into the centre was a wooden trapdoor, a round metal handle sitting in its centre. Jack took a deep breath and then grabbed the metal handle; it was cold and stiff, partially rusted after so many years. He lifted the handle, giving it a firm pull upwards. The hinges creaked, but the door rose up, revealing a set of stairs descending into darkness.

'After you,' offered Jennifer, holding out a torch for him. 'You should be okay to use this down there.'

Jack took the torch and stepped into the hole. The doorway was reasonably tight, but the stairs below were wider. He turned on the torch and descended, followed by Jennifer close behind him.

Chapter 23.

The cellar consisted of a single brick-lined room, about ten feet by twenty. Against the far wall was a wooden desk and chair, and against the side walls were bookcases containing dozens of old books and papers. It was cold down there, and dark, the only light coming from their torch.

'Some kind of study, do you reckon?' asked Jack.

Jennifer ran her hand along the line of books on one of the shelves, wiping dust from them. She didn't recognize any of the names; most were in foreign languages. 'I guess so,' she said. She picked a book at random from the shelf and opened it. She couldn't understand the words, but many pages contained woodcuts and illustrations, depicting strange shapes and symbols, demons and monsters. 'A secret study for researching the occult.'

Jack stepped over to the desk. On one side of it was an oil lamp, on the other a typewriter. In the centre lay a large leather-bound tome. The front of the book had two concentric circles engraved on it, as well as words, hand drawn in red ink: *Custodes Putei*. Jack picked up the book, wiping the dust from its cover, and flicked through the pages. They too were all in a foreign language; from the occasional word here and there, he guessed it might be Latin. Many of the pages were accompanied by sketches, such as maps and symbols, with the occasional drawing of some kind of creature or anatomical part.

'What do you make of it?' he asked Jennifer.

She sighed and shrugged. 'It's all Greek to me...'

'*Latin*,' he corrected, closing the book and returning it to the dust-free square on the desk where it had been. On the floor next to the desk sat an iron waste-paper bin showing clear signs of rust. Jack crouched down to look in it, but it contained nothing but ash – the remains of paper burnt away long ago. He was about to stand up when he noticed something lying on the floor behind the desk – a crumpled up piece of paper. He picked it up and stood up.

Jennifer stepped next to him. In front of her, next to the lamp was a book of matches. She picked them up and looked at them – they were from the Royal Castle Hotel in Dartmoor – not far from them. She thought about lighting the lamp, but looking at it realized it was empty. Any oil would have dried up and evaporated decades ago. She pocketed the matches instead.

'Found something?' she asked.

'I don't know,' said Jack. 'Maybe.' He unfolded the paper and laid it on the desk, flattening it out as best he could; the paper was brown and brittle, and he didn't want to destroy it. On the paper were scribbled several words in scratchy handwriting: *Adam Webber* and underneath that: *Fairhaven* and a date, *15th November, 1929.*

'Does this mean anything to you?' asked Jennifer.

'I'm not sure,' said Jack. 'Fairhaven – I think that's in Massachusetts, somewhere near Boston.' He got out the passenger manifest that Peter White had given him. The date was the 10th November. 'How long did it take to cross the Atlantic back then?' he asked Jennifer. 'About 4 or 5 days?'

'Maybe – sounds about right.'

'I'm guessing he had an appointment with this Mr Webber then.'

'One that quite possibly cost him his life.'

Jack pulled open the drawers in the desk and looked inside; one of them contained a small stone box engraved with the letters RK, just like the one they had found in Robert's crypt. Slowly, his hands shaking, Jack pulled it out and placed it on the desk.

'Go on then, open it,' encouraged Jennifer.

Jack carefully lifted the lid off. It was empty. 'What the...' he muttered. He had been sure that something would have been inside. He checked again, looking in the lid too, but it was definitely empty. He walked back over to the bookshelves and pulled down some of the papers that lay on them. They were mostly written in other languages; some he could recognize, such as French or Latin, others were completely foreign. Even the few that were written in English were barely comprehensible – some appeared to be some kind of hymn or poetry, others just a random arrangement of words, half of which he didn't understand. They looked to be hundreds of years old.

'These are probably some historian's wet dream,' he joked to Jennifer, 'but useless to us. I don't know any of these languages, and I'm a bit old to start learning now. Jennifer was also taking some of the books off the shelf, flicking through the pages to see if any notes had been left in between – but there was nothing.

'Is that it then?' she asked, when they had searched through all the contents of the bookshelves.

'I guess so,' he replied gloomily. 'I was hoping for more.'

'Well, at least you found that name and place. That might lead us to some more information.'

'Maybe... Is that our next stop then?' he asked.

'It's a bit of a long shot, but it's our only lead. We need to find out what happened to Robert in America. I want to know how he died.'

'Okay,' said Jennifer. 'Let's grab some bags and get out of here.'

They turned off their torch and climbed back out of the basement into the pantry. There, they closed the trapdoor, but left the flagstone sitting to the side. They closed the pantry door behind them and then quietly climbed the stairs back to their bedroom, where they found the bags they had used for their visit to France. They quickly and efficiently re-stocked them with clothes and toiletries. Jack packed anything else he thought might be useful: his laptop, phone chargers, a spare torch. As he stood in the master bedroom, he looked out over the grounds.

'Jenn – come take a look,' he called quietly. Jennifer shuffled over to stand by his side. 'Over there,' he said, pointing his finger in the direction he was looking. Parked down the road from their front gate was a black car. The windows were shaded, and in the darkness it was impossible to see if anyone was in it.

'Let's get going before they notice us,' she suggested, and Jack nodded in agreement. They crept quietly back downstairs, their bags slung over their shoulders. Standing in the kitchen, Jack looked around him.

'We haven't been here too long, but I've already grown quite fond of this place,' said Jack with a smile.

'Me too,' said Jennifer. 'Let me just grab something for the journey,' she said, stepping back out into the hall.

Jack opened the back door and stepped out into the night, taking a deep breath of the cold night air. The next thing he knew, he was falling backwards, a blow to his head knocking him to the floor. Above him stood a well-built man, dressed all in black. 'I've been looking for you...' he said.

Chapter 24.

November 9ᵗʰ, 1929. Dartmoor, England.

Robert Knight sat at his desk in the basement of Ash House. On the desk lying next to his typewriter was a first-class ticket to Boston, sailing from Liverpool the next day; he picked it up and put it safely into his jacket pocket.

He reached over and picked up a set of papers from the desk. The title at the top declared it to be his last will and testament. By the light of his oil lamp, he silently read through it. When he had finished, he put it down on the desk and then signed and dated the final sheet. Part of him hoped that this wouldn't be necessary, but he knew well enough what was coming. He slipped the sheets into an envelope bearing the name and address of his solicitor, before licking and placing a stamp in the corner. His affairs were now all in order in case things worked out as he expected. He placed the sealed letter in his jacket pocket alongside his ticket.

From a drawer in his desk he then removed two small stone boxes, the lids engraved with the initials 'RK'. He placed them on top of the desk, and then removed the lid from the first one and looked inside; within was a key on a chain. The second box contained two small white stone cubes sitting in a velvet cloth. He removed one of the cubes and held it in his hand. It was cold, and he felt like electricity raced through his fingers as he ran them over the glyphs carved into its six sides. He gently slipped it into his pocket and picked up the key and chain, placing it in the box with the other cube before replacing the lid on the empty box.

The typewriter on his desk still contained a sheet of paper that he had prepared earlier. He reached over and pulled out the sheet, reading through it again. He hoped he had remembered everything correctly this time; he decided it would have to do. This was a letter that would not be read for another eighty-four years. He stood up, folding the letter and slipping it under the velvet cloth in the open box.

Then, he walked over to his book shelf and scanned through the books until he found the one he was after. He took the large leather tome off the shelf and carried it over to the desk, placing it in the centre. He opened the book, skimming through it, as if to familiarize himself with the contents; then he gently closed it.

Finally, he went to his waste-bin and removed the sheets of typed paper that lay within – earlier aborted attempts to write the letter that now rested in the stone box. From his pocket, he removed a book of matches. He tore one from the packet and lit it, shielding the flame with his hands until it was burning steadily. Once it was fully alight, he held it to the corner of the sheets; when the flame had caught, he dropped them back into the bin to burn away, their light brightening the gloomy cellar, casting flickering shadows against the walls. He waited for the flames to fully consume the pages and then die down again, returning the basement to its previous murkiness, before he went to his desk lamp and turned that out too. In near darkness now, with the only light coming from the trapdoor in the ceiling, he placed the empty box back in the desk drawer and picked up the other, placing its lid gently back into place. He carried it in his hands, walking up the stairs into the pantry.

Around him on the floor lay several piles of flagstones, waiting for the builders to come and finish laying them in the morning. He shut the trapdoor and walked into the hallway. For the last time, he turned and looked up at the portrait hanging on the wall, where it would stay, looking over the house for many decades to come. The face looked down at him from up on the wall, and he could not help but smile back. Then, picking up his bag, he turned and walked out of the door. If he did ever return, he thought, it would not be for a long, long time.

Chapter 25.

December 7ᵗʰ, 2012. Dartmoor, England.

Jack lay on his back in the dirt behind the house. He was dazed, his head throbbing with pain, his vision blurred. Next to him lay his bag; above him stood the man who had hit him, grinning. He took a step forwards and then swung his leg, violently kicking him with a heavy boot. Jack managed to roll slightly, taking the brunt of the force on the side of his hip. He kicked again with the other foot, hitting Jack in the stomach and knocking the wind out of him. The man leant over and grabbed Jack by the collar, lifting his head off the floor.

'You've been sticking your nose where it doesn't belong,' he said, sneering into Jack's face.

'What... what do you want?' said Jack.

'Firstly, we want what Robert Knight left you,' growled the man.

'He left me this whole house,' replied Jack. 'You may have to be more specific.' Despite the pain in his head and his guts, his mind was starting to think more clearly now. It looked like the man wasn't aware of Jennifer's presence – he had to play for time, let her get help somehow.

'If you're gonna play the fool, this isn't gonna work out well for you,' threatened the man. 'In fact, it ain't gonna work out well for you either way, but

131

I can make it much more unpleasant if you don't play ball.' He let go of Jack with one hand to punch him in the stomach. Jack folded up, winded and unable to breathe. He felt like he was going to throw up. 'You've been poking your nose into our business too much for someone who claims he doesn't know what I'm talking about,' continued the attacker. 'You've got something that belongs to us.'

'Are you looking for this?' came a female voice from behind Jack. The man lifted his head up to see who had spoken. He just had time to see a pool cue swinging in a wide arc, before it made contact with the side of his head with a sickening crack. He fell to the side, collapsing on his back in the dirt next to Jack. Jennifer stepped over to look at him. His eyes had rolled up into his head. 'Oh shit!' she said. 'Not again.'

Jack rolled over onto his hands and knees, still wheezing, and crawled over to where the man lay. 'No,' he said. 'He's still alive.' He could see his chest rising and falling as he breathed. He looked up at Jennifer and the pool cue she was still holding. He could see it was cracked. 'That's quite a swing you've got there.'

She looked at the cracked cue as if in disbelief and then threw it to the floor. 'Just remember that if you ever think about cheating on me,' she said, leaning over and resting her hands on the front of her thighs, taking deep breaths of the cold night air. She stepped over to Jack and offered him a hand, which he accepted, pulling him back to his feet. 'Are you going to be okay?' she asked, concern in her voice.

'My head hurts like a bastard and my gut is killing me, but I don't think he broke anything.' He stood up and put his hand into his pocket where the man had kicked him. He pulled out the phone that Peter White had given them; the screen was smashed. 'I don't think this is going to be much use any more,' he said.

'Do you reckon there are any more of them about?' she asked him.

He looked around in the dark. 'Impossible to say.'

'Let's get out of here then,' she said.

'One moment.' Jack leant over the unconscious body, and started frisking him. His trouser pockets were empty. From his jacket pocket he withdrew a phone, small and plain. 'May come in handy,' he said, pocketing it. Then he stepped over to the back door, closing and locking it, taking the key with them this time.

'Are we just going to leave him there?' she asked.

Jack thought for a moment. 'I don't really want to draw any more attention to us,' he said. 'One body could be considered an accident. The police may consider three of them to be a bit of a habit. I'm sure one of his companions will be along to see where he is before long.'

'What if he needs urgent medical attention?' She looked at him again. 'Let's face it – that's quite likely.'

'Isn't it a bit late for that?'

'Oh, I'm sorry. Did you want me to politely ask him not to kill you?'

'Okay...' he conceded. 'We'll make an anonymous call once we get to the car. We can use this,' he said, holding out the phone he had taken from the man. He pressed a button to turn it on and scanned through it quickly. The contacts book was empty; all the call history was from an unavailable number. 'It's got no contacts in it,' he said. 'Not much use to us for anything else.'

Out of the corner of his eye, he saw a light moving in the distance. There was a car stopped by their front gate, its headlights on. Probably the car they had seen parked just down the road he thought. 'Come on. Grab your bag, let's go,' he said urgently.

Half an hour later, they arrived back at their car, tired and panting. They dumped their bags into the boot and climbed into the front. Jack got out the phone they had taken and was just about to call for an ambulance, when it rang in his hand. He was so surprised that he almost dropped it. He sat there looking at it, the phone continuing to ring. The screen simply listed the calling number as *Withheld*.

'Well... are you going to answer it?' asked Jennifer.

Jack pressed the green button to accept the call and then held it up to his ear. 'Hello?'

'Ah! Mr Knight, I presume.' It was a male voice that sounded old and well educated – almost old-fashioned.

Jack said nothing for a moment, and then simply replied, 'Yes.'

'I'm so glad we finally have a chance to talk. You may call me Silas. I'm sorry if some of my associates came across as a bit heavy-handed. They're quite goal-oriented, and ever so keen to impress.' There seemed to be a delay on the line; wherever he was calling from, it wasn't local.

'What is it you want?'

'You have something that belongs to us, Mr Knight. I want it returned. Give it to me and forget all about us. Stop your meddling, and maybe you can go back to living your lives as normal.'

Jack didn't have to think too long about it. He didn't know just how much of what Robert had told them in that letter was true, but he trusted this man and his associates far less. 'Whatever it is, I don't have it.'

'Now, now, don't be like that. I haven't even told you what it is yet.' His voice was charming and jovial. Jack could imagine him being a very persuasive and charismatic leader.

'Okay. What is it that you think I have?'

'That's where it gets a bit tricky,' said Silas, his voice as smooth as silk. 'You see, I don't know precisely. I just know that you have it.'

'Well then, how am I supposed to—'

'It will be something left to you by your great-grandfather, Robert — something you have only recently come into possession of. It will be old, an antique even when your great-grandfather owned it, and it will be quite unlike anything else you own, unlike anything you have ever seen. It will probably be inscribed with symbols or markings that are unfamiliar to you. I could go on, but I imagine that you already know what I am referring to.'

Jack thought immediately of the stone cube that was sitting in his pocket, the one from Robert's crypt. 'No,' he replied. 'I don't.' He was glad this was a phone call; he didn't think his poker face would have been up to the job. He was fairly certain, however, that if he did give it up to this man, they wouldn't be allowed to simply walk away; they had seen too much, they knew too much about them. No, he was certain he couldn't trust this man.

'I see,' said Silas, with a sigh. 'Well, if you're going to be like that, I fear you leave me no choice, Mr Knight. You see, we too have our own legacy, our own inheritance passed down to us over the generations. I know of the events leading up to this point... but I also know of that which has not yet come to pass. We know what you've been up to and you've been far too interested in our activities to be a purely innocent party. If you're not going to cooperate, then we'll just have to switch to Plan B. You can't be allowed to carry on with what you have and what you know. If you're not willing to acquiesce, then we will be forced to eliminate both you and your wife.' And with that, the line went dead.

'Well, fuck you too,' said Jack, and he threw the phone out of the window into a field. He turned to Jennifer. 'Let's get the hell out of here. I hear New England's lovely at this time of year.'

Chapter 26.

November 14th, 1929. Boston, Massachusetts, USA.

It was late in the afternoon as Robert Knight stepped off the walkway from the ship to the shore, feeling the sea breeze on his face, happy to feel solid ground beneath his feet again. The journey from Liverpool had taken several long days. He had never been one for ocean travel, and he was more than ready to adjust to terra firma again. He carried a large rucksack containing his belongings over his shoulder; he was travelling light, as he didn't expect to be around for long. If his suspicions proved correct, he wouldn't be making the return trip on the *RMS Caronia.*

There were butterflies in his stomach as he departed the bustling port, heading towards the town streets in search of the main bus terminal. He was full of fear for what was to happen, but also hope and anticipation – at long last, this could soon all be over. *Once more,* he thought to himself, *just one more time.*

Once he had found the bus terminal, he boarded the bus to New Bedford. The journey was slow and uncomfortable, crawling down the rough country roads, the bus lacking any heating suitable for keeping the cold out. When he arrived, it was just a short cab ride across the river to the small coastal town of Fairhaven, his final destination.

He asked the cab driver to drop him at the Tabitha Inn, which was renowned as the finest small hotel in the town, if not the state. It was a modest Elizabethan style building, built from brick and limestone, a sweeping drive leading up to its grand front door. The driver stopped the cab on the drive in front of the property, and Robert paid the man, giving him a generous tip. He walked up the steps and through the stained-glass door into the reception.

'Good evening, sir, how can I help you?' asked a young gentleman from behind an oak-panelled desk.

'I'd like a room please,' replied Robert.

'I see,' replied the receptionist. 'How long will you be staying with us?'

Robert thought for a moment; he wasn't sure exactly how long his business would take. 'I think just a couple of nights, but I may need to stay longer,' he said.

'Just yourself, sir?' Robert nodded. 'Very good, sir.' He rang a bell on the counter, and a bell-boy appeared from a doorway. The receptionist passed him a key. 'Would you show this gentleman to room twelve?'

In his room, Robert put his backpack down on the table in front of the window and started to open it. He still did not know his final destination, but he knew he was close; he could feel it. This time would be different, he told himself. This time he had a few more tricks up his sleeve. He had not been idle all those years since their last encounter; he had spent the time patiently learning their ways, learning their language, their methods and motives. Carefully, almost respectfully, he removed several objects from the suitcase and placed them gently on the desk. The first was a leather-bound tome, words of some ancient language inscribed on the cover. The next was a fountain pen and a few sheets of plain paper, which he placed neatly next to the book. Finally, he removed a wooden box, which he placed on the end of the desk. He undid the clasps, lifted the lid and looked inside; therein lay a small revolver wrapped in black cloth along with a box of ammunition. He closed the lid and locked the clasps again.

He sat down at the small desk and opened the tome, the old yellowing pages within written in a language that pre-dated most of recorded history.

He gently turned the pages until he found what he was looking for. Then he placed the sheet of paper in front of him, picked up the fountain pen and started to draw on the sheet, copying a diagram from the page in front of him. He closed his eyes, moving the pen slowly across the page, making strange lines and curves; as he drew, he spoke softly to himself, his tongue moving in strange patterns, reciting the same words over and over again in the ancient language. When he had finished, he put down his pen and stood up, admiring his work. He picked up the sheet and carried it over to the bed; as he caught sight of the paper out of the corner of his eye, the lines and curves seemed to slowly glide over the paper, tracing a strange hypnotic pattern, only stopping when he looked directly at it, like some type of optical illusion. He lifted his pillow and placed the sheet of paper underneath, before removing his shoes and lying down on the bed. He closed his eyes and relaxed, slowly drifting off into a deep, dream-filled sleep.

He awoke the next morning, the sunlight creeping in through the gaps in the curtains. He knew now where he had to go, what was required of him. It had been a long time coming, but his journey was nearly over now, and he would finally be able to fulfil his promise. He pulled out his wallet and removed an old worn photograph – the only reminder he still possessed from the love of his life. It had been many years since he had last seen her and held her in his arms, years since she was cruelly taken from him. It had been hard all this time without her by his side, but before the night was over, they would hopefully be together again at last.

He held the photograph in his hands, lying in the hotel room, staring at the ceiling for many minutes. When he had prepared himself mentally, he arose. He changed his clothes and repacked his backpack, leaving it neatly by the side of the bed. He took just two things from it with him – the revolver with its ammunition and a small square cube on a chain. He looked at his watch. It was time to get to the docks; he was going to need to charter a boat.

Chapter 27.

December 8ᵗʰ, 2012. Boston, USA.

The plane landed at Logan International Airport just after two in the afternoon. Jack and Jennifer disembarked from the plane, and joined the lengthy queues at passport control. They knew that the security and immigration checks these days could be extensive and they settled in for a long wait.

'What are we going to do when we get there?' Jack asked Jennifer as they were standing in line. 'We've only got the vaguest idea of where we need to be going.'

'The first thing to do is to find our hotel,' suggested Jennifer. 'I've booked us in to a nice little place in the centre of town.'

'And then?'

'I don't know. Take a tour, see the sights, and look for anything that suggests itself.'

'We know when Robert arrived here,' said Jack. 'We ought to try and find anything that happened in Fairhaven at that time. Maybe the local library will have some records from back then.'

Slowly, they reached the head of the line, and Jack presented his passport. The man scanned it and looked him up and down. 'Is your trip business or pleasure?' he asked.

'Pleasure,' said Jack, very much doubting it would be.

❋ ❋ ❋

They stepped off the bus in Fairhaven later that afternoon, just round the corner from their hotel. They checked in and brought their bags up to their room, before collapsing, exhausted, on their bed.

Jennifer reached for a pamphlet left on the table next to the bed – *Things to see and do in Fairhaven*. She opened it and started reading. 'There are a few places around here that could be of help to us,' she said to Jack. 'There's a library, which could have some information about anything that happened in 1929. There's a local newspaper, over the river in New Bedford. Also, an Office of Tourism, if all else fails.'

Jack opened the safe in the cupboard in their room and put their passports in there. He hesitated for a moment, before taking the small stone cube out of his pocket and putting it in there too.

'You're not going to keep it with you?' asked Jennifer, seeing him place the cube in the safe.

'We're purely on a fact-finding mission here,' said Jack. 'I'm not expecting anything out of the ordinary. I wouldn't want to lose it.'

Jennifer looked at her watch. 'Do you think we have any time to do anything this evening?' she asked Jack.

He closed and locked the safe and then checked his own watch. 'Probably not. What do you say we take a stroll, get the lay of the land and grab something to eat?'

'Sounds good,' said Jennifer. 'I'm starving.'

❋ ❋ ❋

They walked through the streets of Fairhaven as the sun dipped lower in the sky. The part of town they were in was called Oxford Village, although it had been nicknamed Poverty Point at some point in its history. It was an old settlement by American standards; many of the buildings they passed were over two hundred years old, although a large number had been replaced or rebuilt over the years. The houses that remained were large and set in spacious grounds. As they walked west, reaching the end of Oxford Street, they could see the large body of water that was Acushnet River. In the river they could make out several large islands; on one was a large radio tower, on another, further out, was a lighthouse. On the far side, they could see the lights of New Bedford. They walked back east again to Main Street, turning left and bearing north towards I95. After a short distance, they could see a large open area by the side of the road; a sign in front read *Riverside Cemetery*.

'Shall we?' asked Jack.

They strolled along the cemetery path in the dusk, as the sun started to dip below the horizon. They were looking for graves around a century old, hoping to find anything that could be relevant to their investigations. Jack was starting to give up hope, the light levels dropping in the twilight, when he caught a glimpse of a name on an old marble tombstone:

ADAM WEBBER 1879–1934.
NOT DEAD, BUT DREAMING.

'Is that him, do you think?' asked Jennifer.

'Impossible to say for sure,' said Jack. 'It could be...' He knelt down and took a closer look at the tombstone. 'That's an odd inscription,' he muttered to himself. 'Not dead, but dreaming...'

Jennifer nodded in agreement. 'Wouldn't you normally expect "Forever in our hearts", or "Rest in peace"?'

'Nothing about this whole affair is normal,' agreed Jack. 'I think our work here is done for the evening. It'll be too dark to see anything before long. C'mon, let's get back to the hotel and get some food and an early night – it might take a while to adjust to the new time zone.'

Chapter 28.

They awoke early the next morning, not yet fully adjusted to the local time, and were the first down to the restaurant for breakfast. They discussed their plans for the day while they ate, and decided to try the local library first. The waiter who served their coffee was very helpful, telling them where they could find the library – just a couple of blocks from the hotel.

Once they were ready, they wrapped up warmly to protect themselves from the cold wintry wind and set off on the short walk from their hotel to the library. It was an old building, dating back to before Robert's time. It stood out from the buildings around it, having being built in an unusual architectural style, complete with Romanesque arches, recessed entrances and cylindrical towers. They arrived just as the staff were unlocking the front door.

'Excuse me?' said Jennifer to the woman who was working behind the counter. She looked to be in at least her sixties, frail and grey-haired, a pair of tortoise-shell glasses hanging from a chain around her neck.

'Yes? How can I help you?' she replied.

'We were looking to try and track down someone who lived here in the 1920s. I was wondering if you could offer us any advice?'

'Why certainly,' said the librarian. 'There were censuses taken in the area both in 1920 and 1930. If the person was a resident at the time, their details should be present in the records.'

'Do you have the census records here?' asked Jack.

'Of course – they've all been digitized and archived,' she replied. 'You can search them from one of our computers.' She stepped out from behind the counter. 'Come – follow me.' She walked off through an arched doorway into another room, which contained non-fiction and reference items. Jack and Jennifer followed close behind her. Against the rear wall of the room, behind several stacks of shelves, was a bank of four computers, as well as a couple of microfiche readers. 'Please – take a seat,' she offered. She pressed a key on the keyboard of the first computer and the screen came to life. Taking the mouse, she clicked on one of the icons on the desktop and a window opened: *Online Census Search*. She carefully typed in a username and password and a search screen appeared. 'You can enter all the details you know here,' she said. 'If there are any matches, it will show them. If you have any problems, I'm afraid I may not be of much use, but there's a young assistant around here somewhere – he may be able to help.'

'I'm sure we'll be fine,' said Jennifer, smiling at her. 'Thank you very much for your assistance.'

Jack and Jennifer took seats at the computer as the librarian strolled slowly back towards the front desk. Jennifer sat in front of the computer and took control. From the choice of censuses, she selected 1920 and 1930, and entered the name 'Adam Webber'. There was a brief pause as it searched, and then a few seconds later it returned. There were just over a dozen records for 1920 Massachusetts but only one in Fairhaven. He was listed as an American citizen: white, thirty-five years old, able to read and write. There was also a street address where he had lived. 'Could well be our man,' she said to Jack. 'The age matches up with the date on the tombstone.' She looked at the screen to check the 1930 census. 'He still has the same address and details in the 1930 census.' She took a piece of paper and pen from her handbag and scribbled the address down on it. 'Should we go and take a look?' she asked Jack.

'I don't know. What are the chances that anything of interest's still there?' said Jack.

'Well, your house dated back that far, and it still contained items of interest,' she replied. 'I suppose it depends on whether or not the house remained in the family. Have you got any better ideas?'

'Not at the moment,' Jack agreed. 'Okay, let's go take a look.'

Chapter 29.

The house where Adam Webber had lived in the 1920s was about a fifteen minute walk away, over on the west side of the town. As they approached, they could see it was a white wooden house situated at the end of the street, overlooking the river. It was quite a large property, set back from the road and surrounded by a tall hedge. In the yard by the path to the front door was a *For Sale* sign. Jack and Jennifer walked down the path and up to the front door. Jack knocked on the door while Jennifer walked round and looked through a window.

'I don't think anyone's going to answer,' she called to Jack. Through the window she could see that the house was deserted. The living room was almost empty, containing mainly fittings and furniture without any sign of recent habitation.

'I guess no one lives here any more,' said Jack. 'Another dead end.'

'Don't be so defeatist,' said Jennifer. 'Let's look around – it can't do any harm.' She started walking round to the side of the house that faced the river.

'What if someone sees us?' hissed Jack.

Jennifer pointed to the For Sale sign. 'We just say we're looking to buy a property around here, and we're having a look around. Besides – look how quiet it is,' she said, sweeping her arm around to indicate the house's surroundings. The street was empty; it was a quiet residential cul-de-sac, with no traffic or pedestrians. 'Come on!'

They walked round to the garden at the rear of the house, which contained several tall oak trees and a large wooden shed in the corner of the grounds. Against the back of the house was a covered porch encompassing the back door, and further along, a pair of cellar doors. Jack went over to the cellar doors and pulled on them, but they were locked. Jennifer went up onto the porch and knelt down, searching on her hands and knees.

'What are you looking for?' asked Jack quietly.

'A spare key,' replied Jennifer, lifting up the doormat to look underneath. She stood up and started feeling around the tops of the doors and windows, before reaching up into the beams of the porch roof.

'Any luck?'

Jennifer brought her hands back down again. They were covered in dust and cobwebs. She looked at them in disgust, wiping them on her jeans. 'No,' she said. 'Nothing.' She looked around. She could see no movement in neighbouring properties; everything was quiet and peaceful on the street. 'We could break a window and get in that way,' she suggested.

'I've got a better idea,' said Jack. 'Maybe one that won't get us arrested. Why don't we go see the estate agent – see if we can get ourselves a guided tour?'

Together, they walked back round to the front of the house, starting the journey back into town. As they walked back up the path to the road, a man stepped in front of them from behind the hedge. He was tall and well built, in his forties, with short black hair. He didn't look happy to see them. Jack and Jennifer could see that there was a car parked in front of the house that wasn't there before.

'What are you doing?' he asked in a thick American accent.

'Err,' hesitated Jack. 'We were walking past and we saw the For Sale sign. We're thinking of buying a property around here – thought we'd have a look around the grounds before we bothered the estate agent...' The man looked quizzically at them.

'Realtor,' translated Jennifer.

'Anyway...' said Jack. 'It looks nice – we were just on our way to see the realtor now.' He looked at the *For Sale* sign. 'Did you make a note of the number, honey?' he asked Jennifer.

'Already done,' she said. The man was still standing there, looking at them silently. He didn't look convinced.

'So...' continued Jack. He took a step towards the man, who didn't move. 'Nice to meet you. I'm Jack, this is Jennifer. You never know, we may end up being neighbours.' He held out his hand to the man. For a moment, the man did nothing. Then he took Jack's hand and gave it a firm, almost aggressive shake, grunting something unintelligible as he did. 'Let's go, honey,' said Jack, taking Jennifer by the arm and walking off. 'Don't look back,' he urged Jennifer in a whisper out of the side of his mouth. 'Just keep walking.'

When they had rounded the corner, Jack turned to Jennifer as they walked.

'Did you see his hand?'

'No?'

'He had a tattoo on the palm – a tattoo of a six-pointed star. That's *definitely* not a coincidence.'

Back in the town's main street, they found the offices of Fairhaven Real Estate without any difficulty. There were pictures of dozens of properties in the window, although Jack couldn't see the one they had just been at. Looking through the window, they could see several salesmen sitting at desks throughout the office, talking with prospective clients. Jennifer opened the door and they both stepped inside. A middle-aged man dressed in a sharp suit approached them from the rear of the office, a wide smile across his face.

'Well, hello there – how can I help you?' he asked.

'We saw a property over on the west side of town that's for sale,' said Jack. 'We wondered if you could tell us something about it?' He gave him the address.

'Why, sure!' said the man. 'Let me introduce myself – I'm Richard Cousins.' He held out his hand, which Jack and Jennifer shook. He had a firm strong handshake, the grip of a serious salesman. 'Take a seat. I'll just go get the details,' he said, indicating his desk to them. Jack and Jennifer obliged by sitting down at it. The desk was clean and tidy, with just a computer and a small pile of paper in an in-tray. 'Would you like a coffee?' he called from across the room, as he pulled open the top drawer of a filing cabinet and started looking through it.

Jack looked at Jennifer, who shook her head. 'No thanks!' he called back.

Richard Cousins returned, sitting down at his desk and laying two sheets of paper on the desk in front of him for Jack and Jennifer to look at. 'Very nice choice,' he said. 'Four bedrooms, two bathrooms and large spacious reception rooms. It's been well looked after,' he added. 'It's been in the same family for four generations.' Jack and Jennifer looked at each other, exchanging knowing glances.

'How much are you asking?' asked Jennifer, trying to play her part.

'Four hundred and fifteen thousand,' he replied.

'And is that open for discussion?'

'Sure, sure – there's always room for some negotiation,' he said, smiling a broad grin. He leaned forwards towards them. 'You're not from around here, are you?' he whispered conspiratorially.

'No,' laughed Jack. 'We're from England.'

'Ah – I thought so,' said the salesman. 'It's the accent, you see.'

'Several of my ancestors used to live over here,' explained Jack. 'We've come into some money, and we're considering emigrating ourselves.'

'Well, you couldn't pick a nicer place to move to. Say, do you want me to show you around the house?'

They agreed eagerly, and the salesman took them out to the street to where his large black SUV was parked. Jack and Jennifer got into the rear of the truck, and Richard drove them back over to the house. Now that they weren't on foot, it only took a couple of minutes before they were parked in front of the house. Jack and Jennifer both noticed that the car from before was no longer there.

Richard Cousins unlocked the front door of the house and stepped inside. Jack came in behind Jennifer and quietly closed the door behind them. The inside of the house was cold and quiet. The realtor took them through the different rooms, showing them the sights and describing the details of the property. They started in the kitchen, which was clean and empty: a large room, with a range cooker at one end and a large dining table at the other. Besides the furniture and cooker, there was very little here, all the small appliances having been removed.

From the kitchen, they went back into the hallway, and from there stepped into the living room. There were just a couple of old photos on the wall and a few large items of furniture – a couple of sofas and two small tables. There were no electronics – no televisions, radios or computers.

They proceeded up the stairs to the first floor, passing various photos on the wall as they went. The bedrooms upstairs were the same, containing only basic items of furniture. All the cupboards and dressers were bare.

As they walked back down the stairs, Jack stopped to look at the photos they had passed on the way up, one of the few personal touches still remaining. They covered several generations, from portraits that looked like they came from the seventies, dating all the way back to old sepia-tone photographs.

'Can you distract him for a moment?' whispered Jack to Jennifer.

'What are you going to do?'

'Just give me a minute.'

Jennifer walked down to the realtor who was waiting for them in the hallway. 'Does this place have a basement?' she asked him.

'Why sure, there's a wine cellar. Why don't I show you, the door's just over here.'

'So, why are the previous occupants selling?' she asked, as he led her out of the hallway and into the kitchen.

'They're emigrating,' he replied. 'Selling off all their assets and moving abroad...'

With the realtor gone, Jack took the oldest-looking photo off the wall and looked at it. It showed a couple, dressed in formal attire, a serious look on their faces. Jack turned the photo around and removed the back of the frame. On the rear of the photograph, someone had written the names 'Lucy and Rupert' in a faded blue pen, as well as the date: June 1926.

Jack put the first photo back on the wall and pulled off the next. It was a sepia-tone photograph showing two men in thick rain coats, standing in front of a lighthouse. The lighthouse stood next to what looked like a house near the edge of a cliff; even from that single image, frozen in time, he could tell that the wind and rain from the ocean must have been savage. He pulled the back off the photo frame. Written in spidery handwriting on the back of the photo was 'John and Adam, 1928.' Jack pulled the photo out of the frame, and slipped it into his jacket pocket, before putting the empty frame back on the wall. He stepped back to look at it and then took the time to ensure it was straight. He hurried out into the kitchen where Jennifer and the realtor were talking.

'So, what do you think?' asked Richard as Jack joined them.

'It's good, but I'm not a hundred per cent sure,' said Jack. He turned to face Jennifer. 'I think we need to have a chat and discuss it, honey? Plus we've got those other properties to look at.'

'Sure – I understand,' Richard replied. 'Would you like a ride back anywhere?'

Jack looked at Jennifer. 'No – I think we're okay to walk. It's not far, and it'll give us a chance to discuss the house.'

Richard led them back around to the front of the house and pulled out a business card, which he passed to Jack. 'Any questions, day or night, just give me a call!'

'Will do,' agreed Jack. They watched as he got into his SUV and turned around, driving back to town. Once he was out of sight, Jack turned to Jennifer. 'Did you find anything of interest in the basement?'

She shrugged. 'No, just some empty wine racks.'

Jack pulled the photograph from his pocket. 'Look what I found.'

Jennifer looked at it and then at the names on the back. 'One of these is presumably Adam Webber then?'

'That's my guess. I wonder where that lighthouse is?'

* * *

They hurried back to the library, where they found the same librarian behind the counter again.

'Oh, hello again,' she said. 'Anything else I can help you with?'

'Yes,' said Jack. 'We're trying to find the lighthouse shown in this picture.' He showed the woman the photograph. 'We were wondering if you could help?'

'Possibly,' she said. 'We should have some books about lighthouses; maybe you could find something in there. Would that help?'

'Yes – that would be great,' said Jack. The woman led them to a group of tables where they could sit, and then went off to see what reference books she could find.

'Do you think they'll have anything?' Jennifer asked Jack.

'I don't know. What are the odds of someone having photographed this lighthouse? It's worth a try I suppose.'

The librarian returned a few minutes later, her arms loaded with books, which she gently placed on the table. 'Here are the lighthouse reference books we have,' she said. She started passing them to Jack and Jennifer. 'We've got *The Ultimate Book of Lighthouses, Lighthouses of North America, Lighthouse Encyclopaedia: The Definitive Reference, Stories of U.S. Lighthouse Keepers, The Lighthouse Handbook – New England* and *United States Lighthouses – an Illustrated Map and Guide*. There are more, but we'd have to order them in.'

'Err... no. I think these will be fine,' said Jack, flabbergasted.

'Who knew lighthouses were so popular!' whispered Jennifer, as the librarian left them and returned to the front desk. They divided the books between them and started scanning through their respective piles.

'Look!' exclaimed Jack, about fifteen minutes and two books later. Various patrons of the library lifted their heads, disapproving of the sudden loud outburst. He was sure he heard an audible tut from one of them. 'Look,' he repeated, whispering this time. He was looking at *The Lighthouse Handbook – New England.* On the page in front of him was a picture of a lighthouse. It was from a different angle, but still clearly the same building. The text under the picture read 'Cuttyhunk Light, 1891–1929.' He read the accompanying text. 'It's on Cuttyhunk Island, Massachusetts. That can't be too far from here.' He read on and then frowned. 'It was destroyed by a hurricane in 1929. Surely that's not a coincidence?'

'Does it say when in 1929?'

'No. But we should go take a look.'

'If it was destroyed, there may not be anything there any more,' said Jennifer. 'But I suppose there could be remains. Or a new lighthouse built on top of the old one, maybe?'

'Possibly. But first I want to see what's up with this hurricane.' He picked up the books and carried them back to the librarian at the front desk.

'Any luck tracking down that lighthouse?' she asked them.

'Why yes, thank you,' replied Jennifer. 'We think it's on Cuttyhunk Island. I don't suppose you know where that is, do you?'

'Oh yes – it's over across the bay,' replied the librarian. 'Quite a small little place. Head due south from here, and it's the last land you'll hit before you reach the Atlantic.'

'We understand there was a hurricane around here in 1929?' asked Jack. 'Do you know anything about it?'

'Yes, that sounds about right,' said the librarian. 'We have a few of them around here, being so close to the North Atlantic. If memory serves, it was a reasonably bad one, but far from the worst we've ever had. Would you be after some information about that too?'

'If you've got any, that would be great,' said Jennifer.

'Well, we have the local newspaper archives from the time on microfiche. They will almost certainly have lots of information in them. The microfiche readers are–'

'–back over where they computers were – yes, I saw them,' said Robert.

'Do you know how to operate the machines?' she asked.

'I believe so, yes,' he said. 'I've used several before for my research. I'm a journalist,' he added, by way of explanation. Jack and Jennifer went back to sit by the computers, while the librarian went off to find the newspaper archives. She returned a few minutes later carrying a folder in her hands.

'These should have the papers from 1929,' she told them. Jack and Jennifer divided the records between them and started to work their way through the newspapers, looking for details of the hurricane.

'Come look at this,' said Jennifer, after they had both been searching for about twenty minutes. Jack came and looked at the newspaper on the screen in front of her. The headline read:

HURRICANE STRIKES FAIRHAVEN
FIVE DEAD – ANOTHER FOUR MISSING

Underneath that, lower on the page, was another headline:

BODY OF MISSING GIRL WASHED UP IN STORM

'It looks like there was indeed a massive hurricane on November 15th, 1929,' she said, scanning through the text.

'That's just after Robert arrived,' said Jack.

Jennifer nodded. 'It says here it was a freak storm – unexpected. It came in from the ocean, across Buzzards Bay, and caught a lot of people out. I guess their meteorology wasn't as hot back then.' She continued reading. 'As well as all the usual damage, they also found the body of a girl, Mary Reed, who had been missing for a week. She had been washed up on the coast.'

'Does it say there how she died?' asked Jack.

'No,' replied Jennifer, 'just that there was going to be an autopsy.'

Jack had a thought. 'You continue looking through the papers – I've had an idea – let me have a quick search online.' He turned and started typing at the computer next to him. Jennifer had just found another article in the newspaper archives when he called out to her. 'Jenn – have a look at this!' She turned to see what he had found. According to the report in front of him, the lighthouse keeper from 1926 to 1929 was a man called Adam Webber, surely the man in the photograph, the man Robert had come here to see.

'Have a look what I've found,' added Jennifer. She showed Jack another newspaper article about the 1929 hurricane, listing the dead and missing. Included in the list of missing people was Robert Knight, listed as a tourist.

'Well, I guess we've uncovered what happened to Robert,' said Jack. 'Apparently he chartered a boat that morning to go out to the Elizabeth Islands.'

'Is one of those– '

'–Cuttyhunk Island, yes. The remains of his boat were found washed up on the island's shore after the storm. His body was never found. I guess that would explain the death certificate that Peter White gave us.'

'It explains the lack of a body in the crypt too,' said Jennifer. 'Hey! He actually did die at sea.'

Jack gave her a wry smile. 'It doesn't help explain what he was doing out here, and what his business was with Adam Webber – but it can't be coincidence that Jack died in the same hurricane that destroyed the lighthouse where Adam Webber worked. Both at Cuttyhunk Island.'

'What we don't know,' said Jennifer, 'is whether that missing girl – Mary Reed – was mixed up in all of this. Excuse me, are there any other public records for the 1920s?' Jennifer asked the assistant, as she walked past, her arms full of books.

'Well...' said the assistant, pausing to put the books on a table. 'There would be records of births and deaths, marriages and divorces – you could find those at the town hall. Let me see, what else... Oh yes, property ownership and adoptions. I think we may have records of those here, if you would like to see those?'

'Whereabouts would we find the town hall?' asked Jack

'Oh, it's just across the road,' she replied, gesticulating back towards to the front door. 'You can't miss it.'

✳ ✳ ✳

Fairhaven town hall was a large Victorian Gothic building, dating back to the nineteenth century. Inside, they talked to the town clerk, who eyed them with some suspicion when they asked for Mary Reed's death certificate. Jack paid him the required fee, and explained that he was a journalist doing background for a story about the 1929 hurricane, showing him his journalist's ID. The clerk mumbled something about foreigners, but dutifully went off to go and find the document. He returned ten minutes later with a single sheet of paper – a photocopy of the certificate. They took the paper, thanking him, and then went outside, to sit on a bench and examine it.

Jack and Jennifer read through the certificate in silence, sitting in the afternoon sun. Although Mary Reed had been washed up by the hurricane, she hadn't drowned. The cause of death was listed as a single knife wound to the heart.

'It sounds like murder to me,' said Jennifer.

'A single knife wound to the heart,' said Jack. 'Does that sound at all–' He tried to think of the right word, '–*sacrificial* to you?'

'Not conclusively, but yes, it does have occult overtones, doesn't it,' she concurred. 'It says she probably died the day before she was found. Presumably the storm washed her body away from where she was murdered.'

They walked back to the front desk of the library, where they met the librarian one last time.

'You mentioned Cuttyhunk Island before,' said Jack to the old woman. 'Do you know how we'd get over to it?'

'Oh, there's a ferry from over the river in New Bedford,' she replied. She looked at her watch. 'There are a couple of ferries each way every day, but I think you've missed the last one today – you may need to wait until the morning.' She walked over to a rack of assorted tourist brochures in the window, picking up a small paper pamphlet. 'Here, have a brochure,' she offered, handing it to them with a smile. 'It's got the times, prices and a small map of the island in it.'

'Thank you again,' said Jack, taking the brochure.

'No problem,' said the librarian. 'I'd wrap up warm if I were you – the wind out there's a killer at this time of year.'

<h1 style="text-align:center">Chapter 30.</h1>

Later that night, a group of half a dozen men strode purposefully down to the shoreline by the side of the river. The long brown robes they wore were covering them from head to foot, obscuring their faces and brushing through the long wet grass as they walked. As they arrived at the water's edge, one man – their leader – stepped out to stand in the water in front of the others, the river gently lapping over the soles of his shoes.

'The time is nearly upon us,' said the man. He spoke in an educated British accent. 'We will need to leave shortly if we are to arrive for the final ceremony in time. But before we go, we have a loose end to tie up. It would appear that we have some unwanted visitors that need to be taken care of. Gentlemen, if you will...'

The other men started chanting, a chorus of low voices repeating a set of words in a strange guttural language. If anyone had been there to hear them, they would not have been able to understand it – it was a language that had almost become extinct centuries ago, only kept alive by a few secretive cults who fully understood its power. As they chanted, the leader turned to face the water, gently speaking in the same language, before pulling from his pocket a collection of stones; they were smooth and black, a symbol engraved on each. He took two and threw them as far as he could. They flew high in the air before landing in the water with a small splash. Then he returned to the others, joining in with their chanting, holding his hands high in the air.

They continued these incantations for almost ten minutes, until something stirred in the river, not far from the shore. Out of the water crawled two creatures, drawing themselves onto two feet as they came closer. They were humanoid, but like a cross between a man and a frog, with skin that was rubbery and dirty green in colour. They had large round eyes, gills and a mouth full of sharp spiny teeth. With them came an overwhelming stench of fish. The leader of the men walked into the river, stopping in front of the creatures, the water up to his knees. There was a brief exchange of words between the man and the creatures, speaking in the same low and sepulchral tone, before the creatures turned around and walked back, returning to the water, disappearing beneath its murky surface. Moments later, ripples were the only sign they had ever been there. The leader turned around, signalling the others, who stopped chanting.

'It is done,' he said. 'If they visit the temple, they will not find it empty.'

Chapter 31.

The next morning Jack and Jennifer rose, and packed what they needed for the trip to Cuttyhunk Island. Jennifer cleared most of the junk from her handbag, taking only what she thought were essentials.

They grabbed a quick breakfast and then hailed a cab, taking a short ride across the bridge to New Bedford. They arrived at the docks in plenty of time to catch the ferry across to the island. Jack paid for return tickets at the kiosk, and they found a comfortable seat on the deck. It was a large boat, complete with amenities such as a bar for tourists, although it wasn't open today. The ferry was almost empty at this time of year, as few tourists visited the island outside of summer; it was mainly locals. The trip would take just over an hour, and there were two return trips later that day, one in the afternoon, one early evening. Jack hoped that if they found anything there it wouldn't take too long.

The sky was bright and clear of clouds as they set off, but an icy wind came in off the sea, which got worse as they cleared the river and headed into the open water of Buzzard Bay. Beyond Cuttyhunk Island lay the North Atlantic Ocean; only Martha's Vineyard lay to the east, while to the south was nothing but water for a thousand kilometres.

As they arrived, the docks were quiet and the streets were mostly unoccupied as they stepped off the boat. The remains of the lighthouse were on the far side of the island, but that was only just over a kilometre away. Together, they set off, Jack holding the local map in his hands, but once they had passed through the small town, there really weren't that many choices of road to take.

'You know it was destroyed in the hurricane,' said Jennifer. 'I'm not sure what we're expecting to find here.'

'I don't know either,' said Jack as they walked. 'But it looks like something happened on this island, and it's our only real lead. We have to try.'

They reached the ruins of the lighthouse half an hour later. Not much remained now; a large concrete circle lay on the floor, the foundations of the lighthouse, with just a few large stone blocks all that remained of its walls. Next to it were some derelict stone buildings: the lighthouse station and some kind of outbuilding. The wind here was fierce, and spray from the ocean occasionally flew through the air as the waves crashed upon the rocky cliffs below. Jack took the photograph out and held it up in front of him. The landscape and remains in front of him were definitely the same. This was the place.

First, they walked to the concrete circle where the lighthouse used to stand. It was maybe thirty feet across, with large blocks of stone rubble lying around it. There was nothing left to investigate, nowhere for any clues to be hidden. They turned their attention next to the outbuilding. Only three walls remained of this structure, which looked like it used to be some kind of storage shed. Inside was nothing but debris; they took their time searching through the rubble, but quickly realized there was nothing of interest there either. Finally, they turned to the lighthouse station. It too was in a dilapidated state; its roof had collapsed and it no longer had any doors or windows.

'Careful!' Jennifer called to Jack as he stepped inside. 'It looks like this lot could come down at any moment.'

'If it was that precarious, it would have come down years ago,' called back Jack, somewhat optimistically. He looked around. The years had not been kind to the structure; God knows how long it had been open to the elements. There was a black and charred stain on the stone floor inside the hallway – the remains of a fire, probably from local kids. He could see from the inside that most of the internal walls were gone, as well as the ceilings. Only the structural stone walls were still standing to any degree. He slowly walked round the outer wall, looking for anything of interest, but it was use-less; there was nothing that the rough weather had not destroyed years ago.

'There's nothing here,' he said to Jennifer dejectedly, a look of disap-pointment on his face. She was looking at the centre of the building, where the broken remnants of a staircase and large brick fireplace still stood. She was passing her hand over the stone of the fireplace, feeling for anything out of the ordinary. 'Any luck?' he asked. She shook her head.

Jack knelt down in front of the fireplace. A few large lumps of burnt wood sat in the hearth, in a soggy mess of blackened debris. Presumably someone had built a fire here to keep warm, in the not so distant past. He poked through some of the lumps of burnt firewood with a stick, checking for anything of interest, but there was nothing there. He stood back up and walked back to the where the front door used to be, looking out over the barren landscape beyond.

Jennifer walked back over to him, putting an arm around his waist. 'What are you thinking?' she asked.

'There's obviously nothing here any more,' he said.

'It was always going to be a long shot.'

Jack thought for a moment. 'Do we know where Robert's boat was found?'

'No – just washed up on the rocks on one of the islands around here.'

Jack pulled up the collar on his jacket and then strode off purposefully, towards the cliff edge. Jennifer followed close behind him. As they approached the edge, they stopped a safe distance from where the rock fell away. Looking down, they could see that they were on one side of a small cove. Fifty feet below them they could see rough ocean waves breaking against large rocks, which protruded from the water, with just a small gap between them opening onto a small bay. The sea was gentler there, the tide washing up on a rough stone beach perhaps twenty feet wide.

'Can you see a way down?' Jack called to Jennifer over the sound of the wind and the ocean. Jennifer responded by pointing to the other side of the cove. When he looked carefully, he could just make out a small path on the opposite side. Together, they walked around the cliff until they found the top of the trail. It was a thin and winding path leading down the side of the cliff, overrun with plants and crumbling away in several places.

'Are you sure about this?' asked Jennifer.

'No – but I'm going anyway,' said Jack. 'I've come too far to give up now. You can stay here if you like.' He looked at the start of the path, and then stepped along it cautiously, leaning on to the wall with one hand. He progressed forwards slowly, slipping and sliding down the crumbling rock as he went.

Suddenly and without warning, part of the cliff ledge disintegrated under his left foot as he stepped on it. Temporarily unbalanced, he felt for a moment that he was going to slip off the edge, before a hand grabbed him by the arm, pulling him back. It was Jennifer.

'I thought I might come along,' she called to him. 'You know you can't be trusted on your own.' Together they continued, even more carefully now, walking sideways along the ledge, holding hands for balance and support. After a few nervous minutes, they reached the bottom; in front of them lay a short beach of rough pebbles, covered with seaweed, driftwood and other ocean detritus. In the centre of the beach, recessed into the cliff and hidden from view from the top was a small cave. Jack pointed towards it, and Jennifer nodded. Together they walked over the rough pebbles to reach it, the wind and spray stinging their faces, even with the protection of the cove.

The inside of the cave was thin and narrow; as they proceeded deeper into it, the roar of the ocean diminished to background noise. Jennifer removed her torch from her handbag, and turned it on. Around them they could see what might have been signs of human occupancy – rubbish, cigarette butts, empty bottles – but they might also just be debris, washed into the cave during high tides. They pressed on, deeper into the cave. At one point, it was so narrow that they had to turn sideways and breathe in to squeeze through the gap, but finally it opened into a larger area – a round cave with an alcove at the rear.

'Well, if we're going to find anything in here, this is where it'll be,' said Jack. Jennifer shone the torch around the floor of the cave, revealing little apart from sand and stone. The alcove at the rear was raised off the floor. Jack examined it by the torch light and was about to give up when he noticed a small hole in the rear.

'Jenn,' he called. 'Bring the light over here!' By the light of the torch, they could now make out a small star-shaped hole in the rear wall. 'Do you still have the key?' he asked. Jennifer unzipped her coat and reached under her top, bringing out the small star-shaped key on a chain. Wordlessly, she passed it to him.

Jack slotted the key into the hole, held his breath and then twisted. It was stiff; at first, he thought it wasn't going to move, but then it turned slowly with an almost inaudible creak. Jack stepped back in amazement as the rear wall of the cave swung ajar, revealing a passageway beyond. 'What the...' he muttered to himself. He pulled the key from the lock, returning it to Jennifer.

He looked her in the eyes, and she nodded in agreement. 'Here,' she said, passing him the torch. 'After you.'

The opening in the alcove was tight – about two feet square – and Jack had to squeeze through to get into the passageway on the other side. He stood up and brushed the dirt off as Jennifer climbed through behind him. They were standing in a long stone corridor that looked like it had been tunnelled out of the rock. It disappeared into the darkness in front of them, leading towards the centre of the island, twisting and turning gently as it did so.

'Here we go again,' muttered Jennifer.

<h1 style="text-align:center">Chapter 32.</h1>

Jennifer and Jack proceeded down the stone tunnel, Jennifer shining the torch in front of them as they went. In the torchlight, they could see the passage turning and descending before them, a gentle slope at first, before it began to spiral down into the earth below, rough stone steps carved into the floor. They followed the passageway downwards for what felt like several long minutes, the rugged steps twisting like a corkscrew through the stone, descending several stories until it opened out into a room. It was about twenty feet square, and had been paved with stone slabs, although the walls were still natural rock. An old wooden bench was set against the wall on the left, and on the wall to the right were brackets, one of which still contained an old-fashioned wooden torch. A couple of empty barrels and several broken wooden crates were scattered around the edges of the room. In the centre, set into the stone slabs was a wooden trapdoor. Jack went to the torch on the wall and took it down.

'Have you got a light?' he asked Jennifer. She fished around in her handbag until she found a book of matches. They were the ones she had found in Robert's study.

'Try these,' she said. 'Although I don't know if they'll still work.'

Jack retrieved a match from the box and struck it. It burst into flame and he held it up against the torch. For a moment, the flame wouldn't take, the torch just fizzing and smouldering. Then something caught, and it ignited with a small burst of flame, gradually growing until the torch was fully ablaze.

With the increased light in the room, they could clearly see another passageway leading away on the far side now. Jack walked over to it; he could see a tunnel sloping down for a short distance before it opened into what looked like a large natural cavern.

'What do you reckon this was for?' asked Jack, turning back around to face Jennifer. He knelt down to look at some of the crates and barrels; the names on them weren't any that he recognized. 'Some kind of smuggling, maybe? From back in prohibition time?' Jennifer shrugged her shoulders, a doubtful look on her face.

Jack walked to the centre of the room to have a look at the trapdoor, and Jennifer joined him. It was made of a dark wood and had two bolts, one on either side, both unlocked. Jack lifted the door and they both peered through, Jennifer shining her torch through to better illuminate the room below. Beneath them was a smaller room, maybe fifteen feet in diameter; the only thing visible within was water, deep enough to obscure the floor, maybe five feet below the ceiling. He closed the trapdoor again.

Jack looked back towards the passageway. 'Shall we continue?' he asked. Jennifer nodded. They walked down the sloping tunnel, descending down into a much larger subterranean cave – at least sixty feet across. Jack felt like they must have walked a fair way inland, but he could still hear water splashing somewhere nearby. At intervals around the walls of the cavern, stone pillars had been built into the rock, reminding Jack of Greek or Roman temples. Several dark passageways were visible in the walls; where they led to they couldn't even guess. They started to walk slowly across the cave, Jennifer searching the floor in front of them with her torch. After what she had tripped over in the cavern in France, she was being more careful this time. The floor they walked across was damp and slippery, and at the rear they could make out a pool of water, the surface perfectly smooth and still. As they crossed the room towards the pool, they could see the remains of a large mosaic laid in the centre of the floor. Bending over to examine it, Jack could see it was composed of small marble tiles. They were mainly a mixture of black and white tiles, and although many were missing, most were still present. As Jennifer shone her torch around the room, they could make out others now, scattered around the cavern and lying by the cavern walls; small squares reflecting the torchlight and shining in the darkness.

Jack stood up and stepped back to get a better view of the mosaic. Although the mosaic was damaged, there was still a definite pattern visible.

'Does that look like a star shape to you?'

'There *is* a definite solar motif that's becoming all too familiar,' sighed Jennifer.

They started again towards the pool at the back of the cavern. In front of it, they could now make out another shape they recognized – a rectangular, black-stone altar. They approached it cautiously.

'Another cavern, another altar,' shuddered Jennifer. 'At least there's no skeleton this time.'

Jack walked over to it. It was made of a black stone that reminded him of the black granite from his kitchen countertop. He ran his fingers over the side, leaving a white residue on his fingertips. He cautiously licked them – it was salt; presumably the cavern flooded from time to time. Jennifer stood next to him as he turned and looked at the pool in the rear of the cavern. It stretched off for at least twenty feet before it met the rear wall. By the light of their torches, it was impossible to see much below the surface. Jack knelt down and placed his hand in the water. The water was ice cold, unsurprisingly, and the rock underneath was hard and smooth. He pulled his hand out of the water and turned around; out of the corner of his eye, he caught a glint of something below the surface of the water, about half way out.

'Jenn!' he called out. 'Shine the torch over there,' he said, pointing towards the middle of the pool where he had seen the glint of light. As she shone her torch back and forth, he was sure he could see it, something shimmering beneath the surface. 'Here, take this,' he said, passing her the burning torch, before emptying his pockets onto the surface of the altar.

He stepped into the water. The floor sloped steeply; after a couple of steps, his legs were submerged up to his shins. He took a sharp intake of breath – it felt even colder than he was expecting.

'Are you sure about this?' asked Jennifer.

'No,' said Jack, but he continued wading out regardless. He stopped just short of where he had seen the reflection. He was waist deep in the water now. He leant forwards, plunging his arms into the icy darkness, sweeping them around for just a moment before his hands made contact with something solid. He grabbed hold and pulled it out.

He took a step backwards as he saw what it was – the skeleton of a human arm, the hand curled into a fist. There was a white gemstone ring on one of the fingers – the object that had caught his attention in the torchlight. 'Jesus!' he cried, dropping the arm back into the water and taking another step backwards. He was just starting to turn back towards Jennifer when he felt something wrap around his ankles. With a sharp yank, he was pulled down, under the surface of the water.

'Jack!' screamed Jennifer, as he disappeared out of sight.

Chapter 33.

November 15th, 1929. Cuttyhunk Island, New England.

Robert Knight was hiding behind a dense patch of foliage. He peered out from behind it to look at the lighthouse. The rain was torrential now, moving almost horizontally through the air as the wind gusted, stinging his face as the droplets hit it.

As the bright light of the lighthouse swivelled around, intermittently lighting up the grounds around it, he could see men moving about, going back and forth between the keeper's house and the stone storage building. As he sat there spying on their activity, he saw three creatures shambling up towards the group. They were some kind of aquatic humanoid, dark green in colour, with a spiny elongated head and large round eyes, strong and well built with slimy rubbery skin. They were standing vertically, but shambling along as if unaccustomed to walking on two feet. Even at this distance, long claws were visible on their feet and hands. Robert didn't want to have to get up close to any of those creatures.

In the pulsing light, Robert could see one of the men walking over, stopping in front of the creatures. They appeared to converse for a short while, and then the creatures shuffled off towards the cliff edge. Silently, they dived off, splashing into the stormy ocean and disappearing without a trace. Now they were gone, the men hurried back to the keeper's house, anxious to get out of the storm.

Robert sat there, silent and motionless in the rain, waiting for something to happen. The front door of the house opened, and half a dozen men emerged, dressed in brown robes, walking towards the cliff. Robert stepped out from behind the bush, still crouching, and moved slowly towards them. The deluge of rain reduced the visibility, offering him cover but making it harder for him to see where they were heading. He closed the distance carefully, making sure to keep out of the bright light of the lighthouse as it rotated, intermittently bathing the area in light. As he reached the edge of the cliff, he could see the men standing down below in a small cove, walking towards the centre of the beach, oblivious to the raging wind and rain.

Robert shuffled over to the other side of the cove where a path was visible, a rope handrail attached to the side of the cliff. Carefully, he started to descend.

Chapter 34.

December 10th, 2012. Cuttyhunk Island, New England.

Everything was instantly dark and silent as he was pulled under the water. Jack could feel something tightly gripping his foot, trying to pull him further into the pool. Holding on to what little breath he had in his lungs, he reached out for anything he could grab hold of, finding a rock on the floor of the pool. He kicked hard with his free foot and felt it make contact with something soft in the water. The grip on his ankle loosened slightly, and he pulled with all his might, the foot slipping free of its bounds. He rolled over and struggled to his knees in the waist-deep water, his head bursting through the surface, taking in huge gulps of air.

Jennifer saw the thing rise out of the water before he did – some kind of dark green aquatic humanoid, its mouth full of needle-like teeth. 'Look out!' she screamed at Jack.

Jack rolled to the side as it swung a huge taloned arm towards him, splashing through the water where he had been just moments before. He struggled closer to the shore, dragging himself forwards on all fours. The light in the cave was erratic now. Jennifer had dropped the burning torch by the water's edge, frantically looking in her handbag for something; her electric torch was waving about in her other hand as she searched.

Jack looked back at the creature behind him, just in time to see the back of a slimy fist smack him on the side of the face. The force of the blow knocked him sideways and he collapsed onto the floor, lying face up in the water. The room was spinning in his vision. Turning back over, he could just make out the shore a few feet in front of him. He scrambled drunkenly forwards, towards the bright light of the torch lying on the cavern floor.

A bellowing roar erupted from above him. He staggered forwards, dragging himself to his feet in the shallow water, turning to see Jennifer standing next to him. She had retrieved a can of pepper-spray from her handbag, which she had sprayed in its face. The beast roared, waving its arms in front of its face, a foul odour of rotting fish spreading through the air as it did so, bringing a wave of nausea over Jack. He bent over, grabbing the burning torch from the floor.

'Again!' he shouted at Jennifer. She pressed the top of the canister again, squirting another stream of mace towards its face. At the same time, Jack thrust the torch towards it, hoping to drive it backwards. As the aerosolized stream met the torch, it ignited, creating a small fireball in the face of the monster. In the darkness of the cave, the brightness of the flare was intense, causing Jack and Jennifer to avert their gaze. The beast shrieked louder, staggering backwards and collapsing, submerging itself below the surface.

'Go!' screamed Jennifer. Jack stepped to the altar, grabbing his belongings from its surface, not bothering to pocket them until they were out of that cavern. He followed Jennifer, both running as fast as they could on the slippery floor, until they reached the corridor that led back up to the stone-floored antechamber.

In the doorway, they paused to recover their breath and looked behind them; they did not seem to have been immediately followed. Jack hastily stowed his belongings back into his pockets. Then there came a bellowing call from the darkness, followed by another. A third joined it, followed by more voices, until an unholy cacophony echoed from the cavern.

Jack and Jennifer looked at each other. 'Time to go!' said Jennifer, and they sprinted up the slope back into the antechamber. They ran into the room, and then stopped suddenly at what they saw in front of them. Four men stood in the far doorway. One of the men stepped forwards, holding a pistol, which he pointed towards them.

Chapter 35.

'So... we meet in person at last,' said the man holding the gun. He spoke in a well-educated English accent that Jack instantly recognized as belonging to Silas. He was wearing a brown robe, and he pulled the hood down to reveal the face of an old man. He had thin grey hair, a long grey beard and sported small wire-frame spectacles. He was also holding a large automatic pistol, complete with silencer, which he casually pointed at them.

'Just for once, I'd like to meet someone who didn't want to kill us,' groaned Jennifer.

'Ah, I presume you mean my disciples,' said the man. 'Yes – very keen, but not always efficient. I must say, you do seem reluctant to take a hint. For once, I thought I'd come and deal with you myself. If you want the job done properly, and all that...' He paused for a moment, before sitting down on one of the crates, casually holding the gun in his lap. 'In case you don't remember, my name is Silas.'

'I'm...' started Jack.

'Oh, I know who you are,' said Silas. 'Jack Knight. Following in the footsteps of his old great-grandfather, Robert Knight. Trying to carry on and finish what he and his damned *Shadow Watch* failed to stop.'

'Then that would make you... Nazis?' asked Jennifer.

'Nazis!' he laughed. 'Oh, my dear! No – they were but rank amateurs, messing around with things they couldn't possibly understand. It was only unfortunate that their meddling attracted the attention of others to *our* activities. No, we have been around for much longer than that, since man first looked up into the sky and worshipped the gods that lived there.'

'You believe in these gods then?' asked Jack.

'It is not a matter of belief,' replied Silas. 'Not when you have gazed upon them, conversed with them. We are their humble servants. Our masters lie imprisoned, sleeping and waiting for a time when we shall release them.'

'You do realize that you're quite mad,' said Jack. Maybe if he taunted him, he could get a rise out of him, and then – just maybe he would let his guard down.

But Silas just smiled politely back at him. 'We will see about that when the time of their return is upon us.' He looked at his henchmen, who were still standing in the shadows, and waved the gun towards Jack and Jennifer, gesturing for the henchmen to advance. 'That time will be with us all too soon, but I'm afraid you won't be around to witness it.' Two of the men stepped out of the darkness, large and brutish, dressed all in black. They walked around the sides of the room, flanking Jack and Jennifer and moving around behind them. For a second, Jack contemplated resistance.

'Uh uh!' said Silas, obviously sensing the thought in his mind. 'I wouldn't if I were you.' He twitched the gun in his hand. 'You'd never be quick enough.' The men grabbed Jack's arms, roughly pulling his hands behind his back before tying them together with a length of rope. Jack gave only a token show of resistance, and then they repeated the action with Jennifer.

'You've been stopped before,' said Jack defiantly. 'You can be stopped again.'

'By you?' asked Silas. 'No, I don't think so. You're no longer in a position to stop anything. Just like your great-grandfather, these caves will be your tomb. He was unable to stop our ritual, and neither will you. You have failed I'm afraid, and our final ceremony will go ahead as planned, two nights from now.' He stood up, motioning to the man who had tied Jennifer's hands behind her back, who was holding her by the shoulders. He pushed her forwards a couple of steps.

'And speaking of sacrifices, as you may have guessed, we need one for the final ritual. It's all a bit clichéd, I'm afraid, but what can you do...' He shrugged, gesticulating with his gun. 'Since we already have you,' he said, looking at Jennifer, 'there's not a lot of point going to the effort of abducting someone else and risking all the attention that brings. One sacrifice is as good as another.' He stood in front of her, looking her up and down. 'No, you'll do quite nicely.' Jennifer stared him in the face and then spat in it. 'And, oh what *spirit*,' he chuckled, removing a handkerchief from his pocket and wiping his face with it.

'Don't you dare hurt her!' shouted Jack. 'I'll kill you, you bastard!'

Silas turned and stepped towards him, looking him square in the face. 'You? I know men like you, Mr Knight – you don't have it in you. Oh, I'm sure you can defend yourself if necessary, put up a bit of resistance, but kill a man in cold blood? That's not who you are.' Jack opened his mouth to argue, but stopped. In his heart, he knew that what Silas just said was probably true. 'Why don't you untie my hands, and we'll see about that,' was the best he could manage.

'No, I think not,' said Silas. 'I've got better plans for you. A small sacrifice of our own. An offering to some of our allies who live down here.' He looked at his watch. 'Yes, the tide should be coming in now. The timing is perfect.' He looked at the man standing behind Jack who had tied his hands. 'Check him,' he ordered. The henchman frisked him from behind, patting him down and checking the contents of his pockets. He looked at Silas and shook his head.

'Alas, never mind,' said Silas. 'It would appear you don't have the artefact. I don't suppose you'd care to tell me where it is?' Jack ignored him. 'Never mind,' he continued. 'Without you to use it, it is of no consequence. It's a pity you don't have any sons of your own to leave it to, whatever it was. Shame, I would have enjoyed killing them too.' He looked at his watch again. 'But look at the time – we really must be going if we're going to keep to our schedule. Take a final look at your love, Mr Knight.'

Jack took a step closer to Jennifer. The man holding him moved to stop him, but Silas held up a hand. 'No – let them say their final goodbyes,' he said.

Jack moved in close and kissed Jennifer on the lips. 'You know how I like to think of myself as a strong, modern woman?' she said. 'Is it okay to admit that I'm really quite scared at the moment?'

'I'd be shocked if you weren't,' he said. He looked deep into her eyes. Her face was white with fear. 'Don't give up. I'll come back for you. I don't know how, but I will, I promise you.' He lowered his voice. 'And if you get a chance to escape, to take that bastard down... don't hesitate, just take it.'

She nodded. 'Just don't take too long, okay?' she replied, kissing him again.

Silas signalled to his henchmen, and they pulled them apart again. 'Bring her,' he said, turning his back to them and walking off into the darkness. 'You know what to do with him. Your great-grandfather never returned from these caverns, Mr Knight, and neither will you.'

Chapter 36.

Jack saw one of the henchmen dragging Jennifer down the slope back into the large cavern, following behind Silas. The other two grabbed him roughly by the shoulders.

'What are you going to do to me?' Jack asked frantically. The men remained silent, pushing him to his knees on the floor. In front of him, Jack could see the trapdoor in the floor. While one of the men pinned him to the floor by his shoulders, the other walked wordlessly over to the trapdoor, drawing both the bolts back and lifting it up. Then the man holding Jack lifted him up by the scruff of his jacket, and started pushing him towards it. 'No!' Jack shouted, terror gripping his heart as he realized what they intended to do. The first man grabbed Jack's kicking legs as he approached, and together they bundled him through the hole in the floor.

Jack fell feet first into the water that half-filled the small room. His feet hit the bottom, the blow softened by the water. He fell over, his head going under the water, before he stumbled back to his feet, off balance with his hands tied behind his back. Standing submerged up to his waist, he heard the dull thud of the trapdoor slamming shut, followed by the sound of the bolts being fastened. With the trapdoor in the ceiling closed, Jack was plunged into total darkness. The water was rising now as the tide came in; even standing on tiptoes, the ice-cold water was up to his navel. He needed to do something to free his hands. He stretched his arms to see how much slack there was in the rope – he could probably do it, he thought. He took several deep breaths, calming himself even as he could feel the water rising, then he ducked down under the water. He lowered his wrists below his waist as he dropped, until he was sitting on the floor, completely submerged. Then he lifted his hands up over his feet and stood back up, his hands still tied together but at least in front of him now. He grabbed the rope in his mouth and started to pull on it, but it was no good – the knots were too tight. He tried to grab the ends in his hands, but he couldn't reach, and his fingers were turning numb from the freezing water, no use for any kind of delicate procedure.

The water level was rising higher up his chest. He frantically started to search the cave walls, looking for some kind of way out, but save for a low tunnel at floor level where the water seemed to be coming in, it felt like solid rock all round. He considered trying to swim down the tunnel, but he had no idea how long or how tight the passage was, and he would be going against the flow; even without his hands tied he didn't think he was a good enough swimmer to chance it. As it was, he had no chance.

He was running out of time now. He started treading water as the level rose higher, manoeuvring himself so he was under the trapdoor. He forced himself to wait patiently as the room slowly filled, breathing slowly and con-serving his energy, until at last the trapdoor was within his grasp. He tried to push it open, but nothing happened – it was clearly locked again on the other side. He thought of trying to break it down, but while treading water was unable to get any leverage – if he tried pushing hard against the wood, he'd just ended up submerging himself.

His legs were getting tired now, and his fear was starting to turn into panic. There was only a foot of air left in the cave, and he didn't know how much longer he could hold on. He banged on the trapdoor with his fists, yelling in a futile cry for help, but he knew no help would come.

Then, the water was in his mouth, the taste of salt choking in his throat. With the first swallow of water, the panic truly hit him. He tried to scream, but only ended up swallowing more water. His head was submerged in the icy sea as he sunk below the surface, deaf and blind as he felt the last of his energy seep out of him.

Chapter 37.

Just as he was starting to lose consciousness, Jack felt something grab his thrashing hand, a patch of light visible through the water. He was yanked strongly upwards, bringing his face out of the water, and then dragged slowly and roughly through the trapdoor, his body scraping against the edges of the frame. He still couldn't breathe, his lungs full of water, until he spasmed savagely, coughing up the salty water. He felt like his lungs were on fire.

The man who had rescued him rolled him over onto his side, as he spluttered away the last mouthfuls of water. His eyes swam in and out of focus in the dark room, lit only by an electric torch, which lay on the floor. He turned to look at the face of the man who had saved his life, and looked into the cold grey eyes of Peter White.

'You? What are you doing here?' he choked out between coughs.

'Saving your life, obviously.' He grabbed Jack's hands, and starting cutting through the rope with a knife that he took from his jacket.

'But how?' he stammered, getting to his knees, and then collapsing back onto all fours, still coughing.

'There's no time to explain now. We need to get out of here. Is Jennifer...?' He looked towards the trapdoor and the room below, which was now full of water.

'No,' managed Jack. 'I don't know where she is. They took her.' The water was still rising; they were now standing in a thin layer of water spread across the floor.

'C'mon,' said Peter, holding out his hand. Jack took it, and Peter pulled him to his feet, leading him towards the spiralling passageway that went upwards to the surface. In the shadows in the corner of the room, Jack could see a man lying on the floor, face down in the shallow water; it was one of the cultists who had locked him in that watery tomb.

'Won't he drown?' Jack asked Peter.

'No,' replied Peter coldly, not even sparing him a sideways glance. 'He's already dead.'

✳ ✳ ✳

'How did you...?' started Jack, as they climbed out of the cave, back onto what had been the beach. The tide had come in considerably, and they were now wading through a foot of water.

'I'll explain as we walk,' said Peter, heading back towards the path up the cliff. 'We need to get back and get you out of the cold. I chartered a boat to get over here. It's waiting for us at the docks on the other side of the island.'

Jack shook his head and stopped at the foot of the path. 'What about Jennifer? Did you see them taking her away?'

'I didn't see anyone except the guard they left down in the cavern,' said Peter, stopping to face him. 'They must have left before I got here, gone out another way.'

Jack nodded. 'I saw them walking in the other direction, deeper into the tunnels. How are we going to find her now?' asked Jack. He hoped to God she was still all right.

'We'll do what we can,' replied Peter, shrugging his shoulders. That wasn't much reassurance to Jack. 'But first we need to get out of here.' He looked at the rising ocean all around them. 'Come on, we can't wait here any longer. And we can't go back in there.' He started up the cliff.

At the top, Peter took his jacket off and offered it to Jack for warmth. 'Take this,' he ordered.

'Will you be okay?' asked Jack.

'I will,' he said. 'But you'll die of hypothermia wandering about soaked to the skin in this weather. Take it.' Jack shrugged and took his own jacket off, putting Peter's on to replace it. They walked slowly back along the road towards the town and docks just beyond it. Jack was still bitterly cold in the frigid wind, although the dry jacket helped somewhat.

'How did you know?' Jack asked Peter, his teeth chattering. 'How did you find us?'

'After our little talk in Cheltenham, I decided to do some investigation into the death of Ian Williams.'

'Then...?'

'Yes, he's dead – he passed away in the hospital, in his sleep. But, then again, so is the man you killed outside his flat.'

'I didn't kill him – at least I didn't mean too – it was all an accident,' said Jack, trying to explain.

'Either way – he's no longer a threat, and that's what matters. I managed to pull some strings, do some investigation of my own and was able find out who he was – and what he was.'

'What do you mean?' asked Jack, confused.

'I believe he was a member of a cult called *The Brotherhood of the Star*. It's a secret society, dating back hundreds of years – possibly further, no one really knows. They seem to disappear for long stretches of time with no sightings of them, before rumours of their existence surface again, decades later. 'They're also big believers in secrecy,' he added. 'They don't like anyone outside their order to even know about their existence, and they're willing to kill to keep it that way – which is probably how they've stayed hidden for so long.'

'Well, that seems to agree with my personal experience so far.'

'Yes – but it also isn't like them. All my experience and research tells me they like to operate in secret, manipulating others from the shadows. They might have broken into your house and ransacked it, searching for whatever they were after, but interrogating you at gunpoint – that's not really their style.'

'Unless they were always planning to kill us afterwards...'

'Maybe. But they wouldn't be acting so openly if whatever's going on wasn't deadly serious to them. When I found out who they were, and the lengths to which they'd gone, I knew I had to keep an eye on you – if only for your own safety. I tried calling, but you never answered the phone I gave you.'

'It got damaged – when one of them attacked me back in England. We kept our normal phones turned off like you suggested.'

'Are the police sniffing round after you then?' asked Peter.

'Maybe. I'm not sure. If they are, they haven't caught up with us yet.'

They walked without talking for a few minutes, until Jack broke the silence. 'I think I met their leader,' he said. 'Back there, in the caverns.'

Peter stopped and turned to face him, taking him by the shoulder. 'Are you sure?'

'Yes. Well, not really. I suppose I just assumed he was the leader. He was definitely in charge of the group we ran into though,' he explained. 'We also talked on the phone just before we left England. He called himself Silas. He was the one who took Jennifer. He's going to sacrifice her as part of some ritual. They've got some mad idea about trying to free some damned gods.'

Peter nodded at him, as he started walking again. 'They believe that there are creatures,' he explained to Jack. '*Immortal* creatures, by any normal definition of the word, that used to rule here like gods, long before man ever walked on the earth.'

'Sounds like most ancient religions to me.'

'Yes, but they also believe that those same creatures were banished, imprisoned. These creatures, who they revere like gods, could not be released until the stars were in the correct alignment. They believe that they alone have the responsibility to free them and usher in a new era of darkness over the world. How true any of it all is, I couldn't say.' They continued walking in silence for several minutes. They could just see the lights of the town in the distance now.

'How did you find us?' Jack eventually asked Peter.

'I called in a favour with some old friends in Intelligence. They were able to track down your airline tickets and credit card usage without much trouble. It's just a good thing you didn't buy the ferry tickets in cash. I was expecting just to warn you – I wasn't planning on running into any action.'

'I just wish you'd got there sooner. We've got to find out where they've taken Jennifer, and what they're planning to do to her. Well, I suppose I know what they're going to do to her – they're going to kill her. Silas said the ritual was taking place two nights from now, I just don't know where!'

'Jack. Do you trust me? *Really* trust me?' asked Peter, looking Jack in the eyes.

'Well, you've just saved my life, so I suppose so,' said Jack humbly. 'Whatever you need from me, if it'll help save Jennifer, I'll do it.'

Chapter 38.

Back in his hotel room, Jack showered and changed into a fresh set of clothing. Peter had left him while he went and fetched some items that he needed.

Jack looked at Jennifer's clothes and belongings scattered around the room. 'Damn it,' he cursed to himself. He told himself that if anything happened to her, it would all be his fault, although he didn't really believe it. She had been as keen as he had to get into this whole mess – keener, probably. He knew he shouldn't blame himself, but at the end of the day, this was his problem, his family's legacy. If anyone, he should blame Robert for getting them into this danger. He looked again at her possessions, and then gathered them up, packing them into her bag. Then he sat down on the bed, closed his eyes and thought of her; he prayed he could find her in time and make this right, but he had no idea how he was going to achieve this. They could be almost anywhere in the world, and with every passing minute, they could be getting further away.

There was a knock at the door. Jack cautiously approached the door and peered through the spy-hole; it was Peter. He undid the chain, unlocked the door and let him in. Peter entered carrying a leather briefcase and a plastic bag. He put the briefcase down on the table and he pulled out a burger and a can of Coke from the bag. He tossed the burger to Jack. 'I thought you might be hungry,' he said. He was about to pass him the can of Coke when he stopped. 'No,' he said, 'you're going to need to sleep. This'll be better!' and with that, he withdrew a bottle of Scotch whisky.

'Sleep?' said Jack angrily. 'This is no time to sleep; we need to do something–'

'Remember when I asked you if you could trust me?' asked Peter patiently, interrupting him. Jack nodded silently. Peter stepped into the bathroom and returned with two small glass tumblers. He put them on the desk, and opened the bottle of whisky. He poured two large drinks and passed one to Jack, who accepted it gracefully. Peter slumped down in one of the hotel chairs and took a large gulp of the drink. 'I have an idea how we can try to find out where they've taken her. But it's rather... *unorthodox.*' Jack looked at him, a look of uncertainty on his face. 'Remember that I told you this Brotherhood was a cult?' Jack nodded, sipping at his whisky. 'I'm afraid it's slightly more than that. Their ceremonies, their rites – what if I told you they were real?'

'I know they're real,' replied Jack. 'My great-grandfather died trying to stop them.'

'I don't just mean that they actually occurred,' said Peter. 'I mean, what if I told you that there is a real force behind them, a natural power that can be harnessed through the power of words and symbols.'

'Are you talking about magic?' asked Jack incredulously. 'Are you trying to tell me magic is real?'

'Yes,' said Peter gently. 'And I can prove it to you. Here, have another drink – you're going to need it.'

Peter White undid the clasps on his briefcase and opened it. From within he withdrew a small box, made of a dark wood, which he placed on the table next to the briefcase. He gently took the lid off the box, revealing a small square of cloth folded within. Carefully, almost reverentially, Peter removed the cloth, gently unfolding it on the table. At first glance, the cloth looked to Jack like a handkerchief. As he looked closer, however, he could see that, although this cloth was about the same size as a handkerchief, that was where the similarity ended. This sheet was made of a thick cloth, old and browned with age, with peculiar lines and curves drawn on both sides in a faded ink. As he turned his head, viewing the cloth out of the corner of his eye, the lines seemed to move and swirl hypnotically upon the sheet. A memory came quickly to the front his mind – the carvings on the back of the master bed in Ash House.

'What is it?' he asked, his curiosity piqued now.

'Quite something, isn't it,' said Peter, taking the question as a complement. 'Most people think of dreams as random brain activity, subconscious activity trying to make sense of new experiences, filing away new information... and mostly it is.' Jack wondered where he was going with this. 'But in our dreams, freed of our conscious rationalizations, we can open a doorway to... well, I suppose you could call it another level of consciousness. This is the land inhabited by the Great Old Ones that the Brotherhood worship, their method of communication with their mortal worshippers.'

'Not dead, but dreaming,' muttered Jack, thinking back to the gravestone.

'I'm sorry?'

'It was written on the tombstone of Adam Webber,' explained Jack. 'I believe he was a member of this cult back in Robert's time.'

'Ah,' sighed Peter. 'Quite fitting really, for one who uses dreams to commune with gods imprisoned beyond death. Quite poetic.' He picked up his glass of whisky, taking another sip.

'Then this cloth...' said Jack, bringing the conversation back to the present.

'It is a tool, used to help direct dreaming. The incantations written on it can help unlock access to memories and visions.'

'I think I've experienced something similar before,' said Jack. Peter looked at him, curious himself now. 'The master bed in the house I inherited – the house that originally belonged to Robert Knight. There were lines just like this carved into the back of the head board. Some of the dreams I had...' He shuddered, recalling the memories of what he had seen.

'They may have been more than just dreams,' said Peter.

'Well, they certainly felt that way. They were the most realistic dreams I'd ever had. Scared the hell out of me on at least one occasion.' Jack thought for a moment. 'It looked like that bedroom hadn't been used for a long time. I guess I know why now.'

Peter nodded at him. 'There are several different variations of this enchantment. Some allow you to look into the past, while some are more prophetic in nature. Others allow you to explore... well, *other places*, beyond our normal comprehension. The Brotherhood use a version to help them commune with their masters while they sleep. This enchantment here,' he said, indicating the cloth in his hands, 'I came across in India. It's proved itself useful to me in the past.'

Jack was struggling to take this all in. 'Who the hell actually are you?' he asked. 'How do you know all of this?'

Peter took a large swig of whisky, and then put the glass down and turned to face Jack. 'Like my father, I served my time in the military, mainly in special operations, where I learned many of my skills. After I retired, I decided to rent out my skills to the highest bidder.'

'You mean you're a mercenary?' asked Jack, his mouth hanging open.

'No, no,' chuckled Peter. 'A private detective. You'd be surprised how many of the skills were transferable: stealth, interrogation, improvization, patience. Lots and lots of patience. I spent many years unofficially investigating crimes. My big break came when I rescued the daughter of a high-ranking politician who had been kidnapped by a cult. I made quite a few friends in high places that day. After a while I got a bit of a reputation for handling some of the more... *unconventional* cases. Cases with an occult or ritualistic aspect to them. Most of the time, it's all just theatrics, but every so often... well, you get one like this.'

'And that's where you came across the Brotherhood?'

'I never had any direct experiences with them before this, although I had heard stories about them. No... But I have had dealings with similar groups before. I thought I had retired from all of that, but... well, here I am once again.'

'I guess so,' agreed Jack. 'So, do you think we can use that to find Jennifer?' he asked, nodding back towards the cloth lying on the table.

'If she is going to be used as a sacrifice then, yes, maybe it can. She will now be an integral part of their plan, a key component in the upcoming ritual, and that may just be enough.'

'Okay, what do I have to do?' asked Jack nervously. He was getting bad feelings about this.

'Before you start, you should be warned,' said Peter. 'This is not without risk. Your body will be safe here, but the things you may see and experience can still affect your mind. Without training, repeated use inevitably causes insanity in all but the strongest of minds. Even a single use can still have devastating consequences.'

'I understand. If I need to do this to get Jennifer back, then I'm willing to take that risk.' Jack lifted his glass, downing the rest of his whisky. 'What do I need to do?'

'We'll place this close to your head – under your pillow will be fine and then you just need to go to sleep. Concentrate on Jennifer, try and think of her and the Brotherhood – nothing else. With any luck, what you see and experience will help us locate where she is, or where they will be holding this ritual of theirs.'

'And if I find her? Find where she is, where she will be. How do I get back?'

'It's hard to say. You will return when you wake, but to do that yourself – well, it is normally different for every dreamer, different for every dream. I can wake you myself, but...'

'The longer I'm in there, the more chance I have of finding her, right?'

'Right,' he agreed.

'Then don't wake me – for anything!'

'I'll wake you if you look to be in serious trouble,' said Peter. Jack looked at him nervously. 'But hopefully, it won't come to that. I'll only wake you if I have to. Agreed?'

'Okay, agreed,' he said reluctantly.

'Are you ready?'

Jack lifted up his glass. 'I think I could probably do with a bit more Dutch courage,' he said, holding the glass out to Peter. Peter poured him another measure, which Jack downed in one large gulp. Then he took off his shoes and jacket, before climbing onto the bed. Peter came and ceremoniously laid the sheet at the top of the bed and then placed the pillow on top of it. Jack lay down, placing his head on the pillow, while Peter drew a blanket over him, like a father tucking in his son. Jack closed his eyes, thinking only of Jennifer, visualizing her in front of him, and tried to drift off to sleep.

Chapter 39.

Jack awoke in darkness.

'Peter?' he called out, but there was no reply. He felt dazed and confused, his head spinning. He could neither see nor hear anything; all around him was nothing but silent darkness. He didn't even know whether he was awake or dreaming. He felt awake, but that had also been true of some of his earlier experiences. He reached out with his hands to feel around him; he was lying on cold stone, so he definitely wasn't still in his hotel bed. Carefully, remembering the last time he had awoken in pitch darkness, he sat up. This time, however, his surroundings were larger than a coffin. 'Hello?' he called in a quiet voice. He could hear faint echoes and reverberations around him — he was obviously in quite a large area, wherever he was.

He put his hands into his pockets, but they were empty. His wallet and keys were gone. Even the watch from his wrist was no longer there. Slowly and cautiously, he rose to his feet and started to walk forwards. He had to go slowly; in the absolute darkness, he was finding it hard to balance. He continued walking, his hands held out in front of him, until he reached a wall — it was rough stone, hard and cold to the touch. There was an old smell in the air too, a hint of acrid smoke mixed with something damp and mouldy. If this was a dream, it was unlike any he had ever had; everything felt too real, too detailed.

He thought of an old trick he had read about for navigating mazes; he turned to his right, touched the wall with his left hand and began walking slowly, keeping contact with the wall, following it in the darkness. If he kept following the same wall, he should eventually find something. Well, either that or go around and around in circles for all eternity, he thought.

The wall he was touching stopped abruptly – either a passageway or a corner to the left. He turned, following the wall, still running his left hand along it. He followed that passageway for a short distance, before it turned right. He carried on like this, following the wall for a long time, shuffling through the darkness, occasionally stumbling and tripping. He had lost all track of time; he felt like he could have been walking for hours, although his legs did not grow tired.

Just when he was starting to wonder if he would ever find his way out of the infernal darkness, he realized that he could see the faint outline of the passageway ahead of him. He sped up, shuffling faster now, as a faint light – or was it just a lesser darkness – loomed ahead. He was also just beginning to hear something now – the all too familiar sound of a large group of people chanting in an unfamiliar language.

As he continued on down the long corridor, the light grew brighter and the sounds louder. After a few hundred metres, the rough stone passageway opened into a man-made room, paved with red brick. On the walls, there were brackets holding torches, all extinguished. He took one and then looked around. From each side of the square room there was an archway opening into a passage; in the dim light, he could just make out a different symbol carved into the keystone of each. He went up to them and ran his fingers over the symbols – none of them meant anything to him. At each archway, Jack peered down the passageway beyond it. He could not tell where any of them led; they could take him out, or deeper into this subterranean dungeon. However, the light and noise seemed to be coming from just one of the passageways. The symbol above that archway was of two concentric circles. He headed off in that direction, advancing cautiously.

He walked down the passageway for what felt like half a mile. As he walked it twisted back and forth, the rocky stone floor sloping gently downwards the entire way. Every hundred yards or so, a lit torch was secured to the wall by an iron bracket, providing modest illumination. He lit the torch he held, holding it in front of him, both for illumination and for reassurance.

As the passageway opened into a much larger cavern, the chanting was noticeably louder, dozens of voices reciting in that strange language. To his left and right were huge tunnels, easily twenty feet high, leading off into blackness. Rocks and boulders lay scattered around the floor of the cavern, and in front of him, the rear wall was missing. He cautiously advanced towards that opening, stopping behind a large rock that stood there. Before him lay an enormous cavern the size of which he had never seen before. The floor was littered with rocks and the occasional stalagmite, the ceiling dotted with more frequent stalactites hanging down. Around the edge of the cavern, more torches were attached to the walls, providing dim illumination over the proceedings. The space he was in opened up high in the side of that cavern, so that he was looking down on the activities below. In the centre of that enormous cavern was a pit, a deep shaft at least ten metres across. Around the pit, spread out around the area, stood at least a hundred people, all chanting in unison, their arms raised in the air. The voices were low and husky, the language guttural. Men near the centre of the pit were kneeling, raising and lowering their arms as if in supplication. Near the edge were two stone pillars; a naked and unconscious woman hung between them, chains extending from her wrists to the top of the pillars.

On the floor around the pit, stones were laid into the floor to form a tiled circle around it. Carved into these stones in letters a foot tall were the same words, repeated again and again: *puteus mundōrum*. As he watched them chanting and moving around, something about the men struck him as strange and unusual, even for this ungodly rite – their clothes and apparel appeared old. No, not just old but antique – many were wearing robes, or tunics and stockings, which were medieval in appearance.

He watched, mesmerized, unable to draw his eyes away, as the chanting became louder, the gesticulations of the kneeling men more frantic. He found himself unable to move, even as the floor began to shake, as if a minor earthquake was striking the cavern. Small pieces of debris and the occasional stalactite began to fall from the ceiling, but the men below him ignored it, continuing their unholy rite.

Then, from the pit came the sound, an unholy cacophony of screams reverberating through the caverns, followed by an overwhelming miasma of death, the charnel stench of a thousand open graves. He stood there watching, as if hypnotized, as a mass of tentacles slithered out from the pit, rising up from the abyss below to writhe around in the air, slimy and glistening. They were not just gathered around the edge of the pit, but were completely filling it. Then, they were rising up out of the pit – a roiling, writhing expanse of dark green flesh, moving outwards across the floor, before the centre parted revealing a huge deep-red orifice. Tentacles were grabbing the unconscious woman, effortlessly snapping the chains that bound her as she was pulled into that gaping mouth. She was followed by the bodies of the nearby men who seemed delirious, unaware of the horror that awaited them. They were lifted, thrown into that deep-red maw before disappearing with a scream and an explosion of red mist.

Jack found he could not tear himself away, some inner force compelling him closer. He took a step closer, his body no longer under his control. This was the end now. Not just for him, but for everyone. He was falling now, down from where he stood towards that pit, falling... falling...

Chapter 40.

Jack awoke, sitting bolt upright with a gasp. Peter, who had been sitting in a chair next to him, jerked with surprise, dropping his glass on the floor.

'Are you okay?' he asked Jack.

'Yes... Yes, I think so,' Jack replied. His heart was pumping fast in his chest. He was shaking and could feel the sweat on his brow.

Peter picked up his glass from the floor and fetched another for Jack, pouring him a stiff drink. He handed it to him. 'What did you see?'

Jack took a large gulp of the whisky and wiped his forearm across his brow. 'I was underground. Deep underground, I think.' He took a sip of the whisky. 'There was this labyrinth of tunnels, then this huge cavern, and a pit. And... Oh my God, the thing that came out of it.' He gulped down the rest of his drink and held the empty glass out for Peter to refill. 'My God,' he said, his voice quavering with fright. 'If that's what's awaiting Jennifer...'

'Try not to think about that too much. Did you see anything there to tell you where you were?'

'No, it was all underground, most of it in the darkness,' said Jack, causing Peter to curse. 'No – wait,' Jack said suddenly. 'There was something written around the pit... What was it?' He closed his eyes, trying to remember, to visualize it in his mind. 'I think it was *puteus mundōrum*. Does that mean anything to you?'

'Well of the Worlds.'

'I'm sorry?'

'It means Well of the Worlds. And it means we have a problem.'

'Why?' asked Jack. 'Where is this Well of the Worlds?'

'The Well of the Worlds is a place of myth and legend, dating back to the middle ages. A complex of natural and man-made caves stretching deep under the earth. A place where one of the darkest medieval societies known as *The Guardians of the Well* would gather to make sacrifices. The Well of the Worlds was meant to be a place where the barriers between this world and others was weak, where it was possible to cross over to worlds different from our own – or to summon other creatures from them. There are many stories of it over the centuries, rumours of strange rites carried out in absolute secrecy. The cults involved would make the Freemasons and Scientologists look like loud-mouthed attention-whores. John Dee was rumoured to be a member during the Renaissance. Crowley too, in more recent times. If we need to find it then... well, we're in over our head, I'm afraid.' He raised his glass, downing his whisky. 'Precious little is known about the society, even less about its location, except that it was somewhere in Britain.'

'God damn it!' bellowed Jack, throwing his empty glass at the wall, where it bounced harmlessly, landing on the floor. That was their last clue. 'Fuck!' he roared. 'We're so close. That can't just be the end.' He collapsed back onto the bed.

'Well, unless you just happen to have a map detailing its location that you haven't given me, I'm not sure what I can do,' said Peter.

'I can go under again,' said Jack, sitting up again. 'I can try again, look for more clues.'

'I'm not sure that would be safe to do again so soon,' warned Peter.

'I don't care,' said Jack. 'We need to...' He stopped – something had struck him. 'This cult. Would their name in Latin be 'custodes puti' by any chance?'

'*Custodes putei*, but yes. Why? Where did you come across that name?' Peter was looking at him with a serious expression on his face.

'The hidden basement in Ash House – it was some kind of study belonging to Robert. There were various books there, but there was one book in particular – an old, leather-bound tome. That was what was written on the cover – and a symbol, a circular line surrounding a black circle.'

Peter nodded. 'That was their symbol. Where is this book now?'

'Still in the basement, I assume – unless someone from the Brotherhood has taken it. Does this mean we're heading back to England?'

Peter nodded again. 'I think it does. Pack your bags – we can sleep on the plane.'

Chapter 41.

December 11ᵗʰ, 2012. Heathrow Airport, London.

Jack stepped up to the counter at passport control and handed over his passport. The man behind the counter opened it, taking a good look at it and then at Jack. He placed the passport against his scanner and waited. He looked down at something in front of him, and then looked back up at Jack.

'If you could just go with this gentleman, sir.'

Jack turned to see a security guard standing next to him, dressed in a shirt and tie, a security pass hanging from a chain around his neck. 'Is there a problem?' Jack asked.

'If you could come with me please, sir,' the guard said simply.

Jack looked behind him at the line of people waiting. Peter had disappeared. He turned back to face the guard. 'Shall we?' he asked, a nervous smile on his face.

The guard walked him over to an anonymous-looking door simply bearing the label *Private*, taking Jack's bag from him as he did so. He typed a numeric code into a keypad and the door opened with a quiet buzz. Inside, sat several miserable-looking people, most of whom appeared to be eastern European. They briefly looked up at Jack as he entered, before disregarding him as unimportant; just another nobody much like themselves.

Jack was led through into a separate room; this was a small plain area containing just a simple metal table and two chairs – little more than a cell. There was a hatch in the door, which could be opened from the outside to look in. Jack took a seat in the chair furthest from the door.

'Someone will be along to see you shortly,' said the security guard.

'Can I ask what this is about?' said Jack, but the guard was already gone, the door closed and locked behind him.

❋ ❋ ❋

It was over an hour later when the door opened again. This time, it was a police officer rather than a security guard.

'If you could come with me please, sir,' he said, holding the door open.

Jack stood up. 'Can you tell me what this is about?' he asked.

'All will be explained shortly, I'm sure, sir,' replied the policeman calmly. Jack shrugged and walked over to the door. He was led out of the room, through many doors and corridors, before he found himself being led out of the back door, stepping outside into bright daylight. He was standing in a car park. Sitting on the asphalt in front of him was a police car, its rear passenger door open, waiting for him.

'Where are you taking me?' asked Jack.

'Not far, just to the local police station,' said the policeman, holding the door for him. Jack climbed into the back, the door closing behind him. The policeman who had escorted him walked around to the front and climbed into the passenger seat. There was another policeman behind the wheel. They set off silently, travelling for just a couple of minutes before they drew up at the back entrance of a building designated as Aviation Security. He was led inside, which was busy with officials – airport security and police hurrying back and forth on official business. They went down a corridor and into another small room with a table and three chairs, a large mirror on one wall. This was obviously a police interview room. Sat on the far side of the table were two police officers, Detective Inspector Cross and another man he did not recognize.

'Take a seat, please, Mr Knight,' said Detective Inspector Cross, not standing up. Jack did as she asked. 'You're a hard man to get hold of. Detective Sergeant Brooks and I would like to have a few words with you regarding your recent experiences.'

'Am I under arrest?' asked Jack.

'Not yet,' said Cross. 'Currently, you're just helping us with our enquiries – but that could all change, depending on how cooperative you are. I must warn you, however, that we are recording this conversation.' Jack nodded to indicate that he understood. 'Firstly, Mr Knight, where is your partner, Miss Miller? I see here that she wasn't on the flight with you.'

'I'm not actually sure,' replied Jack.

Detective Inspector Cross sighed. 'We're not getting off to a very good start, are we?' she asked. Even now, Jack wasn't sure how much to tell them; a lot of their actions hadn't been entirely legal. He wondered how much prison time he could be looking at already. Breaking and entering, withholding evidence, theft – possibly even manslaughter.

'It's complicated,' he eventually said.

'Isn't it always?' said Detective Sergeant Brooks. 'Why don't you try and explain. Start at the beginning. That usually helps.'

'Okay,' said Jack. 'It all started when we inherited my Uncle Stephen's house. It's been in the family for almost a century. Shortly after we moved in, we were attacked by a burglar, as you know.' He looked at Detective Inspector Cross, who looked back at him impassively. 'He was killed when he attacked Jennifer and she defended herself. That was all just an accident, she didn't mean to hurt him. What else do you want to know?' He didn't want to tell them anything they didn't already know, but he guessed they knew quite a lot, or else he wouldn't be here.

'Tell us about Ian Williams,' said Detective Sergeant Brooks.

'Right,' said Jack. 'The house, you see, used to belong to an ancestor of mine, Robert Knight. After inheriting the house, we hired Ian to look into his history, and background. He used to be in the military you see – my ancestor that is – not Ian. Although Ian may have been too.' Jack realized he was starting to ramble. He stopped and took a breath before continuing. 'Ian told us that he had managed to find some information about my great-grandfather, but then, before he could tell us anything, he was attacked by a burglar himself – as I'm sure you know.' The two detectives nodded, and indicated for him to continue. 'He'd given us an address on a business card, but I wasn't sure if that was a home or office address. We thought we'd go over. We thought that maybe if it was an office, then there might be someone else there who could provide the information.' He hoped this was close enough to the truth to be believable. He was starting to feel hot now, his face starting to flush. He coughed. 'Could I have a glass of water, please?'

The two detectives looked at each other, and then Brooks stood up and went over to the door. He opened it, spoke briefly to someone outside and then sat down again. 'Continue, please,' he said.

'Well, the two of us went over to the address on the business card. We didn't realize until we got there that the address was the crime scene where he had been attacked.'

'And did you go in?'

'How could we? The door was locked. At least, I assume it was locked, it was closed at least – and there was tape over the door.' He thought of the key, still on the key-ring in his pocket. He shuffled uncomfortably in his chair.

'So what happened then?'

'This guy jumped out on us, all dressed in black. Waved a gun in our faces. Made us go with him.'

'This man,' said Brooks, 'had you ever seen him before?'

'No.'

'And did he explain *why* he wanted you to go with him?'

'No. All he said was that somebody wanted to talk to us. He told us that he was willing to kill us if we didn't come with him.'

'I see.' Just then there was a knock at the door. Brooks returned to the door, and opened it. He took a small white cup from a man standing in the doorway and returned to the table, putting it in front of Jack.

'Thank you,' said Jack, picking up the cup and drinking the water down in one. It was cold and refreshing. He could do with another, but he didn't want to push his luck.

'Then what happened?' asked Cross. She had been silent for a while now.

'The road was busy. Jennifer went across first. Then I went across. I misjudged the speed of the lorries – I was lucky, I guess he wasn't.' The two detectives looked at each other again.

'Why did you run from the scene of the accident?' asked Cross.

'We were scared. I think I was in shock – I'd almost been killed. I didn't know if he had any... associates nearby. We just ran, to get away.'

Brooks leaned over and whispered something into his colleague's ear.

'What do you think they wanted?' asked Cross.

Jack thought of the stone cube currently in his hand luggage. He wondered where that was now. He really didn't want the police to take that away from him. Robert had told him he needed to keep it close to him to protect himself. He didn't know how it could do that, but at this stage he trusted his great-grandfather. Every bit of information Robert had left him seemed to be slotting into place. 'I don't know,' he said. He looked them in the eyes, trying to look convincing. 'I really don't.'

'Okay,' said Brooks. 'You ran – I can see that, you were scared, panicking. Personally, I would have called the police, but...' He shrugged his shoulders. 'Why America? Running home is one thing, but fleeing the country? You've got to admit that sounds suspicious.'

'We weren't fleeing the country, we were just...'

'Yes?'

'We'd been meaning to get away anyway. We'd been planning to go to New England for a while.' He hesitated for a moment. 'I was going to write an article about light houses of New England,' he said, trying to blend some reality in with his lies, trying to sound plausible. The two detectives looked surprised. 'It was a commissioned piece, for a magazine,' he said by way of explanation. 'We didn't feel safe here, thought we'd pull our trip forwards.'

'And your wife? Sorry – your partner – Miss Miller?'

Jack thought for a moment about what to tell them. 'She's still in America–' he started, when there was a sudden knock at the door. It opened, and a serious-looking man in plain clothes stepped in. He was older than both Cross and Brooks.

'Can I have a work with both of you?' he asked, looking at the two detectives.

'We're just in the middle of–' began Cross.

'No, this needs to be now,' he interrupted. They both stood up and walked out into the corridor, where they talked in hushed tones. The door was open a crack, and Jack could just hear whispers and murmurs.

'You've got to be fucking kidding me!' Brooks suddenly exclaimed. What the hell was going on, Jack wondered. Moments later Detective Inspector Cross walked back into the room.

'Someone up there obviously likes you,' she said. 'You're free to go.' She started to pick up her papers off the table, the annoyance on her face obvious. Jack didn't understand what was going on. Brooks grabbed a uniformed officer who was walking past. 'P.C. Jackson here will show you out. You can collect your bags and passport at the front desk.'

Jack didn't know what had just happened in the corridor, but he wasn't going to turn down a chance to get out of here, and back to finding Jennifer.

'Thank you,' he mumbled at the two detectives, unable to make eye contact, as he walked out into the corridor, where the police constable was waiting to take him to the front desk.

Once he was gone, Detective Inspector Cross and Detective Sergeant Brooks both sat back down in their chairs.

'Do you believe him?' asked Brooks.

'Not a word of it,' said Cross. 'He's definitely hiding something. I don't care what orders have come down from above, I want eyes on him twenty-four seven. No one moves without authorization, but I want to know the minute anything out of the ordinary happens.'

Chapter 42.

At the front desk, the police had both his hand luggage and suitcase waiting for him. He simply had to sign for them, and then they were returned to him, along with his passport. Ten minutes after he had left the interrogation room, he found himself standing outside the Aviation Security building, wondering what the hell had just happened. He wandered back to the main road, where he hailed a cab to take him back to his car, which was parked in the long-term parking.

He put his luggage in the boot, and then sat in the car, the engine turned off. He had no idea what to do next. Where did he go now? Was it safe to go home? He decided that he needed to speak to Peter. He opened the glove compartment and retrieved his phone from where he had stored it. He took the back off, replacing the battery before turning the power back on again. There was no point trying to hide from the police at the moment; they knew exactly where he was. He held the phone in his hand as it booted up and connected to the network. He was just about to ring Peter when his phone buzzed in his hand, indicating a new message. It was from an unknown number. He opened it.

Meet same place as before. 20:00. P.

It looked like it was from Peter, who obviously wanted to meet up in Cheltenham again. Jack looked at the time on his phone – it was 17:13, which gave him almost three hours; it ought to be plenty.

Jack parked in a dark street in Cheltenham, just around the corner from the Imperial Square and Gardens. He looked at the time on his dashboard – it was five minutes to eight. He got out of the car and locked it, before he turned and hurried across the road, back to the bench where they had met Peter before. It was empty; the whole park was practically deserted. He sat down and tried to wait patiently, but he was too full of nervous energy. Instead, he stood up and started pacing back and forth along the path. Suddenly he was struck by a terrible thought. What if the message wasn't from Peter? What if it was from the Brotherhood, trying to lure him out? He stopped pacing and turned towards the exit. He was just about to leave, when he saw someone striding purposefully towards him. It was Peter.

'Am I glad to see you,' said Jack, the relief almost palpable.

'Me too,' said Peter, grinning at him. 'Let's walk.'

'I don't know what happened,' said Jack as they walked through the gardens in the moonlight. 'When they stopped me at passport control, the police took me in for questioning. They were grilling me and then in an instant it was all over, they released me. Do I have you to thank for that?'

Peter grinned. 'I called in a couple of favours. Big favours. You remember I told you that I rescued the daughter of a politician from a cult a few years ago?' Jack nodded. 'He was sympathetic to your situation, having been there himself. He appreciates that sometimes you have to go around the official channels for the sake of expediency.'

'What did he do?'

'The story the police were told is that the security services are watching you. The two men who attacked you are both part of a criminal gang, and they're hoping to draw them out by using you two as bait. By holding you for interrogation, they were jeopardizing the bigger operation.'

'And they believed it?'

'Well, they let you go, didn't they? I don't know whether they might still try to follow you, but I'm assuming they won't have organized anything just yet. It might be hard for them to make it an official case – at least for now. If they dig too deep though, the story won't hold water.'

Jack stopped walking in front of the fountain. 'So what now?'

'We need to head back to your place. See what we can find in that book of Robert's.'

'If it's still there.'

'Well, we'll just have to see.'

'Do you think it'll be safe? Last time I was there, one of them jumped me. If it hadn't been for Jennifer…'

'Hopefully they think you're dead. And if not, you've got me covering you this time.'

They drove back to Ash House in a convoy, Peter following Jack in his car. They could see no one watching the house, so they used the front gate this time, driving up the driveway and parking in front of the porch.

Jack opened the front door and looked inside. It was dark and deserted; nothing seemed to have changed since he was last there. Peter came in behind him, closing the door behind them, and they headed straight for the kitchen. The signs were good; the back door was still closed and locked, the door to the pantry still shut. Jack opened the door, and together they pulled on the trapdoor and lifted it up. Jack grabbed a torch and started down the steps, Peter following closely behind. Descending down into the cellar, he could see that nothing seemed to be disturbed. He walked over to the desk and picked up the book, handing it to Peter.

'Is this what you were hoping for?' he asked.

Peter looked at the cover and then opened the book, scanning over the first few pages. 'I think it is. Let's take it upstairs into the light to get a better look.'

Sitting in the study five minutes later, Jack turned to Peter. 'Does it mean any-thing to you?' asked Jack.

'Well, I speak some Latin, but I'm not great. However, I can understand enough to think that this is the real deal. It's probably worth a fortune to the right people.'

'If you can use it to help me find Jennifer – it's yours,' said Jack. Peter nodded back at him, a wide grin across his face.

Peter leafed through a few of the pages. 'I'm going to need some time to decipher this,' he said.

'How much time? I don't have to remind you we're working against the clock here.'

'Hard to say. I don't need to understand everything in here, just enough to find where the Well of the Worlds is.' He looked at the books lining the walls of the study. 'Can I use your laptop?'

'Sure,' said Jack, opening it up and turning it on. 'Whatever you need.'

'You might as well try to get some rest while I get on with this,' said Peter. 'I could probably do with some peace and quiet to help me concentrate. I'll give you a shout if I need anything from you.' With that, he turned to the first page of the book and started reading. Jack left him working and went to the kitchen to make himself some food. He quickly realized he wasn't hungry. He tried sitting on the sofa in the living room and watching something on the television, but it all just seemed too mundane; he couldn't concentrate. They only had one more day to find Jennifer. He prayed that Peter would find something, anything, in that damned tome. He turned the volume down on the TV until it was almost inaudible, just a faint background noise to distract his mind. He lay down on the sofa and closed his eyes, racking his brain for anything that might help, any slight hint or clue that they had overlooked.

He woke with a start to look into the face of Peter, who was shaking him awake. 'Glad you managed to get some sleep,' he said. 'I wasn't sure whether you would or not.'

'I guess I was more tired than I thought,' replied Jack, trying to stifle a yawn. He looked at his watch – it was eight in the morning. 'Any luck?' he asked. 'Do you know where the Well of the Worlds is?'

'I think so,' said Peter, who handed a cup of coffee to Jack. 'There isn't a big map with a red cross on it, but there are quite a few references to it. As far as I can tell, it appears to be in Scotland – somewhere below the Glasgow Necropolis, to be exact.'

'The Necropolis – I've heard of that,' said Jack. 'Isn't it supposed to be one of the most haunted places in Britain?'

Peter chuckled. 'If it's sitting on top of the Well of the Worlds, then I'm sure that reputation is thoroughly deserved. Who knows what has come crawling out of there over the centuries.'

'Are you sure it's the right place? If we're wrong...'

'I know what's at stake here. I can't be completely certain... but yes, I think it's the place.'

'So – we go to Glasgow?'

'Yes. I'd suggest we grab something to eat and then set off – if what you said is correct, we've no time to lose. We can take my car.'

'You don't want to fly?'

'Not after last time – it's too much of a risk in case anyone's been digging into your story. It's all too easy to grab you at the other end. No, we drive – it's far more anonymous.'

They set off shortly after half-eight, driving north up the M5 and then the M6. The weather was bad, rain and spray reducing visibility and forcing everyone to slow down. They went as fast as they could, but a combination of weather, accidents and road works kept getting in their way. By the time they pulled up in Glasgow it was just after six in the evening. The sun had gone down and the gates to the Necropolis had been closed for the night.

Jack was reaching for the door handle, just about to get out of the car, when Peter grabbed him by the arm. 'Jack,' he said. 'Before we do this, I've got something important to tell you. Have you ever killed a man?'

'No! Of course not!' spluttered Jack.

'There were the two cultists...' Peter reminded him.

'But both of those were accidents – and the first one was Jennifer, anyway...' His voice trailed off.

Peter reached over to the glove box and opened it. He took out something wrapped in cloth and held it out to Jack. 'I want you to have this,' he said. Jack reached out and took the object from him, unwrapping it. It was a hunting knife in a leather sheaf. Jack undid the clip on the sheaf and withdrew the knife. It had a solid wooden handle and a six-inch blade that gleamed in the dim light. 'Before this is over, you may very well have to kill someone,' Peter told him.

'I'm not sure I can,' admitted Jack. 'Silas told me as much, and I fear he may be right. I did self-defence when I was younger, but that's just it – it was defence, not attack.'

'You'd be surprised what you can do, when you really need to,' said Peter. He sighed and looked Jack in the face. 'You know how you're always told that there are no absolutes, no pure good or evil, just shades of grey?'

Jack nodded. 'One man's terrorist is another man's freedom fighter – that kind of thing?'

Peter nodded in agreement. 'Well, I'm telling you now – fuck that shit. They're bad, you're good. If it comes down to a choice of them or you, you need to remember that.'

Jack swallowed. 'I'll try to bear that in mind,' he said, nervously, slipping the knife back into its sheath and then putting it in his inside jacket pocket.

Jack and Peter clambered over a stone wall into the cemetery, using a rubbish bin to get them up. They stood in a dark corner of the grounds behind some trees and looked around in the dim light.

'This place is huge!' exclaimed Jack. Around them, lights from neighbouring streets provided enough illumination to see by, but further into the cemetery it appeared much, much darker. 'Just how many graves are there?'

'Over fifty thousand,' replied Peter.

'How on earth are we going to find where this place is?' asked Jack. 'No one's found it for hundreds of years and we've got...' He looked at his watch 'Six hours – at the most?'

'We've got the advantage that we know it's here. We've just got to do what we can.' Jack drew his torch out of his pocket. 'No,' said Peter. 'If there's anyone here, we don't want to draw any attention to ourselves.' Jack nodded and put the torch away again.

They set off, walking along the paths, looking in the twilight for anything unusual, any clues or hints relating to the Well of the Worlds. They had been walking for about ten minutes when Peter grabbed Jack by the arm.

'Shh!' he whispered, putting a finger to his lips and pulling him behind a large stone monument of a winged angel sitting on top of a stone sarcophagus. 'Look over there,' he said, pointing forwards into the darkness.

'What?' said Jack. 'I don't see anything.' Then he spotted movement in the shadows. About a hundred metres in front of them stood a man dressed in a black robe, a hood drawn over his head. He was pacing back and forth, looking around. 'A lookout?' he asked. Peter nodded. 'What do we do?'

'Stay here,' said Peter. 'Any sign of trouble, come running. Don't forget your knife.' Jack swallowed and nodded. Peter hurried off, crouching, into the darkness.

For Jack, the next few minutes felt like an eternity. He sat in the cold and the darkness, watching the man, waiting for something to happen. He was just starting to wonder whether anything had happened to Peter when he saw movement in the shadows next to the lookout. One second he was standing there, the next he was lying on the floor. Just a moment later, his body slid into the shadows, his feet the last thing to disappear into the darkness. Jack saw Peter appear out of the darkness, beckoning him to come forwards. Cautiously, he crept forwards until they were together again. He looked in the direction of where he had seen the body being dragged. 'Is he dead?' he whispered.

'No,' replied Peter. 'But he'll be out for a while. We need to find what he was guarding.'

They split up, searching the nearby monuments and tombs. After a couple of minutes, Jack quietly called Peter to him. 'Come and have a look at this!'

Peter shuffled over. 'What have you found?'

Jack pointed to the archway over the front door of a mausoleum. Engraved into the keystone was a circular line around a filled circle, the symbol of the *Custodes Putei*. 'That's their symbol, isn't it?' he asked Peter. 'The Guardians of the Well of the Worlds.'

'It certainly is,' said Peter. 'This has to be it.' He stepped up to the door of the mausoleum, which was made of dark wood reinforced with thick metal bands. Cautiously, he tried the handle; it was unlocked. He opened the door and stepped in.

The room inside was octagonal in shape. Stone coffins lined the walls, and in the centre was another stone coffin, raised off the floor on a block of marble. Its lid had been removed and was leaning against the far side of the room.

Jack stepped over to the coffin in the centre and looked in. As his eyes grew accustomed to the dark, he could see that this was no coffin. Instead, there were steps leading downwards, into total darkness. 'This has to be it!' he said. 'Peter, come take a look.' He turned around to face Peter, who was standing silhouetted in the doorway, motionless. Then, without a sound, he dropped to his knees, a thin trail of blood running from the corner of his mouth. As he fell forwards, he revealed another cultist behind him in the doorway, dressed in the same black hooded robe as the first. He held a large knife in his hand. Even in the dim light of the mausoleum, Jack could see that the blade was coated in a dark, thick liquid, dripping from the point. He staggered backwards with fright. He reached into his jacket pocket, pulling out the knife that Peter had given him, his hands shaking with fear. He pulled the blade from its sheath, but it fell from his trembling fingers, falling to the floor with a clatter.

The cultist took a step forwards. 'I'm afraid this is the end of the line for you,' he said. 'Time for you to die.'

Jack tried to take another step backwards, but bumped into the stone coffin in the middle of the room. This was surely the end now. He looked down at the knife lying on the floor in front of him, and then up at the cultist who was advancing towards him; he would never make it in time. His legs gave way underneath him, and he slumped to his knees as the last of his will left him, his head bowed. He had failed, just when Jennifer had needed him the most.

Suddenly he heard a whack, and the sound of metal hitting stone. He looked up to see someone standing behind the cultist holding some kind of stick. The knife was gone from his hand; it now lay at his feet. The cultist span round as another blow came down, striking him on the side of the head this time. His knees buckled, and he fell to the floor, where he lay, motionless. Jack looked up into the face of Detective Inspector Cross, who was holding a telescopic metal truncheon in her hand.

'What the hell are you doing here?' asked Jack.

'I could ask you the same thing,' replied Cross. She knelt down next to Peter, rolling him over onto his side so she could examine his injury. She cursed, pulling a handkerchief out of a pocket and pressing it hard against the wound. A significant amount of blood had already pooled on the floor. 'I've been keeping an eye on you ever since you were released from custody.

Good thing for your friend here that I was willing to put in a bit of unofficial overtime.'

'Then you're alone?'

'Not for long,' she said. She had already pulled a mobile out of her pocket with her free hand and was dialling 999. 'Police,' she said a few moments later, as she was asked what emergency service she wanted. She quickly but calmly explained who she was, and that they needed backup and an ambulance.

'Will he be okay?' asked Jack.

'Maybe. I've managed to stop the worst of the bleeding, but it depends on how badly his organs are damaged, and how quickly an ambulance can get here.'

Jack stepped back over to the coffin. 'I need to go,' he said. 'They've got Jennifer and they're planning to kill her. I have to stop them.'

Cross looked at him. 'Go then – quickly.'

'You don't think I'm guilty any more, then?'

'I'm sure you're not completely innocent, but at the moment I'd consider you the lesser of two evils. If you get out of this alive, I expect you to turn yourselves in. Both of you.'

'Agreed,' said Jack. 'I don't care what you charge me with any more; I just need to save her.' He looked back at Peter. 'You'll take care of him, won't you? It's all my fault he's here.'

Cross nodded. 'Go on – before I change my mind. I'll send in the cavalry as soon as they arrive.'

Jack drew his torch out of his pocket and turned it on. Then he climbed into the coffin and started to descend the stairs. 'I'll see you again soon,' he said to Detective Inspector Cross. He couldn't have been more wrong.

Chapter 43.

Jack stepped down the stone stairs, his descent illuminated only by the light of the torch. The first few stairs were made of marble like the coffin and were narrow enough to fit within it, but they soon widened out and were replace by plain brick. The steps were old, crumbling and missing in places, descending steeply into the earth. There was no railing or handholds; Jack had to proceed cautiously, one hand holding the torch, the other against the wall for support. The passage turned continuously to the left as he made his way, spiralling downwards into the depths of the earth.

After descending for what felt like several storeys, the brick corridor opened into a T-junction of natural rock – what looked like a man-made tunnel mined out of the earth. It stretched left and right, with no clues as to what lay in either direction. Jack looked both ways carefully, shining his torch first one way then the other. To the left, the passageway seemed to rise slowly; to the right, a gradual descent. He chose to descend deeper; that was surely where the Well of the Worlds was. He carried on down this passageway, the rough stone floor uneven and rocky, making it difficult terrain in the darkness. The corridor continued to descend at a gradual pace.

After walking for maybe ten minutes, he stopped. He could feel a faint draught blowing into his face. He wasn't sure how this could be possible so far underground. As he stood in the dark and the silence, he felt he could just make out some kind of noise carried in the wind, too indistinct to recognize what it was. He carried on, and before long the passageway opened into a larger cavern. Three tunnels lay ahead of him. He approached them, and held out his hand, holding it in the air in front of him. From the right-hand passageway, he could feel that slight breeze again, and when he strained his ears, could hear just the faintest hint of a sound. He took that passageway and continued.

This passageway again descended, steeper than before. In some places, moisture was dripping down the walls, making the floor slippery and danger-ous underfoot. He continued, until the room opened up into a man-made room, paved with red brick. It now appeared much older, the bricks worn and crumbling, the brackets on the wall broken and rusted, but it was clearly the same room he had encountered in his dream – or his vision – or whatever it had been. Above each of the four arched passageways out of the room, however, he could still make out the symbols carved into the head-stone. He headed down the same passageway he had taken in his dream, the breeze growing stronger, the noise getting louder. It was now distinguishable as voices, chanting in a language he did not understand but which was never-theless all too familiar.

He followed the same path as before, through the caverns with their huge tunnels until he again reached the cavern overlooking the Well of the Worlds. A feeling of déjà vu sent a shiver down his back. He had arrived at last.

Below him was the same vast cavern he remembered. The pit still lay in the centre of the cavern, dark and inviting. Illumination was provided this time not by burning torches, but by electric lamps, which lay all around the edge of the room.

Next to the pit was a large star, painted onto the floor with white paint, and adorned by symbols and signs all around the lines that comprised it. Eight cultists were standing in a wide circle around the star, all chanting loudly. Between them, within the circle, a huge whirling maelstrom of light was swirl-ing and pulsating in the air above the star, growing in size and intensity as the air flew around them. The wind was whipping up the dust from the floor, scattering it around the cave like a sandstorm, reducing the visibility. Behind the cultists and the pit, he could just make out someone else through the swirling dust. He couldn't be certain, but was pretty sure it was Silas. He was standing behind a black altar, upon which lay a woman dressed in white – Jennifer – her hands tied behind her back.

As he looked down at them, Jack could feel something warm in his pocket. He thrust his hand in and pulled out the small square cube left to him by Robert. It felt warm to the touch now, no longer milky white but pale red, glowing and pulsing in time with the maelstrom of light. He knew it had to mean something, but didn't know what – a warning perhaps? Could it somehow be used to stop whatever was going on down there? He put the stone back into his pocket and looked down. The way down to the cavern below had been a sheer drop in his dream, but since then someone had carved a path into the rock wall of the cavern, leading steeply down to the floor below.

The path before him was narrow, barely wide enough for one person, but he raced down it, towards a space in front of the chanting cultists. Jack used his momentum to carry himself down, running as fast as he dared, almost but never quite stumbling. He was desperate to break their circle, to get to Jennifer and disrupt their ceremony before it was too late. As he reached the bottom and sprinted towards them, the cultist nearest to him turned, facing him down and still continuing to chant. His legs were bent, and he was holding his hands out in front of him, in some kind of martial arts stance.

Jack smacked into him at full speed, the cultist twisting as they collided, keeping his footing and managing to grab him by the arms. Jennifer watched, helpless as they grappled with each other, the cultist still continuing to chant through gritted teeth as they struggled. For several long moments the two of them wrestled for control. Jack appeared to be gaining the upper hand, pushing the cultist down to his knees, when all of a sudden he twisted, rolling and throwing Jack over his shoulder into the centre of the circle. Jack stumbled forwards, falling into the maelstrom of light and wind.

From her place on the altar, Jennifer looked on in horror as there was a brilliant flash of blinding red light, causing her to momentarily shut her eyes. When she opened them again, Jack had disappeared. 'No!' she screamed.

Silas looked down at her. 'There is no one to help you now,' he said, a wide grin forming on his face.

Chapter 44.

Jack felt excruciating pain wrack through his body; he felt as if every part of him was being wrenched apart in all directions. Blinding white light filled his eyes, burning into his brain. The sound of tearing wind rushed through his ears. Then all faded to black.

Jack woke up lying on the floor; his face was pressed against cold damp stone. His ears were ringing, and all he could see were stars flashing before his eyes – bright white pinpoints flickering in and out. Gradually, his senses began to return to him. He rolled over and started to sit up; a wave of nausea came over him, forcing him to stop. He closed his eyes and counted to ten before trying again. Another wave of dizziness swept over him, but less intense this time. He forced himself to sit up and appraise his situation. Wherever he was, it was dark – no, more than that, this was pitch black, absolute darkness. He felt around on the floor – it was rough, uneven stone, which felt like natural rock. The only sound he could hear was the ringing in his ears.

Gradually, he raised himself up and stood, trembling, on unsteady legs. The darkness was overwhelming, he could feel himself swaying at he tried to stand straight. He attempted to take a step forwards and stumbled, his leg almost buckling under him. He stood there, leaning forwards with his hands on his thighs and breathed deeply, trying to get his breath back and to regain composure. For several minutes he waited and recuperated, trying to make sense of his surroundings. There were no stars, no breeze... He couldn't be outside, and with the rough stone floor, he must be underground, in another cave somewhere – but where?

As his eyes gradually became accustomed to the dark and his vision cleared, shapes slowly became visible in the darkness. He definitely was in a cave – in the far wall he could just make out the faint shape of a passageway, illuminated by a dim light from far down it. He started to walk towards the light, his strength slowly coming back to him now, his legs stronger with every step. As he moved further from where he had lain, the dizziness also subsided, the ringing in his ears reducing to a gentle low-pitched hum. From down the passageway, he could hear the sounds of chanting now, several voices all intoning together in that same damned language he could not understand. But this was not the same as the cultists he had been fighting with just a few minutes ago – the voices were different in number and in tone.

He moved slowly and cautiously down the passageway, a corridor of natural stone that twisted and turned as it wound its way onward towards the lights and sounds. It finally ended at a ledge, which he cautiously approached – the voices were loud now, he must be right above them. He peered over the ledge, a drop of maybe ten feet to a cavern below. Below him, a circle of six hooded men dressed in black robes were chanting, standing around a familiar six-pointed star painted on the floor. Behind them stood a seventh man, also dressed in a black robe. His hood was down, and Jack could not make out his features from the dim light provided by a handful of torches mounted to the walls of the cavern, but he was certain this wasn't Silas. This was another ritual in another place. Beyond the man was a black altar with a deep chasm behind it; in front of him on the floor was the body of a woman in a white dress; she was not moving. As he watched, the seventh man drew a long knife from the altar and held it aloft above the woman, the chanting growing ever louder.

Jack felt in his pockets for something, anything, to use as a weapon. He felt for the stone cube in his pocket, but it was no longer there, only a handful of dry dust – something had caused it to crumble. In desperation, he pulled out the only other thing he had in his pockets – his wallet. Then, from below him rang out an almighty blast – a gunshot, echoing and reverberating wildly in the enclosed cavern. Jack dropped the wallet in shock; it tumbled through the air before bouncing on the floor and disappearing somewhere in the darkness. 'Damn!' he cursed.

He looked up; a man had stepped into the cavern below, and one of the cultists had gone down, shot by his bullet. The other five cultists who had been in a circle broke rank and charged him, another screaming and falling as he ran, cut down by another round. He glanced towards the floor, but his wallet had gone. All that he could see was a photograph that had fallen from it. He quickly picked it up and looked at it – it was a black and white photo of Jennifer. How he wished she was here by his side. He knew he had to act now. 'Please God, don't shoot me by mistake,' he prayed silently, and then he leapt from the ledge, aiming for a nearby cultist who was running towards the armed intruder. He landed ungracefully on him, both of them falling to the floor, the cultist bearing the brunt of the blow. Jack pulled himself to his knees, but the cultist he had landed on wasn't moving – either knocked unconscious or dead from the impact.

He turned round to see one of the others charging at him, a dagger held aloft in his hand. Jack managed to step to one side as the man slashed at him with the dagger, hitting only air. Jack felt panic rising in him, but tried desperately to remain calm, to remember his self-defence training from his youth. He scrambled to his feet, facing the man who had now slowed and was pacing towards him slowly and cautiously. Out of his peripheral vision, he could see the intruder scuffling violently with a cultist of his own, and another slowly advancing towards him. In the background, he could still hear the seventh cultist continuing to chant, his voice now rising to a crescendo. The cultist lunged at him with the knife. Muscle memory kicked in for Jack, a reflex from repeated self-defence training all those years ago. As the cultist's arm came down wielding the knife, Jacks came up, grabbing his forearm with his left hand. He twisted it back and the cultist's eyes grew wide in surprise, cursing as the knife fell from his hand. With his right hand, Jack punched the man as hard as he could in the side of the head. The intensity of the pain as his fist made contact with the cultist's head surprised Jack, but it shocked the cultist more; he reeled back, staggering. Jack took a step forwards and punched him again, this time in the gut; the cultist wheezed and bent over double. Jack kicked up violently with his knee; it collided sharply with the man's face, and he dropped to the floor, no longer moving.

Jack looked around and saw the dropped dagger on the floor; he bent over quickly and retrieved it. Another cultist was advancing towards him slowly, cautious now that Jack was also armed. Still, Jack could hear seventh cultist chanting, almost shouting the words now, as if oblivious to their battle. Jack could feel a chill wind, rising from where he did not know. Dust from the floor began to swirl in the air, the torches flickering madly, making the dim light even more erratic.

The cultist and Jack circled each other. The cultist made a feint with his dagger – once to his left, then once to his right. Jack tried to stay calm, to stand his ground. Without warning, the cultist moved in a swift sweeping motion, taking Jack by surprise. His arm went up to protect him, but failed to deflect the blow; the dagger struck his arm, slicing through his clothes and cutting his flesh deeply. Pain surged through him, and his own dagger fell to the floor. Jack staggered backwards, tripping over his feet and falling to the floor, landing painfully on his back. He winced as the man stood above him, raising his dagger, an evil grin on his face.

Suddenly, the arm holding the dagger was grabbed by someone standing behind him. The cultist twisted around just in time to see a fist smack him in the face. Stunned, he dropped his dagger to the floor. The man swung his fist again, but this time the cultist was prepared and he stepped backwards, dodging the blow. The cultist aimed a punch back at the man in retaliation, but he too ducked away, stepping to the side and grabbing the cultist by the arm. The two men were grappling now, locked in each other's arms.

'Go!' shouted the man at Jack. 'Get out of here while you still can. I'll hold him off.' Jack froze, lying on the floor. All his energy had left him. The man managed to free his arms and pushed the cultist back. He swung his fist and it connected with the cultist's jaw; his head jerked backwards from the impact and he collapsed to the floor. Jack looked up at the man who had saved him, silhouetted by the light of the torches as he stood above him. 'I thought I told you to go,' he said.

Then there was another almighty bang as a gunshot went off, and then another. A third shot rang out, and a small crimson circle appeared on the man's chest, a thin mist of blood spraying over Jack. The man dropped to his knees and fell forwards, Jack just managing to roll out of the way before the body fell on him. Dragging himself to his feet and clutching at his arm, he looked across the room. In the dim light, he could just make out a cultist lying on the floor, left for dead by his ally when he had come over to rescue him. He was holding the pistol that the man had dropped. He pointed it towards Jack and pulled the trigger, but there was only a small click. Jack picked up his dagger from the floor and staggered back towards the cultist, but by the time he reached him, he had already slumped to the floor again, a trickle of blood running from the corner of his mouth. Jack prodded him with his foot, but he didn't move. He was dead.

Jack picked up the gun and returned to the man who had saved him. He was lying on the floor, a small bloody hole in his back. Jack threw the empty gun on the floor next to him and knelt down, turning him over onto his back. He froze, unable to believe what he saw. The face he was looking into was Robert Knight's, clearly recognizable from the photograph in his army records.

'Oh fuck,' thought Jack Knight. 'I've just killed my great-grandfather.'

Chapter 45.

November 4ᵗʰ, 1918. Novéant-sur-Meuse, France.

Jack knelt there motionless. Surely there must be a mistake. He felt around Robert's neck and drew out a set of dog-tags. Stamped on the tags was the name: *Robert Knight*. No, there was no mistake.

He knelt there, momentarily oblivious to all that was going on around him. Then his gaze fell upon another item on the chain next to the dog-tags: a small key, its end in the shape of a six-pointed star. In a moment of clarity, it all came flooding into his mind – he knew where he was now. He knew what had already happened; he knew what he had to do. He slipped the chain with the dog-tags and key over his neck. He stood up in a daze; he felt numb all over.

He turned back to face the rear of the cavern. The high priest – for that was surely what he was – had his hands raised above his head, shouting to the heavens in that infernal language. He could see now a large patch of crimson on the body of the woman who lay at the priest's feet; killed at some point during his struggle with the cultists.

The wind was rising higher, billowing out of the chasm, raising dust and dirt from the floor into the air. As Jack stumbled towards the priest, there was a deep rumble from far below; the cave shook as if there was an earthquake. He picked up speed as he moved towards him, first limping on aching legs, then jogging, before breaking into a muscle-straining sprint. He made contact with the priest, just as his chanting was reaching its crescendo. They fell back against the altar, knocking the wind from both of them, silencing the chanting.

Then he saw it, rising from the chasm below; a seething mass of tentacles, swarming over the end of the cavern. They pulsated as they swept along the floor, seeking life, seeking food. As they moved, they left behind a slick black ichor, glistening in the torchlight. Jack fell backwards, scrambling on his hands and knees, trying to get away but unable to avert his eyes. A thick black tentacle had wrapped itself around the priest, squeezing the life out of him; his chants turned to screams, which turned to silence.

Jack froze. He was unable to move as he watched it rise out of the chasm. An infernal monster, some eldritch mockery of life, summoned forth from the dark depths where it had lain hidden for God knows how long. He watched as the body of the priest was raised high into the air in front of the creature, before the tentacles threw him into its mouth, where he disappeared with a sickening crunch. The enormous red eyes of the creature turned to face Jack. He saw reflected in those eyes the depths of his own insanity, and he knew this was the end; not just for him, but for everyone.

Then, something changed. The shaking ground shook harder and the wind grew stronger, but Jack could see now that the wind had changed; it was flowing back into the chasm. The tentacles whipped through the air more furiously than ever. As they came flying towards Jack he put his arms in front of his face and closed his eyes, weeping with fear, but they stopped short. Looking down, he saw he was lying in the centre of the six-pointed star; tentacles writhed all around but seemed powerless to cross its boundary. The woman's body as well as those of the dead cultists were being dragged away by the tentacles, towards its open mouth.

An ungodly cacophony of screams erupted from the belly of the beast, drowning the cavern in sound, dwarfing the volume the gun had achieved. Jack felt like his brain was being crushed from the sound echoing in his head and feared he might never hear again. In actuality, it was a sound he would hear again and again in his dreams until the day he died. The beast was being dragged back down again; the ritual had not been completed, its release was only temporary.

As the monstrosity dropped back below the chasm's edge, Jack picked himself up and ran. He ran as fast as his aching legs would carry him, never stopping, never looking back.

The French forces found him the next morning, lying in the church graveyard in a pool of his own blood. He was catatonic, unable to tell them who he was, or what had happened to him. The only thing to identify him was his dog-tag around his neck, his only possession a small photo, clutched in a vice-like grip in his hand.

Chapter 46.

November 15th, 1929. Cuttyhunk Island, New England.

Jack could hear the cultists now. He had to get the timing right. Too soon and the gateway would not be open. Too late and – well, he thought, who knows how bad it could be – especially for Mary Reed. He hoped he wasn't making the wrong decision.

He put down his lantern. He could see well enough now by the torches attached to the wall. He crept out of the antechamber and down the passageway to the main cavern. The scene within was familiar from what he could remember from eleven years before; there were a group of cultists standing in a circle in the middle of the cavern, standing on a stone mosaic. They were chanting in unison, with their leader standing behind them, standing in front of an altar. In front of him with her back to Jack stood a woman dressed in a white dress, her hands tied behind her back and a cloth bag over her head; Mary Reed, presumably. In the space between the cultists, the air was glowing and whirling, twisting into a seething whirlpool of wind. The wind whipped around the cavern, lifting dust and debris from the floor. Waves in the large pool of water at the rear of the cave started growing in intensity along with the wind, buffeting against the rocks.

Jack cursed under his breath; they were further though the ceremony than he had expected. He had anticipated having time to plan an attack, but he was going to have to move quickly. The hurricane was growing in intensity as their ritual progressed, and what else was coming along with it, Jack dreaded to think. He didn't intend to stick around to find out. He felt inside his shirt; against his skin lay a stone cube, attached to a chain. It was glowing red now, pulsating slowly and warm to the touch. He reached inside his jacket and pulled his pistol from the inside pocket. Then there came the scream.

'Shit,' he cursed. Looking up, he saw a shiny spike of metal poking through the back of the woman's dress, a crimson circle spreading out around it. 'Shit!' he cursed again. There was no time left. He prayed he wasn't already too late.

He ran into the room, towards the circle. He saw the woman drop to the floor. Behind her, the leader turned to face Jack as he ran. From his belt he drew his own gun, which he now pointed at Jack. Jack could see now that it was Adam Webber, still recognizable from that photograph he had seen all those years ago – or would see many years in the future, depending on your point of view.

'Fuck!' screamed Jack as the gun went off and he felt something fly past his face – the shot must have been close. He hadn't been expecting enemy fire. He stopped, facing the leader, aiming his own gun at him. They both stood there, looking each other in the eye, each aiming at the other – a standoff. The other cultists continued to chant.

'We seem to be at an impasse,' said Adam Webber.

'You know I can't let you get away with this,' said Jack.

'And you know that I can't let you leave.' Adam Webber advanced slowly, and Jack moved in unison, the two of them tracing a circle in the dirt, Jack being pushed slowly towards the vortex of air.

'It's all over,' said Jack. 'I know about your rituals. I stopped the first one, and I intend to stop this one too.'

Adam Webber grinned as they slowly moved across the cave. 'You still don't understand, do you?' he laughed.

'I know more than you think,' said Jack. 'I have been watching you from afar, learning your secrets. I know there's a third ceremony still required, decades from now. I've taken steps to ensure that when the time comes, someone will be there to stop your cult, and they will be armed with what they need to defeat you. I know about your magic and your rituals. You should know that you're not the only one with access to those ancient arte-facts.' Jack thought he saw the confidence waver on Adam Webber's face, but only momentarily.

'Oh really,' sneered the Adam Webber in reply. 'You're very confident for a man who's surrounded with no means of escape. And you're sure about this, are you? Is this the Prophecy of the Great Robert Knight?' he laughed. Jack didn't feel like correcting him over the name.

'Quite sure,' replied Jack coolly. 'I've left it in the hands of someone I can rely on.' He smiled a grin of his own now. He stopped walking, and quickly glanced to either side. The cultists had retreated towards the edge of the cavern, and he was standing with the whirling maelstrom of air behind him. 'I've made sure that when the time is right, they'll have everything they need. So really, you might as well give up now, save us all the trouble.'

'Oh, Mr Knight,' replied Adam Webber. 'I find this all rather hard to believe. You're just a small man, well out of his depth. You see, these are not isolated rituals, but each an integral part of a larger plan. Our masters don't perceive time and space in the same way that we do, with our limited senses. They exist outside of what we would consider linear time, and in dimensions beyond the three we are aware of. No, what is needed is not one successful ritual, but the three of them together, performed when the stars are right; the one you interrupted in the past, this one now, and the one to come, almost a century from now. These three rituals will become connected across time and space, and set up the necessary conditions to forever free our masters. All that's really required is the sacrifice, and the proper spell at the right time to link the three rituals together. In my opin-ion, the rest is all just... window dressing. You see, despite all your heroics, you have achieved nothing of any true importance. The first two rituals are complete; killing me now will have no effect on our plans. Once the third sacrifice is complete, the time of mankind will be over, and our masters will be free to return. Even if you kill me now, it will change nothing.'

Jack considered this. It might be true, but it still didn't change his plan. He placed his left hand into his jacket pocket, his right hand keeping hold of the gun, which was still aimed towards his adversary. Adam Webber nodded towards his cultists, who each drew a dagger and started to advance on Jack, the circle tightening around him.

'No, Mr Knight... I don't think I'll be the one giving up. I think you will be the one to die here, and your legacy will die with you.'

'I'm sorry to disappoint you,' said Jack, as the cultists grew even closer, 'but I'm afraid that won't be possible.' He could feel the stone cube against his skin, not just warm now but almost hot enough to burn him. He drew his hand out of his pocket, revealing a hand-grenade. The pin had been removed, but his hand was still on the safety trigger. The approaching cultists stopped as they saw this, more apprehensive now. 'You see, I have an appointment somewhere else,' he said, dropping the grenade, letting it roll gently towards Adam Webber, into the circle of cultists. He just had time to see a look of panic grip Adam Webber as he dived for cover behind the altar, before he turned and leapt into the whirling pool of wind and light. There was a blinding red flash of light followed by a deafening explosion. When Adam Webber raised his head from the floor, the room was full of dust and smoke. A couple of the cultists were picking themselves up from the floor; others were not so lucky and were either screaming in pain or lying motionless. As he gazed through the dust and debris, he could see no trace of Jack Knight – he had disappeared.

Chapter 47.

December 12th, 2012. The Well of the Worlds, Glasgow.

Silas stood over Jennifer holding a long dagger in his hand. Dust was still swirling all around in the air as the cultists continued to chant. 'You are all alone now. In the end, the efforts of you and your husband were to no avail,' he said. 'He is gone forever, his body scattered throughout the depths of time and space. Now it is time for *your* life to end, to herald in the glorious new reign of our masters.' He lifted the long blade high in both hands. 'Prepare to meet your maker,' he said, an insane grin spread across his face.

Then, everything happened. There was another blinding flash of red light, accompanied this time by a crash of thunder. Out of the sky above the cultists flew a body – a man. He rolled as he fell onto the floor, bouncing off the wall before coming to a stop.

'No!' said Silas, stepping backwards, lowering his knife. 'I can't believe it... Aloysius was right!' he muttered under his breath.

The man staggered to one knee, wobbling as he did so. In his hand he held a gun; he lifted it towards a cultist who was moving towards him and took aim with a shaking hand. He squeezed the trigger and there was an almighty bang, the cultist falling back with a bloody red hole in his chest. Another cultist started towards him; there was a second blast from the gun and he too fell over. The other four cultists who had been chanting broke and ran for the exits, self-preservation overwhelming their loyalty to their masters. As they did so, the swirling maelstrom of wind and light stuttered, and then folded in on itself, winking out of existence. As it did so, the wind died down, the dust in the air falling slowly to the floor, but there also came a deep rumbling from below, echoing up from the pit, and the floor started to shake gently.

Silas pulled Jennifer up in front over him for cover, holding his dagger to her throat. 'Don't you move!' he shouted at the man.

Jennifer looked into the face of the man and gasped. Of all the people she might have expected, this would have been the last on her list. His face was the face of Robert Knight from the portrait in Ash House, old and with a thick grey beard. But looking into his eyes, she could see that somehow, impossibly, it was Jack – *her* Jack. As she looked at him, he looked back into her eyes and smiled.

'I'll kill her!' said Silas. He no longer sounded confident, but instead uncertain about what was going on around him.

'Oh, I don't doubt you,' said Jack with a measure of composure. He held up the pistol, pointing it towards Silas and Jennifer. It was shaking in his hand; he looked as if he was struggling to stay vertical.

'There are things you don't know – things you don't understand,' said Silas, the tone of his voice almost pleading now. 'If you kill me, you will never find out. I can explain. I can tell you about Aloysius.'

'It's too late to talk your way out of this. You need to let her go.'

'I can't do that. You need to put away your need for revenge. I understand how you must be feeling, but you need to understand the bigger picture of what's going on, and your place in it all.'

Jack said nothing, simply pulling back the hammer on his pistol.

'Drop the gun! I mean it! Do you want your wife to die?' shouted Silas, his voice rising to a higher pitch, panic obvious in his voice now.

'She's dead either way,' Jack mumbled, more to himself than to Silas. One of his legs buckled, dropping him to one knee, although he still managed to keep the gun aiming towards them. Jack looked into Jennifer's eyes. There was fear in them, but also a sense of peace.

She silently mouthed something to him: 'I trust you.'

Jennifer had been silent ever since she had seen Jack disappear, but now she spoke up. 'There's one thing you need to know about me Silas,' she said, quietly and calmly.

'Oh yes?' said Silas. She could see that the hand holding the knife was shaking.

'Yes. I'm not his wife,' and with that, she stamped on the instep of one of his feet with the heel of her shoe, twisting to the side, away from the knife. For Jack, time seemed to slow to a crawl. He closed one eye to aim, the trembling in his hand subsiding as he held his breath. All his attention was focussed on this single act. With a silent prayer, he gently squeezed the trigger.

The sounds of the gunshot echoed loudly through the room. Jack dropped the gun and collapsed forwards, the last of his energy spent. Jennifer felt a searing pain in her cheek, then felt Silas collapse behind her. Her cheek was burning, and she could feel blood running down her face. She turned and looked down at the body of Silas on the floor, a deep bullet hole in his face, a crimson pool of blood growing beneath his head. He had taken the full force of the bullet. On legs made of jelly, she ran over to Jack, her hands still tied behind her back. She rolled him over onto his back using her shoulder then looked into his face. He looked like he was at least ten years older than when she had last seen him, and the years hadn't been kind to him. His eyes were closed, but he was breathing. He slowly lifted his eyelids to look at her.

'You shot me!' she exclaimed.

Jack looked at the blood on her cheek. The bullet had just grazed her skin. 'You'll live,' he whispered, with a smile on his face.

'You?' she asked nervously. He didn't look good.

'I'll be okay. You'll just have to give me a while. When you travel that far across time and space, the jet lag's a real bitch,' he chuckled.

She looked into his eyes. 'I was right about that beard,' she whispered to him. She leaned over him and kissed him first on the forehead and then on the lips. To Jack, it felt like the finest kiss of his life, like their first kiss all over again. 'How long has it been?' she asked him.

'Over ten years – but I promised you I'd be back. I've had a lot to time to think things over.'

Jennifer looked around them. The rumbling noise was growing louder, and the shaking was getting stronger. Dust and small pieces of stone were falling from the ceiling. 'We've got to get out of here,' she said, standing up again. 'Before this whole place comes down.'

Jack nodded in agreement and pulled himself up onto one knee. 'There's something I've got to say first.'

'What do you mean? Can't it wait?'

'Knowing I was the one that got you into this mess, and was the only one capable of saving you – it almost tore me up inside. In the end though, it only made my decision easier.'

'What–'

Jack looked up into her eyes. 'Jennifer, will you marry me?'